D1026231

MORE THAN A KISS

"Christmas isn't far off," Flint said. "I hope I'll be gone by then, but if not, I don't want to be exchanging glances under the mistletoe."

That stopped her thoughts from going in circles. Damn right. He wasn't going to be exchanging *anything* under the mistletoe with her, she thought. She nodded, withdrawing her hand from his in embarrassment. A finger lifted her protesting chin until Casey was forced to look into his face. He was smiling that devastating smile that had always been reserved for others. She caught her breath at the potency of his charm.

Was she about to be kissed right now?

Searching For Santa

JANET DAILEY

ZEBRA BOOKS
Kensington Publishing Corp.
http://www.kensingtonbooks.com

ZEBRA BOOKS are published by

Kensington Publishing Corp.
850 Third Avenue
New York, NY 10022

All Kensington titles, imprints, and distributed lines are available at special quantity discounts for bulk purchases for sales promotion, premiums, fund-raising, educational, or institutional use.

Special book excerpts or customized printings can also be created to fit specific needs. For details, write or phone the office of the Kensington Special Sales Manager: Attn. Special Sales Department. Kensington Publishing Corp., 850 Third Avenue, New York, NY 10022. Phone: 1-800-221-2647.

This title was originally published in 1980 as *Boss Man from Ogallala*.

ISBN-13: 978-1-4201-0306-9
ISBN-10: 1-4201-0306-7

First Printing: October 2008
10 9 8 7 6 5 4 3 2 1

Printed in the United States of America

Chapter One

"Got a kiss for the old man today, Casey love?" the weak voice asked from the hospital bed.

"Sure do." A determinedly happy smile curled the corners of her mouth upward as Casey Gilmore dodged the hanging ropes and weights that held her father's leg in traction. His orthopedist considered the treatment the best way to go for her father's hip fracture—it had been a messy break and a hip replacement wasn't an option at this point. She brushed her lips lightly over his cheek, noticing how pale he was under what was left of his tan. Not even the steady dose of painkillers had erased the reflection of pain in his brown eyes, only dulled their brilliance.

"Sorry to be so late, Dad." The cheerful smile on her face didn't match her troubled eyes. Casey glanced briefly at her mother seated in a chair next to the bed before she herself sat in the adjacent chair.

"We were just beginning to worry about you." Her mother studied her closely, her teasing voice revealing concern and apprehension growing underneath. These last few days had been rough.

"I had lunch with Johnny before he went back to North Platte," Casey explained, keeping her voice purposely light so her father wouldn't know how disappointed she was with the results of that talk. She brushed her short-cropped brown hair away from her equally dark eyes in a nervous gesture, sensing that despite the lightness of their greetings, her parents had been having a serious discussion before her arrival. "I see you haven't started chasing the nurses yet," she joked to fill the silence.

"Not likely to, either," John Gilmore sighed. His dark hair, just beginning to become flecked with gray, moved restlessly on the white pillow. "I hate this contraption—I didn't know they still used them. Old-fashioned treatment for an old guy, huh?"

"Dad, you're not old."

"I'm feeling every year of my life." He looked at the ceiling in desperation even as he muttered what amounted to a curse. "Of all the times to get thrown by a horse, this wasn't the best. I guess I should count myself lucky that it didn't happen before Thanksgiving. At least we had that time together, without a worry in the world."

Casey knew what he meant. They'd followed the cherished ritual of taking turns to say what they were most thankful for, and her dad had looked around the table at his family and said he was thankful for them most of all, and after that, health and happiness.

Everything had been in its place on the snow-white tablecloth, right down to the cut-glass bowl of cranberry sauce and the little paper turkeys she'd made in grade school that her mom had kept ever since, embarrassingly. A day of convivial feasting with a few good friends; then, after the groaning about eating too much and the cleanup, there was major-league football on TV for the guys and a few of the women. Her mom dragged out her beloved scrapbooks and set to work with the most recent photos, decorating them with little doodads from the hobby shop. Being a good sport, Casey had bounced between the scrapbooks and the game.

It seemed like an awfully long time ago.

Her father cleared his throat to get her attention. "How are things at the ranch, Casey?"

She had trouble meeting his earnest gaze. How glad she was that her mother had spent the last few days in Scottsbluff with her father so that she didn't know the latest crisis that had occurred. Her mother was open about her feelings and couldn't have kept a thing from her husband no matter how hard she tried.

"Outside of everyone missing you so much, everything's fine." Casey's fingers were crossed and hidden in her lap. She refused to think about the broken water pump or the ten head of cattle missing from the Burnt Hollow pasture.

"You wouldn't be keeping anything from me, Casey?" he asked with his usual perception at reading her mind.

"You're a worrier! The most serious thing that's happened since your accident is that Injun threw a shoe." Casey grimaced. "At least he didn't break a leg."

The soft chuckle at his tenderhearted daughter's vehement statement couldn't compare with his usual robust laughter. "That horse isn't worth the hay he eats." His expression grew more serious as he glanced briefly at his wife, then back to Casey. "Fred Lawlor from the bank stopped in this morning after you and Johnny left," he said.

Not more problems, Casey groaned inwardly, knowing how precarious their position had become financially since the cattle market had taken a nosedive. Some of the local farmers had done well planting corn for ethanol, taking advantage of the boom in biofuels, but the Gilmores hadn't been able to even think about switching over. And with the up-and-down swings in the value of farmland, there had been plenty of foreclosures in the county.

She looked at her father's face—something told her that Fred, his oldest friend, hadn't stopped by just for old times' sake.

"Nice of him," she said to be polite.

"Yes, yes, it was." John Gilmore moved uncomfortably in the bed. The white hospital gown looked unnatural covering his chest. "He made a suggestion that your mother and I have been talking over."

Casey stiffened unconsciously, waiting to hear what that was.

"He knows I'm going to be in traction for some time as this broken hip mends. Then a wheelchair. And after that—well, I'm not a young man anymore. Even with the surgery that inserted the steel pin, it's going to take time for my creaky old bones to heal. And the doc thinks I'm going to need months of physical therapy, and that costs a mint."

"Our insurance will cover it," her mother said soothingly.

"I hope so," he said.

"I'm filing a claim for preapproval right this week," her mother reassured him.

Casey nodded. "Mom's been up to her ears in paperwork, Dad. She gets around to it when you're sleeping, just in case you didn't know."

"Is that right? Lucille, you just gave me another reason to love you." He gave his wife a fond look, then turned back to Casey. "In the meantime, the running of the ranch has pretty well been dumped in your lap."

"I can handle it, Dad," Casey said quickly. "We already finished all the dipping, branding, and vaccinating before you got hurt. Mark will be out of school soon and he can lend a hand, even if he is only fifteen. You'll be up and around to supervise the fall work."

The sympathetic exchange of glances between her parents told Casey that her arguments weren't successful.

She forged on. "Sam's there, too. And if I need extra help, you know Smitty will always come over. Dad, I am twenty-one. I know every inch of the ranch. I've lived there all my life."

"I'm not doubting your ability, Casey. And I've never pulled any punches with you or your mother. You know how hard we got hit last year between the late spring blizzard and the cattle prices. If it wasn't for the rising land values, I don't know if I could have got another loan from the bank. Fred Lawlor knows you pretty well. If it was his choice, he'd trust you to take care of things." He couldn't meet her eyes any longer as his gaze shifted to his right leg dangling in the air. "But the bank manager suggested that we bring someone more adult in to run the ranch until I'm in a position to take over myself."

Casey's teeth bit hard into her lower lip to keep it from trembling. Staring down at her well-worn but much loved jeans and the hopelessly scuffed toes of her roping boots, she took a deep breath. "I get it. I'm too young. And female. If Johnny were home it would be different, wouldn't it?"

"We don't really know the reason why, dear," her mother said quietly. "But the bank gets to decide whether they give us a loan or not. It's just not that easy to get one, even though our credit rating's pretty good."

John Gilmore frowned. Like everyone who had to make a living despite the vagaries of nature, he'd had good years and bad. He was the kind of man who hated to owe, but he'd been overextended more than once, and even though he'd kept to a strict repayment schedule, the rating wasn't solid-gold perfect.

"Just because the banks made a zillion bad loans to other people doesn't mean we Gilmores are a bad risk." Casey attempted to laugh, but only a bitter sound came out as she rose from her chair and walked to the window, her face clouded over.

"If there was a chance that I could recuperate at home, they probably would've considered it, maybe even given us decent terms. You have to face facts, Casey," her father said, "you can't consider a two-hour drive each way as being close in an emergency."

"Well, we can call you if we need you, right? C'mon, even a dinky rural hospital like this one has phones."

John Gilmore frowned. "Yes, but I can't be there

to make decisions for you. What if a cow needs doctoring and you don't know what to do?"

"Call the vet, what else?"

He shook his head. "You haven't heard? The last one actually living in the county retired and he's not going to be replaced anytime soon. Folks have had to let stock die because the nearest large-animal vet is a hundred miles away, trying to help someone else who's just as desperate."

"All right." She had to concede the point. Doctoring big, dirty cows that had to be caught on sprawling farms just wasn't as profitable as, say, neutering poodles in a lucrative suburban veterinary practice. Her dad was right about there being a shortage of vets.

"So someone else has to run our place," he said. "Someone who can handle a few everyday disasters on his own when it comes to the animals, at least until help arrives."

"But I can manage their care," she protested. "You showed me a lot of basic animal medicine and I learned some in 4-H, too."

"4-H didn't teach you everything you'd need to know," John Gilmore said quietly. "You're pretty tough, Casey, but there's only your mom and teenage brother there to help you. It takes serious muscle to do a lot of things that need doing around a ranch."

She wanted to sulk, but she controlled the impulse. It wasn't right, not when her dad had to be in the hospital for so long.

"And here I am, strung up like a country ham." John Gilmore sighed. "I feel so darn useless."

"Don't say that," his wife remonstrated.

"Why not? It's true." He looked up at his leg as if

he were mad at it. "Anyway, you'll have less to worry about with a take-charge type of guy."

"You're the only boss man the Anchor Bar has ever had," Casey protested. "I don't know if I could take orders from anyone else but you. Can't you talk to Mr. Lawlor again? You could persuade him to—"

"He knows a man from Ogallala," John Gilmore interrupted firmly, "who's extremely experienced and capable. I've already told Fred to get hold of him and send him out." A little more gently, he added, "I'd like to know I can depend on you to help things run smoothly for him."

"You want me to just shut up and take it like a man, huh?" Casey didn't bother to hide her annoyance. She and her father were too close for him not to know it was there. Her chin jutted out determinedly as she turned from the window toward him. "You can depend on me, Dad, but you knew that all along."

"I was pretty sure of it," he said, smiling, "but I feel better now that I've heard you say it."

"Besides, honey, we want your dad home for Christmas. And he'll still have to take it easy even then," her mother pointed out. "He can't come back to a slew of problems that could have been avoided."

A nurse walked into the room carrying a tray. "It's that time again, Mr. Gilmore." She glanced at Casey and her mother.

They nodded to her and rose. They could take a hint. Hospitals had routines, and patients who couldn't get out of bed needed a lot of care.

"I'll say good-bye now, Dad." Casey walked over

to kiss her father's cheek. "I want to get home before Mark does." She paused. "Um, about the man who's coming, when should I expect him?"

"Fred said he'd try to get him out there the first of the week."

Casey raised her eyebrows and then smiled. Okay, that was five days at the most to make sure everything was in order. "Mark and I will be down Sunday," she promised, giving him a thumbs-up sign as she followed her mother out the door.

Outside she paused to look at her mother, taking in the pinched lines around her mouth and the way her dress hung loosely around her waist. Casey had often admired her mother's devotion to her husband. Now she could see the toll that love had taken in the four days since the accident. The serene composure of Lucille Gilmore's delicate features faded as she turned to her daughter.

"You do understand, don't you, Casey, that your father was in no position to argue with the bank?" she said.

"I can understand it without liking it."

"To be truthful, I'm glad he put his foot down," her mother sighed, "metaphorically speaking. Obviously he can't, poor soul, in real life." Her blue eyes glanced apologetically at Casey. "I didn't like the idea of you shouldering all that responsibility alone, not when things are so difficult."

"Everything's going to turn out fine, Mom. You just worry about Dad and leave the ranch and the new boss man to me to worry about."

"All these years I've been so concerned about you being such a tomboy in some ways. Now with Johnny working for the railway instead of taking over the ranch like your father and I had planned, I guess we can be glad you're the way you are. When this is all over and John is back home—" There was a catch in her voice.

Casey laughed with the same tight sound to her voice that her mother had. Neither one of them could discuss the subject most prominent on their minds, that of the man lying in the hospital room with a broken hip. Even when Lucille Gilmore talked about wanting to be home with Mark, her youngest son, her husband's injuries were foremost on her mind. She'd been sleeping at the hospital on a cot in her husband's room and seeing that he had everything he needed. The small rural hospital didn't have enough nurses to go around, especially when a trauma case came in.

After exchanging parting kisses, Lucille promised, somewhat reluctantly, that she would be returning home with Casey and Mark when they came to the hospital on Sunday. Casey could tell that her mother was torn between her desire to be at her husband's side and to be with her children. The subject had probably been discussed thoroughly with her father and the result had been decided. There was no need for Casey to try to persuade her that apologizing wasn't necessary. Lucille didn't have to be at the ranch every minute, not with grown children.

Well, *she* was grown, Casey amended that. Mark, at fifteen, was still self-centered and could be a real pain.

As Casey left the hospital, she toyed with the idea of making a side trip to North Platte to meet with her older brother again, to renew her earlier pleas at lunch that he return to the ranch to help out in this new crisis. She had only to remember his forceful refusal of her suggestion. During his teens, John had tried to live up to his father's wishes that he learn ranching so that he could take over one day, but after he had finished school, he'd enlisted in the army. Two tours of duty overseas had changed his mind about living in the same place he'd grown up in.

He'd told Casey first that he had decided not to go back to working for his father. His enlistment had ended in late summer of last year and he had wasted no time in letting his parents know that he was taking a job with the Union Pacific Railroad in North Platte.

The disappointment had been a bitter pill for her parents, combined with all the setbacks they had suffered, but whatever they felt had been concealed. Casey could only guess at how upset her father had been when he stoically accepted the fact that his eldest son intended to make his own future. She'd secretly hoped that she would be able to persuade her brother to return, even temporarily. Johnny had been sympathetic and ashamed when he refused.

"I made the break once," he had said. "I know Dad would never stand in my way. But don't you see how guilty I feel about letting him down? I know how much he was counting on me. If I came back now, I'd be building his hopes up again. Let's face it, Casey, you think more of that ranch than I do."

But he'd added something else that forestalled Casey from contacting him again about the news that someone was coming to take over control of the ranch.

"If things get too much for you, Casey, you and Dad can hire someone a lot more experienced than I am," Johnny had finished. "You know Mom will agree with whatever decision he makes."

Her journey back to the Anchor Bar was made with a combination of anxiety and anger. The thought of her father confined to that hospital bed when he was needed so badly at the ranch weighed as heavily as the revelation that some stranger would be in charge of their future.

And the thought of Christmas coming didn't exactly make her feel merry and bright.

She would be up to her knees in muck and old hay, cleaning out stalls when most of her friends would be shopping in Omaha, she thought glumly. The prospect wasn't thrilling, especially not in cold weather. Nebraska winters were brutal, and this one promised to be no exception.

The fields for miles around were a patchwork of gray and brown cornstubble, tipped with frost from the severe but snowless weather of the last weeks. The landscape was dreary. Of course, a great big howling blizzard would make everything picture-postcard pretty once it was over. Casey loved the way the old red barns stood out against the massive white drifts. But she really did know that a blizzard could and would do a lot of damage. Her father had good reason for her not to go it alone.

When she'd been a kid, she'd never thought twice about who'd had to do the shoveling out and road clearing. Her father had taken care of that before his kids even struggled out of bed when they were little.

They usually overslept on those days, even though they fully intended to go out and play, because of the profound quiet cast by a deep snowfall. Still in pajamas, they would watch him from an upstairs window, riding around like a king on his tractor. He used the plow mounted on the front with skill and took pride in his work, creating neat banks with angled edges on either side of the scraped asphalt.

The gorgeous sprays of snow to the left and right were a thrill to watch. Her dad made snow mountains and built huge forts just for the three of them, and she'd been delighted with those too. Yes, she'd been a very happy tomboy, happier hanging out with her brothers than being with most of the girls she knew then. And she considered herself a lot more capable than most of the guys she knew now. She could drive a tractor as well as any of them, but she probably wouldn't do as precise a job as her father when it came to snow clearing.

Patience wasn't her strong point. But maybe it was time she got better at it. John Gilmore wasn't going to be the king of the snow mountains this year, that was for sure.

She was almost surprised that he would let another man take over his domain.

Whoever was coming might or might not give her a chance to prove herself. Casey fully intended to give him a hard time if he didn't. He might be the most capable ranch boss on earth, but he didn't know the Anchor Bar the way she did.

Even if Dad made it home by Christmas, he'd probably still want the guy to stay on. Casey wasn't looking forward to the holidays this year at all, not with a stranger around.

Don't stop believing.

She smiled, remembering her father saying that every Christmas until, at the age of six, she'd finally managed to convince him that there was no Santa and that she knew where presents came from. He'd only sighed and said she was growing up too fast.

Chapter Two

Three miles after turning on the graveled road that led to the ranch lane, Casey saw a pickup truck just turning out of the Smith ranch. Both horns honked at the same time as Casey slowed her car to a halt. She rolled the window down and smiled her hello at the young guy in faded denims and battered straw Stetson who hopped out of the cab of the truck.

"Just gettin' back from the hospital?" Smitty asked, lifting the hat from his head long enough to wipe the sweat off his forehead as he leaned against the car.

Casey nodded, gazing up into the deeply tanned face, boyishly handsome with its eagerness for life. His eyes were a warm brown that had a perennial twinkle. His hair was brown and shaggy, growing long and thick to below his ears, where it mingled with his sideburns. It was long enough to have been in style somewhere around 1970 but not long enough to give Willie Nelson a run for his money. As far as Smitty was concerned, muttonchops were back. He got teased for looking so much like his father in the framed wedding picture over their fireplace but it didn't bother Smitty.

Smitty, or more correctly, Don Smith, was the only child of Robert and Jo Smith, the Gilmores' nearest neighbors. Smitty, at twenty-three, was the same age as Johnny, Casey's older brother. Ever since Casey could remember, she had been tagging after the two of them, an unwelcome addition to their adventures. And then she'd turned seventeen and Smitty had suddenly taken an interest in her. Unlike Johnny, they both shared a love for ranch life, sports, and animals.

"Dad's doing a lot better. He's still in a lot of pain, but you know him, he never complains." Casey smiled, her pride showing with the love for her father.

"We're driving down Sunday," Smitty said. "How's things at your place?"

"The water pump broke at the number ten well. Sam tried to fix it, but he's no good with motors. I was wondering—"

"If I'd come over and take a look at it," Smitty finished with a laugh. "Sure I will. My old man told me to go over anytime you need me. Were you able to talk Johnny into coming back?" Casey had confided in him the previous day that she was going to try.

"No." The deep sigh that accompanied her negative reply told him the futility of the attempt.

"Got it." He'd figured as much already, judging by the unsurprised look on his face.

"That's not all, either." Casey's hand clenched the steering wheel in a nervous, angry gesture. "Fred Lawlor from the bank is making arrangements for a man to come in and take over the ranch operations until Dad is on his feet."

Smitty's eyebrows went up at the announcement and he exhaled a silent whistle. He had known Casey too long not to know what her reaction to that news had been.

"They don't trust someone my age, apparently," she added, her forehead knitting together in a frown.

"Uh-oh. Independent little Casey is going to have to take orders from some big boss man," Smitty teased. At her glowering stare, he reached out and let his fingers follow the gathering of freckles that bridged her nose before his finger ended up under her chin. He lifted her face to his as he leaned inside the window and planted a firm kiss on her lips. "I'm glad. I wouldn't want my girl tied down to a ranch twenty-four hours a day. Especially not with winter coming on."

"I'm not your girl. I'm not anybody's girl." Casey knew she should have felt flattered by his pronouncement, but the idea of someone other than a Gilmore holding the reins of the Anchor Bar ranch was more than she could tolerate. Her sense of humor completely deserted her on that subject.

"Okay."

"How would you feel if someone came in and started bossing you around on your ranch?" she retorted.

"Anything that'd get me out of chores—"

"Forget I said it. You're not a woman, so it probably would never happen to you."

"Ah, come on, Casey, don't take it as a personal insult." He had heard her before on the subject. "Are you going to step up to the podium again and go on and on? If someone steps in to replace your dad, it's not going to be forever."

"I thought you'd understand," she accused.

"I do. It's just no good getting upset about something you can't change. Which reminds me, I was flying over the west pasture today. I think I saw those ten head of cattle you were missing mixed in with our own herd over there," he informed her.

"That means there's a fence down somewhere." Casey sighed, relieved that the cattle had been found and weren't rustled as she'd feared.

"I'll meet you out there tomorrow and we'll check it out," Smitty offered.

"Thanks. I want everything in apple-pie order when this . . . this man comes."

"Who is it?"

"Somebody from Ogallala." Casey shrugged. She had been too upset to get any details. "I'd better be going. I want to be home before Mark gets in."

"The school bus went by about a half hour ago." He tapped the car lightly with his hand as he moved back toward the pickup. "Say, we had a date for Saturday night. Is it still on?"

"I have to go into Scottsbluff with Mark. Why don't you just come over and we'll watch TV or something?" Casey suggested, shifting into reverse and backing onto the road as Smitty waved his agreement. "We get nine thousand channels with that satellite dish. There has to be something good."

"World Wide Wrestling?"

"I was thinking more of a romantic comedy."

He pulled a long face to make her laugh. "There is absolutely nothing funny about romance."

"Oh, shut up," Casey said crossly. She wasn't

saying yes to wrestling. She really didn't want to watch two huge guys in spandex slam each other around and roar.

"Sure will, Casey girl. Just as soon as you lighten up."

She gave him a wry smile, just because he was trying to be nice, and waved good-bye.

Two miles farther on the graveled road, Casey turned onto the lane leading back to the ranch house grounds. She instinctively studied the rolling hills, the sturdy prairie grass long since drained of its spring green color, punctuated by dried-up shrubs. The colorful rusty red hides of the Hereford cattle brightened things up some. The hills stretched out interminably from horizon to horizon, the skyline broken occasionally by towering windmills. Following the curving track around one deceptively larger hill, Casey saw the small valley open before her. The buildings that signified home nestled against the bottom of the north side so that the hills could shelter them from the blasts of the cold north wind.

Bounding out from under the wooden porch at the sound of the slowing car came a dog of such mixed parentage that he always proved a topic of conversation. His ears were erect and pointed; his coat was long and shaggy; his forehead was wide and his nose was long; and the bushy tail wagged happily. Everyone agreed there was a shepherd breed somewhere in his ancestry, based on his black and tan coat, but one look at his lean body and sly grin led everyone to speculate whether he was mixed with a coyote.

But Shep was a member of the family and had

been since the day he wandered into their yard, a frightened, skinny puppy. He was no longer skinny. All ninety-five pounds of him launched at Casey, the most cherished member of his adopted family.

Mark appeared on the porch as Casey greeted the exuberant dog and gradually quieted him to a more controllable state. She smiled at her ungainly brother. He was wearing jeans that stopped above his ankles, betraying the way he had suddenly grown this year. His sweatshirt looked almost empty but he was in there somewhere. Mark had the same sandy hair and blue eyes as their mother and promised to be as tall as their six-foot father. He was already taller than Casey, who was five foot four inches.

"About time you got home," Mark grumbled in a voice that threatened to break into a squeak with each word. He more or less collapsed into one of the porch chairs and picked up a worn pair of boots sitting beside the door. "I'm starved. Can't we go into town tonight and have a pizza?"

"Are the chores done?" Casey asked, ignoring her younger brother's never-ending pleas for food.

"No, I just got home."

"Smitty said the bus went by his place a half hour ago, which means you've had time to finish those cookies Mrs. Barker sent over and the half gallon of milk in the refrigerator," Casey replied perceptively. "That should give you enough energy to do chores."

"I was hungry." He shrugged, pulling on his boots. "How's Dad?"

"Better, I think."

"Do I have to go to school tomorrow? Can't you take me in to see him and write me an excuse?"

"Hey, Mark, tomorrow is Friday. One more day

isn't going to hurt you. Besides, it's the last day before winter sets in for real, according to the almanac." She walked up the steps onto the porch. "I have a list of things that need fixing before the first snowfall, want to sign up for repair work?"

"No. It's not going to snow soon."

"Think so? Okay, then, I'll do the chinking and check for loose siding and roof shingles and all the rest of it by myself."

"No, you won't. You're only a girl."

"What's that supposed to mean?" she asked a tad belligerently.

"It means you need a guy to help with the heavy work."

"Too bad that's not you."

He only grunted an affirmation.

"Never mind. Hurry up with the chores."

Mark was still grumbling as he clomped down the steps toward the largest of the three buildings that, with the house, comprised the only ranch structures.

"Don't forget to bring that saddle in tonight so you can soap it down," Casey called after him as she swung the screen door open to enter the house.

The empty milk pitcher and the white-filmed glass stood silently on the kitchen table amidst the cookie crumbs. Casey shook her head as she cleared the table and wiped it off. There was no doubt that she'd be glad when her mother came back. Next to cooking and cleaning, she hated washing dishes the most. She and Mark had been lucky with the neighbors pitching in to provide precooked casseroles and desserts after their father's accident on Monday and their mother's departure to Scottsbluff. She hadn't had time to cook and freeze; she wanted to be at his side during the recuperation from the operation to insert a pin in his hip.

Tonight, however, Mark had devoured the last of the neighbors' offerings. Casey walked to the sink, then groaned as she realized that she had forgotten to get any meat out of the freezer for the evening meal.

If that had happened to her mother, which it never would, Lucille Gilmore would have been able to raid the refrigerator of its leftovers and the shelves of their canned supplies and come up with a delicious meal. Casey took one look inside the refrigerator at the depressing leftovers and knew she could never do it. Bacon and eggs and hash browns, she decided. A person couldn't go wrong with that, Casey thought, as she removed the dish of cold potatoes from its shelf.

Nearly an hour later, she heard two large thumps coming from the barn that doubled as a stable. That meant Tally, her buckskin horse, had just finished his grain. Ever since he was a yearling, he had kicked the back of his stall twice the minute he had finished his oats, another personality quirk that made horses into individuals. If Mark was on schedule, he would show up for dinner in fifteen minutes.

Casey turned the fire on under the grated potatoes, flipped the sizzling bacon over in the second skillet, and added a spoonful of lard to the third skillet. The table was already set, the toaster sitting to one side with slices of her mother's homemade bread in the compartments. Opening the refrigerator, she placed six eggs in a bowl while juggling the jar of preserves in her other hand.

She was beginning to feel very efficient as she sat the bowl of eggs by the stove and the preserves on the table. She popped the slices of bread into the toaster, stirred the potatoes around so that they browned evenly, and straightened out the curling bacon. Remembering that Mark liked his eggs turned over easy so that the yolks remained runny, Casey lit the fire under the last skillet and removed a small saucer from the cupboard to break the eggs in as she had seen her mother do many times before.

When she tapped the first egg on the saucer's edge, it broke smoothly, then she dropped the shell into the saucer accidentally. The ragged edge of the shell broke the yolk of the egg. Grimacing but thinking that she didn't really mind eating hard-cooked eggs, she slid it in the skillet. But when the second, third, and fourth eggs met the same fate under different circumstances, Casey lifted her hands in despair, vowing that Mark could eat scrambled eggs and like it. Hurriedly she broke the remaining eggs into the skillet and began stirring them together as fast as she could with a fork. Simultaneously she smelled the bacon burning and heard the toast pop up. As quickly as she could, she transferred the charred bacon strips onto a towel to drain, stirred the increasingly crisp hash browns, and ran to the table to butter the toast before suddenly remembering the eggs.

Mark walked into the kitchen, took one look at Casey as she muttered to herself between trips from the stove to the table, and shook his head in disbelief.

"It would've been a lot easier to go to town and get some decent food." His sad eyes met Casey's angry gaze before returning to the too-crisp hash browns, the burnt bacon, the globs of unmelted butter on the cold toast, and the scorched eggs. "I don't understand how Mom ever had a daughter who cooks like you."

"Just hush up and eat!" She jerked her chair away from the table and sat down, trying not to look too closely at the unappetizing food before them.

"It was bad enough last night." Mark's voice croaked as he rose from his chair to open the refrigerator door and take out a bottle of ketchup. "I had to nuke a frozen taco dinner because you boiled the potatoes dry and forgot to turn the oven on to heat Mrs. Gordon's meat casserole." He came back to the table. The hash browns snapped like potato chips when he touched them with his fork. "But an entire meal cooked by you?"

Casey was chewing the rubbery eggs with false contentment, wondering if she swallowed them whether they would go all the way down. She glanced over at her brother just as he picked up a thoroughly charred piece of bacon and it crumbled in his hand. "When's Mom coming home?" he moaned.

"Whining doesn't help. And the answer to your question is not until Sunday," Casey replied in an equally depressed tone.

They rose from the table at exactly the same time.

"With both of us helping, we can clean the kitchen up in ten minutes and be at the restaurant within an hour," Mark vowed.

"Okay."

He got to work. "So, uh, who's going to do the Christmas baking?" he asked. "Mom always got started weeks ahead. You know, homemade fruitcake is, like, a ritual."

She shot him a glare. "Not my thing."

"You sure?"

"Positive. You don't even like fruitcake, Mark."

"No," he mused. "But I like the way it smells when it's baking. I bet you could do it."

"Never have. Never will. If you want a fruitcake that much, we can order one from a catalog or online."

He shook his head. "It's gotta be homemade. How hard can it be? It's basically a big chunk of gummy cake with weird-colored fruit, as far as I know. You mix it, bake it, and pour whiskey on it once a week."

"Dad used to tell her it was a waste of good liquor," Casey said.

"That didn't stop Mom. And don't forget about the Christmas cookies. Icing, sprinkles, gingerbread, and plain, the whole nine."

She folded her arms across her chest and glared at him. "Anything else?"

"Eggnog?" he said hopefully.

"We're barely into December. Besides, you can get that at any store."

"Just asking."

"Mark, I'm not that domestic."

"You'll probably never get married, you know," he said gloomily.

"Not to someone like you," she retorted.

"You mean you want a guy who wears an apron?"

"Turn on the Food Network. Guys look great in aprons."

He looked down at his sloppy jeans and Cornhuskers sweatshirt. "Not me. I just want a fruitcake."

He held up a hand when she started to talk. "I know I'm being childish. You don't have to tell me."

"Okay, I won't, then. But cookies and stuff like that are a lot of work," Casey said briskly. "I know because I helped her make them one year when I was old enough not to eat them all."

"What a honor. I never got asked."

Casey burst out laughing, remembering the cookies he'd just demolished. "That's because you're still eating them all."

Mark laughed too. "Yeah, I guess so. But it still would be nice to uphold some of the traditions."

Casey gave him a curious look. "What's got into you?"

Mark shrugged. "Well, you know, Thanksgiving was pretty great, what with us all being there. I got to thinking that we shouldn't take the holidays for granted, especially when Dad got hurt."

"Well, this isn't going to be the bestest Christmas ever, Mark—" She stopped, not liking the edge in her voice.

"Hey, don't get all big-sister on me. I wasn't expecting a shiny new bike and a PlayStation, okay?"

"Good," Casey said. "I think Mom and Dad are more worried than they let on and there may be unforeseen medical expenses."

"We have health insurance—"

It was her turn to interrupt. "Sure. If the claims aren't denied because they say there was a pre-existing condition or something."

"How can getting thrown off a horse be a pre-existing condition?" Mark wanted to know.

Casey sighed. "An insurance company isn't always your best friend, let's put it that way. Dad's getting older. They could say he had arthritis or something—oh, hell, Mark, I don't know. I could be worrying about nothing. But money's tight and the situation isn't likely to improve. We're going to have to buckle down and do what needs doing. "

Mark gave her a wary look. "So you're in charge?"

Casey pressed her lips together into a thin line. "Not entirely."

"Fill me in."

She let out her breath in a long sigh. "Dad wants someone to come in and run the ranch—he's already arranged it. I don't know anything about the guy besides that Dad and Fred Lawlor picked him. With luck he'll just do what needs doing and leave us alone. Not like we have to celebrate Christmas with him or anything."

"I want Dad home," Mark said. "That's all." There was a suspiciously watery look in his eyes.

"Me too," she said calmly, deciding to tease her younger brother so as not to embarrass him by noticing his tears. "But I didn't have you pegged for the sentimental type."

Mark shrugged. "What did you think I was all about?"

"Dude, you're only fifteen. So what you're all about would be eating, sleeping, and—"

"I can't get a girl to take me seriously," he complained. "I get called a beanpole a lot. Hurts my feelings."

"Poor baby," she said soothingly. "Not that the girls are wrong."

"You're no help, Case."

"What do you want me to do?"

He shot her a mischievous look. "Learn to bake cookies."

"Nope, I don't think so. Seen one gingerbread man, you've seen 'em all."

The next day, Casey waved good-bye to Mark as he set out on his bay gelding. It was nearly four miles from the house to the graveled road where the school bus picked him up. The reliable bay would make his way back, and Mark believed whole-heartedly in the Western motto: "Never walk when you can ride." He was counting the days until his six-teenth birthday when he could get his driver's li-cense and not be forced to take the bus. That time wasn't a long way off, either. Casey sighed. Just five months. Spring would've arrived by then.

Then there would be a whole new set of worries when it came to Mark. In a rural area, a license to drive was like getting a license to drink as far as a lot of teenagers were concerned. Her mother could be clueless about how prevalent that was. Casey was the exact opposite. At twenty-one, she didn't think get-ting bombed was a real big thrill, but she was pre-pared to get on Mark's case about it if she had to.

The idea of taking on that much responsibility wasn't a thrill, either. She hoped he wouldn't take it into his head to practice his driving without a permit, or get into any other illicit activities he didn't want to tell her about.

With both parents gone, he was likely to act up some. Her father was a kind man, but he made all his kids toe the line. She'd very rarely questioned his authority—but what if Mark questioned hers, or sidestepped it entirely?

The new boss man from Ogallala wouldn't be expecting to play papa to someone else's son, Casey was sure of it. She allowed herself a long sigh, just thinking about it. There was a lot to running a ranch, just as her father had said, and it occurred to her that maybe caring for the critters on it would be less trouble than riding herd on her teenaged brother.

She saw Sam Wolver, their hired hand, hammering away at a horseshoe beside their portable blacksmith equipment. Casey glanced at the horse tied to the nearby post. It was Injun Joe, the horse that had thrown her father. Studying him from the rear, she admired again the almost perfect quarter horse conformation. His coffee-brown coat gleamed in the morning sun while his nearly black tail swished idly at the flies.

He should have been a bay horse with black points, but his legs were snow white from his hooves to about four inches above his knees. The horse swung his head around as he heard Casey's boots making their soft sound on the mixture of sand and gravel. She couldn't suppress the shudder that went through her as she stared at the almost totally white face with just a small amount of coffee brown color visible on his cheeks. A changeling, her father had called him, and Casey agreed, especially when she looked into his eyes. One was brown and one was blue.

Just meeting the horse's gaze was unnerving. She had often argued with her father about the horse and said he ought to sell him, but he had always pointed out what a good cowhorse he was. It was true. Injun Joe was probably the best cutting horse on the ranch. Any time he was near a herd of cattle, it was a joy just to sit back in the saddle and let him work. It was the rest of the time that Casey was uncomfortable with him. He was totally unpredictable at any other time and couldn't be counted on to perform the simplest task.

The day of the accident, Casey had tried to persuade her father to take her buckskin out to check the well in the near pasture since his favorite mount was lame. But he had insisted on taking Injun Joe, who hadn't been ridden since a roundup nearly a month before.

She hadn't liked the way the horse had set off with such a stiff-legged walk. Casey knew she never wanted to relive the moment nearly three hours later when she saw the empty saddle on the horse when he wandered into the yard. The terror that had gripped her with its ice-cold fingers had practically numbed her voice. Her knees had shaken so badly when she mounted her own horse that she had trouble holding him. Thankfully Smitty had been there. It was his calmness that had finally settled her down enough so that she was able to find her father's trail while Smitty followed in the pickup.

Together they had found her father trying to crawl back to the main track in the pasture. His face white with pain, he had told them what had happened, how the horse had done some minor bucking when they first reached the pasture meadow. John Gilmore had been lulled into thinking that the friskiness, or whatever it was, was over, then without warning the horse had suddenly lowered his head and began bucking in earnest. In the first jump, her father had lost a stirrup, and by the second, he had already started his flight through the air. Only his retelling of the escapade wasn't so mildly worded.

Casey shook off the unpleasant memory with an effort. She hurried quickly toward the corral where her buckskin waited, already saddled and ready to go. The rich golden yellow color of his coat was beautifully complemented by his black mane and tail and black-stockinged feet. Docile, he followed her as she took his reins and led him out of the corral to the waiting horse trailer.

The dog Shep was sitting beside the pickup, somehow managing to have all four feet beating an anxious tattoo while still not moving from his place. Once she had the horse securely tied in the trailer Casey gave the command for Shep to get into the back of the pickup. He needed no further word, obeying the command with alacrity.

Once Casey hopped into the cab of the truck, she tooted the horn twice at Sam to let him know she was leaving. He had been working for them for years, so long that he no longer needed to be told what to do or when to do it. As long as it wasn't mechanical, Sam Wolver could do anything on the ranch, and ably, too.

Silent Sam, Mark called him. The Gilmores didn't really know very much about him. He didn't seem to have any family that he cared about. He had refused offers to sleep in the bunkhouse, choosing instead to park a ramshackle trailer alongside one of the ranch's so-called lakes, which were really more like large ponds. Sam never talked much, hence his nickname, but when he did, you could bet it was important or informative.

He had an "Old West" attitude toward women, treating them with the utmost respect and courtesy. Casey had more than once thought his behavior toward her mother was almost worshipful. She had the feeling that he was the last of the men who had shaped the Western frontier. Long and lean and shy and well versed in the vagaries of Mother Nature's plants and animals, he had told Casey of the different plants that grew in the Sand Hills, of the uses that they had been put to by the Indians who once roamed the area, and of the time when the bison had ruled these prairies, their numbers mounting into the millions.

Casey remembered how Smitty and Johnny used to tease her when she was younger that Sam was an orphan from a wagon train that had been raided by the Indians long, long ago, that Sam had been captured and raised as an Indian himself. His nearly ageless appearance and his amazing lore had convinced her for a time until her father had at last explained that it was impossible. Still, that was the way Sam Wolver appeared to her and always would—a throwback to a bygone era and another breed of men.

Casey was almost to the gate at Burnt Hollow pasture when she saw the dust of Smitty's pickup approaching from the opposite direction. By the time he had parked his pickup and trailer behind hers, she already had Tally unloaded and was opening the gate. Smitty, like Casey, wasted no time in unloading his horse and leading him through the gate. They both knew work came first and talk afterward. Once the gate was firmly closed, they mounted, both horses setting out in a ground-eating trot with Shep's feathery tail waving merrily in front of them.

They followed the fence for some distance before Smitty broke the companionable silence.

"What did Mark say when you told him about the new man coming?"

"You know Mark. The biggest catastrophe in his life was when he thought he was never going to grow any taller." Casey laughed easily before a slight frown that had nothing to do with the bright morning sun creased her forehead. "He seemed relieved that he wouldn't have so much work to do once this winter closes in. I guess it's a natural reaction for someone as young as he is."

"So says all-grown-up Casey," Smitty teased, "with the learned wisdom of her years."

Casey blushed lightly, recognizing the patronizing note that had been in her voice. The slight budding of color in her cheeks gave her a very feminine glow that seemed at odds with her boyish jeans and boots and plain blouse. She wore no hat, even though the air was chilly, but her thick hair shone in the sun, which illuminated the brown color with a golden sheen. The unseasonably gentle breeze fluffed the close-cropped curls so that dainty swirls kissed her face.

Her dark, naturally arched brows had never known a tweezer to ensure their graceful shape, and her brown eyes that sometimes seemed to snap with angry fires were warm and almost shy. The sprinkling of freckles across her nose and cheeks seemed to have been dusted on her tanned skin to give her the air of pert innocence. Although her mouth was small in keeping with the rest of her features, her finely shaped lips were pleasingly generous.

"There's the break in the fence!" Casey pointed.

Directly ahead of them stood a tree beside the fence. Hard cold winters and hot dry summers had shorn it of its foliage and stripped it of its bark. The whiteness of its sun-bleached trunk stood out sharply against the monotony of the rolling prairie. One large limb had been torn from the tree and now lay at its base, taking with it a section of fence as it fell.

Quickly Casey and Smitty secured their ropes around the branch, wrapping the free end around their saddle horns and towing it away from the fence. Once it was out of the way, they cleared away the tangle of snapped barbed wire. As they remounted and rode their horses through the gap, Smitty indicated the direction where he believed he had seen the Anchor Bar cattle.

The deceptively flat hills stretched out before them. Any depression could successfully hide a full-grown cow from view, or a horse and rider. Here and there, wind had eroded away the sturdy prairie grass from the side of a small hill, exposing the tan-colored ground that gave the Sand Hills their name. A meadowlark that had forgotten to migrate called from a wire while a sharp-tailed grouse burst into the air a few feet ahead of them.

A godforsaken land, Casey had heard it called by some people who stared at the vast expanse of sky and the unbroken rolling hills and cried out at the isolation it implied. But Casey heard the whisper of wind, the melodic calls of the birds, and the quiet shuffle of her horse's hooves as it moved over the grass and sand.

Especially in summer, she loved to rise early in the morning and watch the sun penetrating the mists and the kaleidoscope of colors as the sun settled on the western horizon at the end of the day. This was her home; there was no loneliness. How could there be when she was surrounded by the people she loved and the sights and sounds that were set on this earth by God?

As the two riders topped the crest of a hill, they both saw the small group of cows grazing on what was left of the rich grass that had grown in the hollow. The white faces lifted warily as Casey and Smitty slowly approached the herd. Shep trailed silently behind them, his mouth opened in a happy grin as he panted from the warmth. His bright eyes studied the cows thoroughly as he waited very patiently for his mistress to signal to him to round them up. "I count seven Anchor Bar brands," Casey said softly.

Smitty nodded agreement as they circled the herd and saw three more that had wandered off from the main group. Casey's hand swept out before them and Shep darted forward, snapping and biting at the cows as he began his work of bunching them together. The dog was a whirlwind, dashing and springing from one to another until they were all together in a loosely grouped circle. Now Casey and Smitty nudged their horses forward, separating the Anchor brands from the Bar S. Shep lay silently in the grass, moving only when an Anchor Bar cow threatened to join a retreating member of the Bar S.

"I swear that dog can read brands," Smitty declared, when the last cow had been cut away and they began to drive the ten head back toward the gap in the fence.

"He gives you an awfully eerie feeling sometimes," Casey agreed, smiling at the dashing black and tan dog racing alongside the cattle.

The pace back to the fence was brisker than the first. In half the time they were back and had driven the cattle onto the Gilmore ranch. Another hour was spent patching the broken strands of barbed wire so that the fence was once more secure.

"I've got a thermos of lemonade in the pickup," Casey invited as Smitty shoved a pair of pliers back in his saddlebag.

"And I can use it!" he exclaimed, wiping the perspiration from his forehead with the back of his hand. "I'll race you back."

Casey didn't bother to accept his challenge verbally. She just grabbed the buckskin's reins and vaulted into the saddle with Smitty only a split second behind her on his mount. Her horse nearly jumped out from under her as she drove her heels into his flanks. Smitty's bay was as fast as her own fleet Tally. Most of the way back to the trailers they raced stride for stride, dodging the clumps of withered bushes or jumping them when they had to save time. But Casey's lighter weight eventually forecast the winner and she began to draw away as they neared the pasture gate. When they reined in their horses, she had won by more than a length. "Loser cools the horses!" she announced with a gleeful hoot.

"As long as the winner pours out the lemonade, I don't mind." Smitty took her reins with a grin.

Casey rejoined him a few minutes later, exchanging a cup of cold lemonade for the reins of her horse, then fell in step with him as they made the slow circle to cool their heated horses.

"I was telling my dad last night about your father's arrangement for a ranch man while he's in the hospital. When Dad plagued me for more specific details that I couldn't supply, he called the hospital himself last night. Do you know who's coming out here?" Smitty asked, looking down at the grim-faced girl walking beside him.

"No, I don't. And I don't care," she retorted, keeping her face expressionless.

"I do."

"Goody for you," she said with annoyance.

"Flint McAllister." Smitty paused, letting the name sink in. Casey continued walking, staring blankly ahead of them without commenting on his statement. "You know who he is, don't you?"

"I can't say that I know one thing about him." Her reply was cool, letting him know of her dislike of the subject.

"The McAllister Land and Cattle Company of Ogallala? Every cattleman in the midwest has heard of their outfit."

"Oh, them." Casey's nose turned up disdainfully.

"Don't try to tell me you're not impressed by the news," Smitty persisted. "You've heard talk yourself of how old man McAllister and his son could have taken the whole Sand Hills area and acquired the biggest cattle empire in the United States during the drought years. Instead he went out of his way to help every rancher he could, even extending them credit when he couldn't afford it himself. He very nearly went under along with some of the others. Flint McAllister is his grandson."

He noticed the grudging expression of admiration on Casey's face. "Don't you remember a couple of years ago when Flint McAllister took part in that exchange program and spent a year in Australia studying their methods of ranching in the outback on—what do they call their spreads—stations?"

"I remember," Casey muttered. "It's really going to be a comedown for him to be in charge of our measly sixteen thousand acres."

"Good grief, Casey! This could be a hell of an opportunity, you know," Smitty exclaimed. "Think of how much you could learn while he's here. Why, it's rumored that his father is stepping down this winter and giving Flint complete control of the company."

"I'm not impressed!" Casey hurled her angry words at him. "I can just imagine how the great man is going to lord it over us."

"Casey, you're going to need all the help you can get—"

She forced herself to sound calmer. "The holidays are coming. I agreed to the arrangement for my dad's sake, so he wouldn't have to worry."

Smitty studied her for a long minute. "Right."

"Well, I want him home on time, and that means nothing can go wrong."

"Nothing? You'll find that life tends not to cooperate. Don't forget Murphy's Law."

She tossed her hair. "Okay, a few things around the ranch aren't working at the moment, but everything else is under control. You're looking at one girl who isn't going to be bossed around by some know-it-all."

Smitty compressed his lips grimly. It was absolutely useless arguing with her. She could be so bullheaded and obstinate that it would only lead to more harsh words. Instead he determinedly led his horse over to the trailer and loaded him up, knowing that the slightly muffled sounds indicated that Casey was doing the same.

"I'll follow you to the ranch and pick up that motor that broke down," he said curtly before climbing into the cab of his truck.

Casey nodded an angry agreement, shooting the bolt that held the trailer's loading chute in place.

Chapter Three

Flint McAllister—Flint McAllister—Flint McAllister! Casey felt if she heard that name one more time, she'd explode. The entire weekend everyone who'd visited her father at the hospital had been talking about him. Her father had become more and more pleased with the thought that this man was going to run his ranch. He seemed to take pride that someone as well known and respected as Flint McAllister was the new boss man for the Anchor Bar.

The enthusiasm of his fellow friends and ranchers added to his satisfaction. The awe and reverence in their voices when they spoke his name had disgusted Casey. They were referring to him as if he was the president of the United States, a movie star, and God all rolled into one.

Johnny had come down Sunday. He had been particularly elated by the news since it removed the feelings of guilt that had been plaguing him. Casey had been right when she had decided there was no use appealing to her older brother to prevent the new man from coming. Johnny was one hundred percent in favor of it. Even Mark had caught the contagious rush to praise this paragon called Flint McAllister. He'd bugged Casey on the drive home Sunday with their mother with all the tales he had heard about him. Her mother was the only one who noticed her silence as Casey fought to control her rising annoyance. But there was no comfort in meeting the sympathetic glance. She knew too well that Lucille Gilmore was happy about who was coming to run the Anchor Bar.

This morning Casey had been in her father's office calling to check with Smitty about the broken pump for the number ten well. It was deemed an office since it housed the ranch's records and a desk. It had been intended as a dining room, situated just off the kitchen, but it had never been used as such. It had just naturally become the ranch office where John Gilmore had installed his gun cabinet, decorated the walls with his hunting trophies, and moved in his favorite easy chair. And oh yeah, a computer—he'd given in when he saw how easy it was to run spreadsheets and keep accurate records. In recent years, an old daybed was added as the bookwork increased and her father kept late hours. He preferred his vintage rotary-dial phone, but Casey used her own.

Just as Casey had clicked her cell phone shut, her mother entered the room, her arms loaded with dust rags, mops, and polish. Casey hadn't paid much attention to her until she was halted in the doorway by her mother's words.

"There are fresh sheets and blankets on the hallway table, Casey. Would you bring them in?"

"What for?" She watched her mother remove the coverlet from the daybed.

"So I can change the bedding," her mother replied. There was a slight pause as Mrs. Gilmore looked dubiously at the exposed mattress. "On second thought, why don't you take the mattress outside and air it for me instead?"

"Sure. No problem. It only weighs five hundred pounds and I don't care that it's freezing out." Was her mother seriously expecting her to lug a giant folding mattress outside in early December? Casey wasn't going to do it.

Her sarcasm was lost on her mother, whose hand reached out in an absentminded gesture. "And you'd better lend me a hand to bring that cupboard of your grandmother's in from the bunkhouse. We'll need Sam to help with that. But you and I can manage that small dresser in the attic." Her mother's eyes drifted around the room in studied concentration as Casey slowly realized what was happening. "I think we can arrange the furniture so that it will fit in satisfactorily and still give him plenty of room for his clothes."

"You mean *he* is going to stay here in *this* room?" Casey asked. "What's wrong with the bunkhouse where all the rest of the hired help stay? Why does he have to live in the house with us?"

"Flint McAllister is not exactly hired help, Cassandra." There was a sharp reprimand in Lucille Gilmore's quiet voice. She only used Casey's given name when she was particularly upset with her daughter.

"But this is Dad's room!" Unwelcome tears pricked her eyes as Casey realized that McAllister was not only usurping her father's position but his personal office as well. Harsh words rose in her throat, only to be stopped by the pitying and reproving look in her mother's eyes.

"I thought you'd gotten over this feeling of antagonism. We're very lucky to be getting such capable help," she said firmly to her angry daughter. "And where's your Christmas spirit? Peace on earth, goodwill to—all men but one? In case you've forgotten, it's not far away."

"I still don't want him in the house—I can't stand the idea of him taking over from Dad." Casey's words were drawn through her clenched teeth.

"Cassandra Gilmore!"

The shock in her mother's tone spun Casey around and sent her speeding out the door. She was not going to hear another lecture on the paragon Flint McAllister.

She shouted to Sam at the barn that he was wanted at the house before she hopped into the cab of the blue and white pickup and slammed the door shut. As the wheels churned up the sand in response to the sudden demand for acceleration, Casey had a brief picture of Sam walking to the house porch, respectfully removing his hat as Mrs. Gilmore walked out, her hand shading her eyes while she watched Casey speed down the lane. She didn't remember turning onto the graveled road and was only half conscious of the squealing of her tires as she turned south on the highway.

Not until she reached the turnoff for the Agate Fossil Beds did her rage burn away to leave ashes of suppressed emotion. She braked the pickup to a stop near the bridge over the Niobrara River, made

a U-turn, and headed back for the ranch. Flint
McAllister could go to hell, all dressed up in one of
those beautifully tailored western suits with a fancy
white Stetson hat and kangaroo-hide boots she
imagined him in. He'd probably be wearing one of
those fancy string ties with a diamond-studded
clasp in a longhorn design, just to be extra tacky.

She'd heard about these big cattle barons before,
of their loud bragging talk about the money they'd
made and how much they'd blown in weekend ex-
cursions to Las Vegas. More than likely McAllister's
father had been glad to send him off to Australia
for a year so he wouldn't run through the family
fortune. She had known a few of those spoiled
scions of early pioneers. This man had probably
learned long ago how to throw his family name
around. It wouldn't work with her.

In her side vision, she spotted a small herd of
pronghorn antelope grazing in a pasture near the
road. She tooted her horn, watching their delicate
heads rise before they took off with bounding
leaps. Her speedometer read nearly sixty and, as
they raced alongside the fence, they still kept
abreast of her until they finally veered away. The
white, targetlike circles of their rumps were in view
for only a few seconds before they disappeared.

She kept her windows open, liking the energiz-
ing effect of the cold air. Casey was just cresting a
hill when she turned her attention back to the
highway. Suddenly there in front of her was a horse
trailer and a pickup going at a much slower speed.
She had two choices, to slam on the brakes and
hope she didn't run into it from the rear, or to pass
it. In the split second that it took her to glance

ahead to see the highway stretching clear of any
traffic save the vehicle ahead of her, Casey turned
the wheel out and stepped on the accelerator to
ensure her passing the pickup and trailer cleanly
before the next hill came up. She had no doubt in
her ability as a driver, having started her lessons
when she was nine, driving the ranch's tractor and
graduating to the pickup as soon as her legs were
long enough to reach the pedals and she could
handle the gearshift.

There was a small smile of satisfaction on her
face as she passed the pickup with plenty of room
to spare before the hill loomed before her. The
deafening roar of wind from her open windows
filled the cab, giving her an exhilarating feeling of
victory so that she didn't slacken her speed. On the
downhill slope the needle crept to eighty. Without
warning, Casey heard a sickening thud at the same
time that the steering wheel was nearly wrenched
out of her hands. A blowout! With all her strength,
she held the wheel on a straight course, removing
her foot from the accelerator and slowly applying
the brake.

The pickup finally rolled to a halt on the shoulder of the road. Her arms and legs were trembling
so badly that she couldn't move. She just rested her
head against the steering wheel, mentally chiding
herself for speeding, and at the same time trying to
cheer herself up. She sure hoped that the spare tire
was in good condition. In the next instant her door
burst open and she was staring into the angriest
pair of stormy gray eyes she had ever seen. For one
ridiculous moment she was reminded of the dark,

rolling thunderclouds that sometimes covered the Sand Hills' skies.

"You crazy, idiotic—what was the idea, going that fast? What were you trying to do, kill yourself? You damned crazy cornhuskers are a menace to every sane driver on the road!"

"Well, thanks a lot," Casey jeered, her own short temper rearing up to strike back at this jerk. "But no, I'm not hurt. It was kind of you to ask."

"It's usually the other guy that is," the man replied, undaunted by her sarcastic rejoinder. "Where's your tire jack?"

"I'm perfectly capable of changing my own tire," Casey answered, pushing her way out of the cab to reach back behind the seat for the jack. With the clanking tool in her hand, she gave him a haughty look to see if it would change his expression of arrogant amusement and mocking disbelief. Nope. She stalked around the pickup to the right front wheel.

She didn't attempt to hide her glowering expression as she heard his footsteps following her. She had the jack assembled in seconds and quickly raised the front end of the pickup truck, then began to unscrew the lug nuts holding the wheel of the flat tire in place. The first one popped loose immediately, but the second one refused to budge. Casey could feel the stranger's eyes watching her. Unwilling color crept into her cheeks as she hit it to try to knock it free. Her palm stung sharply with the blow, but the lug nut refused, despite all her hard efforts, to budge.

Before she could stop him, he had pushed her out of the way.

"I can do it!" she protested angrily.

"So I see," he said as he deftly hit the handle of the wrench and unscrewed the nut. "If you want to be useful, you can get the spare tire."

Casey's fists doubled up in anger as she went to retrieve the spare. His authoritative tone rubbed her the wrong way. By the time she returned, he had the flat tire removed and expertly rolled the spare in place. For the first time Casey had the opportunity to study the man who had forced his assistance on her.

A dark Stetson with a wide brim was set well back on his head, revealing thick brown hair interlaced with burnished red highlights. His profile was strong and masculine from the smooth forehead and straight nose to the square-cut jaw and finely honed chin. His eyebrows were dark like his hair and the left seemed to be perpetually arched. And his eyes were so dark a gray that in the shadows they nearly appeared black. His skin was deeply tanned from many hours outdoors, making a sharp contrast to the white shirt he wore under his down jacket.

Casey remembered that he had been quite tall in that brief moment that she had stood beside him, six feet or perhaps an inch or two more. Long and lean, she thought, studying the muscular spread of his back and the slim-hipped and well-worn Levis.

"There you are." He rose to his feet, went over, released the jack, and disassembled it before handing it back to her. There was the barest hint of a smile on his face and two creases that could have been called dimples on any other person. But on him, Casey felt, they emphasized the mockery in his eyes.

She watched him effortlessly place the flat tire in

the back of the pickup while she quietly stowed the jack away.

"And *you're* very welcome, too," he drawled when Casey failed to thank him for his help.

"I never asked you to help me," she retorted.

"My mistake." He touched his hat, faking respect. "I won't make it again. Drive a little slower. Next time you might not be so lucky."

Casey jumped quickly into the truck, turning the ignition on hurriedly. She grinned into the side mirror as she trod on the accelerator and drove away. Nobody, but nobody told her how to drive.

After she had put some distance between herself and the pickup and horse trailer, Casey slowed down to a more moderate speed. Not for anything would she have admitted to that infuriating cowboy that the blowout had frightened her a little. Why did it seem as if the whole world was against her sometimes?

The truck's pace when it finally turned up the lane that led to the house was considerably slower than when it had left. Casey drove it over to the ranch's fuel drums to fill the nearly depleted gas tank. Along with all their other mounting expenses, the price of gas had shot sky-high. She felt a little guilty about driving over the speed limit and wasting fuel, now that she had to keep track of paying for every drop of it.

She noticed Sam at the corral, his gentle hands calming one of the yearlings he had begun to halter break. Evidently her mother had completed all the various shiftings of furniture to prepare for the arrival of Mr. Flint McAllister. Once the tank was filled, Casey drove the truck over to the one big shade tree in the yard and parked it there out of habit. Not like there was a leaf left on it. Shep appeared from his wanderings to welcome her home with enthusiasm.

Casey had just put one foot on the porch step to enter the house when she heard the sound of another vehicle coming up their lane. For the first few minutes a dust cloud obscured it from her vision as it rounded the curve of the hill. Shep's acute hearing failed to recognize the motor's sound as any that had been to the ranch before. The long hair on his back raised up as he bravely raced forward to challenge the intruder.

Her hands moved to rest on her hips in a disgusted and angered stance as Casey recognized the pickup truck and trailing horse van. The curve of her mouth turned down. The pickup braked to a stop in front of the house and the tall stranger who had helped her change the tire hopped out, undaunted by the ferocious warning from Shep.

"It wasn't necessary for you to follow me," Casey said. "I was quite capable of making it back without your assistance."

"This is the Gilmore ranch, isn't it?" There was a husky quality to the low, baritone voice that carried a commanding tone.

"Yes, it is. But if you're looking for work, you can just climb right back in your truck and move on, because we aren't hiring," Casey replied sharply. "And if we were, we wouldn't want any drugstore cowboys."

Their two pairs of eyes clashed in silent challenge while Shep growled menacingly at the stranger. Even though there was an irritated look in the man's gray eyes, Casey was surprised to see a glint of amusement as well, as if she were a kitten trying to prevent a mountain lion from crossing her path. This stranger was nothing more than a common trespasser, Casey thought with undisguised contempt.

"Did I hear a car drive in?" her mother's voice asked a second or two before the screen door to the house swung open. Before Casey had a chance to reply, Lucille Gilmore saw the stranger standing in front of the snarling dog. Her hands clapped together sharply as she called the dog away and cast her daughter a scolding glance. The stranger politely removed his Stetson, revealing again the thick brown hair that occasionally mirrored the sun's fire.

"Mrs. Gilmore?" He stepped forward.

"Yes, yes, I am. What can we do for you?" Her mother's melodic voice instantly revealed the open-hearted friendliness that was so natural to her.

"My name is McAllister, Flint McAllister."

The announcement took both of them by surprise. But it was Casey's reaction that he was watching. Her hands slid off her hips while her squared shoulders sagged in disbelief. If her mouth had dropped open, her astonishment couldn't have been more obvious.

"We didn't expect you until the middle of the week," her mother was saying, while Casey continued staring at the stranger who bore no resemblance at all to the Flint McAllister she had imagined.

"I hope I haven't inconvenienced you."

"Not at all. I just took some homemade bread out of the oven, and the coffeepot is always on. Won't you come in?" Lucille Gilmore smiled.

"I'd like to take care of my horse first." He motioned toward the trailer. "Then I'd be happy to."

"My daughter, Cassandra, will show you where you can stable him," her mother offered, much to Casey's disgust. For one thing, her mother had used that hated given name of hers, and second, Casey wasn't interested in showing this man anything around the ranch. However, she was in no position to disagree.

Her rebellious eyes met his amused glance for a brief instant before Casey moved away from the steps toward him. The sound of the screen door closing told her that her mother had gone back into the house. Her gaze remained fixed on the ground as she walked to the rear of the trailer where the stranger Flint McAllister had already disappeared.

All the antagonism she had felt for the man McAllister before she had met him, and now for the stranger who had so arrogantly thrust his help on her, had suddenly been rolled together into one giant ball of serious dislike. Her eyes were two bright pieces of coal, throwing off dark sparks as he led his horse out of the trailer.

Any other time Casey would have fallen in love with the horse. It was a blue-black Appaloosa, with a white rump that showed the circular spots of black. Now all she could think about was that anyone could have an animal like that *if* they had the money to buy one. If she had thought about it before, Casey was sure she would have picked a horse like this for McAllister to own, an expensive mount to draw attention to himself.

"I imagine you'll want a stall to keep him in,"

were the only words she could say aloud. "Our ranch horses just run loose in the corral with a shed for shelter."

"He's a stallion. I prefer to have him penned separately," Flint McAllister replied, his tone just as short and to the point as Casey's. "A stall won't be necessary."

"Sam, our hired man, can fix up something for you." She motioned toward the barn. "He's working with some of the yearlings this morning."

The Appaloosa followed docilely at the end of the lead rope as they walked toward the building. Sam was leaning against one of the corral posts, a homemade cigarette dangling out of the corner of his mouth as he talked softly to the yearling colt standing beside him.

Casey never liked to interrupt these intimate sessions when the colt's ears were perked, hastening intently to every word that came from Sam. There was no need to let him know they were standing on the other side of the corral because Sam would already know. She glanced at Flint out of the corner of her eye, half expecting him to show impatience. He wasn't. He was watching with the same rapt attention that she usually had when the wizened cowboy performed his magic on the young horse. Finally Sam straightened and led the horse to the pasture gate, removed the lead rope, and swatted the horse on the rump as it sprang through toward the open field.

When Sam turned back toward them, Casey watched his face eagerly, anxious to see his reaction to the new boss man. Whatever Sam thought as he shook the hand extended to him after Casey's

introductions was securely hidden behind his ageless face. The meeting of the two men was over in a
matter of minutes with Sam walking away leading
the Appaloosa.

The toe of her boot dug into the sand as Casey
turned reluctantly toward the house. She had hoped
to rid herself of McAllister's company by pawning
him off on Sam. She had been sure that he wouldn't
allow Sam to care for his valuable horse without him
watching. But Flint turned with her.

"I saw your father this morning. We went over
quite a few things, but I'm going to be grateful for
your help over these next few weeks, Cassandra."

Casey gave him a malevolent glance. What was
she supposed to do, grovel at his feet for throwing
her a little bit of respect?

"Nice of you to say so." Her lips tightened. "Especially since I live here." She ignored the raised eyebrow and spoke to Sam. "Hey, tell my mother that
I'm going into Harrison to get the tire fixed. I'll
have lunch there."

Casey wheeled abruptly away. Let the others make
him welcome, she thought bitterly. She wasn't going
to; there were going to be no false words from her.
He was an interloper, unwanted and distrusted.

As she turned the truck toward the lane, she saw
him staring after her. She could see by his stance
that her rudeness had gotten to him. Yet his head
was tilted slightly to the side in what seemed like curious amusement.

Never mind that. She wasn't at all curious about
him.

* * *

Returning from town, Casey met Smitty en route to her ranch. He honked his horn and motioned toward the rear bed of his truck. She had a fleeting glimpse of a motor sitting in the back. He had evidently fixed the pump motor for the number ten well. She waved for him to follow her and set her course for the track leading off their lane to the number ten well.

"What are you looking so glum about today?" Smitty asked as he unloaded the motor to restore it to its former position.

"*He's* here," Casey said meaningfully, a serious frown marring her features.

"McAllister? Flint McAllister?" He exhaled slowly in a silent whistle as he paused in his efforts. "Now that you've met the big boss man, what do you think of him?"

"He's not big," she snorted. "He's just tall, that's all." In despair, she turned away and leaned against the pickup's fender. "Oh, Smitty, he's even worse than I imagined!"

Gently Smitty coaxed her into explaining her statement. All the while she told him about the meeting on the highway, he maintained an outward calm, his hands busy fastening the motor in place. He could hear the trembling dismay in her voice and her anger toward Flint McAllister. Smitty knew how Casey hated anyone to watch her when she succumbed to the more feminine side of her nature, treating it as a form of cowardice.

"It was just awful!" she ended in a defiant flare of temper. "He talked down to me as if I was a feather-brain without an ounce of sense. I can just imagine what he thinks of a woman my age running a ranch.

I could tell what he was all about the second he so patronizingly asked for my help."

"Now, how do you know that's how he felt?" Smitty accused, coming to stand beside her. "Why can't you accept the fact that the man wants your help? You're the one who has a paranoid inferiority complex."

"Spare me the armchair psychology, cowboy. I do not!"

"Then why do you take every comment so personally?" Smitty smiled to take the sting out of his words.

"That's just not true! How did this situation come about in the first place? Because I wasn't a man!" Casey trembled in anger. "That's why Dad had to hire someone else to come out here—to please that old bank manager who doesn't think I'm capable of running a ranch! And McAllister agrees with them. I can tell."

"You're not exactly open-minded." Smitty shook his head in despair. "Take me back and introduce me to this tyrant who's taken over your ranch."

"With pleasure."

But Casey didn't have an opportunity to do so. When they returned to the ranch, Mrs. Gilmore informed Casey, a little sharply, that Mr. McAllister had gone on a self-conducted tour of the property.

"It was really your place to show him around, Casey," her mother reprimanded.

Despite the rebellious glint in her eyes, Casey did lower her gaze guiltily. Lucille Gilmore's gentle reproof made pinpricks of discomfort at her childish behavior. Although Casey hated to admit she had been in error, she did manage a mumbled apology.

"You don't need to apologize to me," Mrs. Gilmore said, "but to Mr. McAllister."

"When will he be back?" Casey asked grimly.

"I told him supper would be at six."

"Well, I can't stay that long," Smitty stated. "I may stop back this evening to meet Casey's new boss man." A lopsided grin was turned teasingly on Casey, who wrinkled her nose in answer. "Walk me to the truck?"

"What's he look like?" Mark persisted, hanging over the side of the manger where Casey was milking their cow, MooMaw. She liked to keep in practice and MooMaw hated being hooked up to a milking machine, regarding it as beneath her bovine dignity.

"Oh, I don't know. He's tall, probably six foot one or two, taller than Johnny." She tried to stem her growing exasperation over her brother's questions. "Good-looking in a conceited way. What does it matter what he looks like?"

Mark shrugged off her question. "How old is he?"

"How should I know? I didn't ask for his vital statistics."

"Ah, come on. Take a guess?"

"In his early thirties, maybe." Casey slapped the cow on its side as she moved the bucket away and rose from her stool. "Been everywhere. Done everything. Or so everyone seems to think."

"He sounds awesome." Mark smiled at the answering grimace on his sister's face when she handed him the milk pail.

"Good grief, Mark, you act as if he's Brad Pitt or something! He's just the arrogant son of a wealthy rancher who's playing at being a cowboy," Casey retorted. The sound of a vehicle in the yard was accompanied by Shep's frantic barking. "That's probably the great man now."

Mark started for the door, slowing his pace when Casey reminded him not to spill the milk. She dawdled in the barn as long as she could, fussing with the horses that Mark had already grained before finally heading toward the house. It was nearly six o'clock. And when her mother said supper would be ready at six, it was. Her delaying tactics had evidently worked, for when she finally stepped into the kitchen there was no sign of Flint McAllister. Casey quickly set to work, washing her hands before helping her mother place the hot dishes on the table. Seconds later Mark walked into the room, directly followed by Flint McAllister.

Casey took pains to keep her glance from sliding toward him. Inside she felt her anger, frustration, and self-pity warring against each other. Yet all her senses were keenly tuned to his presence. The scent of soap and shaving lotion seemed to rise from the crisp white shirt that contrasted with the darkness of his hair still glistening wetly from a shower. She heard the scrape of the chair as he seated himself at the table and the clear, rich tone of his voice as he patiently, but interestedly, answered Mark's questions.

When all the dishes were on the table, Casey had no option but to seat herself. The only vacant chair was on his right. She managed a polite smile vaguely in his direction, knowing full well that the falseness showed in her eyes. His own gray eyes captured her gaze before he nodded condescendingly in acknowledgment. There was an answering aggressive thrust to her chin as she passed the potatoes to him. Casey was sure her silence didn't go unnoticed by anyone at the table, but her brother Mark's questions were endless, filling the void that she created.

"Tell us about Australia," Mark urged, shoveling a large portion of potatoes onto his plate despite the reproving glance from his mother. "What are the cattle ranches like down there?"

"The two ranches I visited were both in central Australia, the outback," Flint answered amiably. "The land there is basically flat and arid with little vegetation. The actual work isn't much different from what we do here. Mostly it was a matter of adjusting to the different terms they use. Ranches are called 'stations.' Roundups are called 'musters' and because of the reverse seasons, they take place in the spring instead of the fall. The biggest difference is that they don't finish their cattle like we do on corn and grains. Consequently when you order a steak, the meat isn't as tender as you're accustomed to here in the States, although it does have a good flavor."

"Did you see a lot of kangaroos?" Mark asked.

Casey glanced at Flint with a look that plainly dared him to continue monopolizing the conversation with his exploits. His jaw tightened perceptibly at her gaze even as he turned back toward Mark with an indulgent and, Casey was forced to admit, gentle expression.

"Yes, a lot of them, but they're considered a nuisance. There's also wild turkey and wild pigs. The pigs that I saw looked plump enough for a barbecue, but Benedict, the station owner, assured me that they were no good to eat." There was no mistaking the fascinated look of interest on Mark's face and Flint continued, "The most unwelcome form of wild life is the dingo."

"That's a breed of wild dog, right?" Mark interrupted, eager to show off his own knowledge, however meager it was. His attention was all on Flint.

"They breed with domestic dogs, and it makes them way too intelligent and hard to catch. They travel in packs, roaming wide areas, attacking calves and weaker stock. You could compare them in nuisance value to the coyote, although a dingo is much more vicious and fiercer in combat."

The meal seemed to pass swiftly as Flint McAllister continued to relate happenings during the year he was in Australia. In spite of herself, Casey discovered she was just as interested as her mother and brother. During the short space of time it took to consume their supper, she had learned more about Australia from Flint's comparisons to life as she knew it in Nebraska than she had ever learned in a geography class. But she maintained an expression of studied disinterest.

"Well, Mrs. Gilmore," Flint said, draining the last of his coffee from the cup, "that was a delicious meal."

"This family operates on first names, Mr. McAllister," Lucille Gilmore inserted, a genuine smile lighting her face. "Call me Lucille."

"Then you'd better forget the Mr. McAllister and call me Flint." Casey watched his smile transform his face from mocking sureness to devastatingly charming good looks. "Since this is my first night here and I might not ever get a night with no paperwork, I'd like to show my appreciation for the meal by helping with the dishes."

"I take care of that for my mom." With this statement, Casey broke her self-imposed silence.

"And she hates every minute of it!" Mark laughed.

His remark was all too accurate, but it was a chore that Casey's conscience had insisted she undertake to make up for her lack of help in other household duties.

"In that case, she'd probably be glad of some help for a change." For all the lazy regard in Flint's eyes when they rested on her, Casey could feel the piercing challenge in his gaze. She was ready to refuse any assistance from him, but the picture of him in front of a sink full of dishes was too beautiful to deny. The thought of him with one of her mother's decorative aprons tied around his waist brought an audacious twinkle out of the depths of her dark eyes.

The dishes were started in silence with Flint electing to wash since Casey would know where the dishes belonged once they were dried. Strangely enough, Flint didn't look in the least out of place standing in front of the sink. He seemed to sense Casey's desire to keep a businesslike distance between them.

"I noticed the hay field in the west section will need fertilizing come spring." He finally broke the silence.

"Okay. Put that on the to-do list," Casey agreed stiffly, not wanting to agree with him on anything. "We did do that field the second week of May last year."

"Your plane is out of commission. I'd like to get an aerial view of the ranch so I can get a better idea of the layout." Casey felt his glance rest on her for a minute. "Would it be possible to borrow a plane from the neighbors?"

"I'm sure the Smiths would lend me theirs. I don't know how they'd feel about lending it to a stranger, though." She enjoyed getting her little dig in even if it didn't seem to penetrate his thick skin.

"I didn't intend to fly it myself. Your mother told me you were just as much at home in a plane as in a saddle." The gray eyes met her startled glance with only the slightest betrayal of amusement. "I can't get a good overview of the land if I'm behind the controls."

"I see." She saw all right. She saw that she was going to be at close quarters with that man for two or three hours. And with growing irritation, she also knew that his inspection of the ranch would be very thorough. "When did you want me to arrange this tour?"

"Tomorrow."

Casey's hand paused as she started to withdraw the meat platter from the rinsing water. He certainly wasn't going to give her a chance to get used to the idea.

"I'll check with them to see if their plane will be free. They might have something scheduled."

"They might," Flint agreed, but Casey could almost visualize him winking, though he didn't.

She had been attempting to stall and she was uncomfortably aware that he knew it. The damp towel refused to wipe over the already dry platter again, its dragging feel bringing Casey back to the work at hand. On tiptoe, she stretched her arms toward the third shelf of the cupboard above the sink. Holding the platter in one hand, she tried to push the bowls out of the way with the other. A group of plastic lids cascaded down on her head just as she pulled the glass bowls too close to the edge and they started to fall. Casey leaned heavily against the sink, trying to gain all the extra inches she could, angrily aware that her shirttail was dragging in the rinsing water. As she was trying to figure out how to set the platter down and still rescue the bowls, she glimpsed Flint reacting to her predicament.

His superior height allowed him to reach the third shelf easily. But to do so, he had to stretch his lean frame over the top of Casey's head. The muscular hardness of his body pressing against her brought an incredible rigid tenseness as she tried to control the tingling of her body where it came in contact with him. From outside there was the slamming of a door and Mark's jubilant cry of welcome.

"Hey, Smitty! I figured you'd be over tonight," Mark called in a voice that rang all too clearly in the kitchen. "The new dude's giving you some competition. He's already in the kitchen helping Casey with the dishes."

The bowls had been rescued and the platter was in place behind them. Casey's face had turned an amazing shade of red as Flint turned his speculating gaze on her and stepped back. She had one fleeting thought of running out on the porch and strangling her loud-mouthed brother before she chose instead to pick up the lids scattered around the floor.

"I take it your boyfriend is here," Flint stated, returning to the sink and the remaining pan.

"Yeah, that's Smitty," Casey tried to say with some degree of composure. She didn't succeed, probably because there was too much free-floating testosterone in the air. His very masculine virility was one of the most annoying things about him. "Our nearest neighbor."

"The one you're going to borrow the plane from?"

"Yes."

"Good. We can find out if it's available."

The man didn't waste any time, Casey thought crossly. "Mind if he sits down and has pie and coffee with us first?"

"Not at all." Flint gave her a look that was the equivalent of a pat on the head. "Wouldn't mind some myself. What are my choices?"

She smirked at him. "Not humble pie, that's for sure."

He let the jab go by without responding. "I'm a traditionalist. I'll take apple. If your mom made it, it has to be good."

Casey stiffened. It was harder than she thought to get under his skin. "Okay. We have apple. Give me a minute." She got everything back into the high cabinet as Flint nodded to her mother, who came into the kitchen just as he was going out.

Lucille beamed at him. "Thanks for helping, Flint."

"No problem."

Casey could hear his cheerful, satisfied whistle as he headed, she guessed, toward the living room.

"Isn't he something?" her mother said.

"If you say so."

"You're determined not to like him, I can see that." Her mother seemed disappointed.

"It's not that simple."

"Hmm. Maybe I don't even want to know why he gets on your nerves. Now let's get the pies cut and served up," her mother said.

She went to the old-fashioned pie safe, which Casey's great-grandfather had built back in the day. It was framed with honey pine and its insert panels were of pierced tin with screening behind it. Her grandmother had done the piercing as a girl, using nothing more than a nail and a hammer to make whimsical designs of hearts and stars.

Grandma Gilmore had always bragged that the pie safe was flyproof and dogproof, but not man-proof. The safe, which an antique dealer in a nearby town said was a valuable piece of real Americana, had been handed down in the family, along with recipes, including Casey's favorite, shoofly pie.

Lucille turned the wooden latch and took out an apple pie and a plum kuchen, made from her mother's recipe, which had been handed down from the German ancestors who'd settled in this part of Nebraska.

"I want you to be nice to him," she said to her daughter without looking directly at her.

"Whatever you say, Mom."

Casey could see her mother frown and regretted her tone of voice. Her mother had enough to worry about without dealing with her daughter's overreaction to Flint's arrival.

Her mother set the pie and kuchen down on the kitchen table, then opened a drawer looking for a knife. She found it and a triangular pie server, and began cutting the pie into perfect segments.

"There's a reason for it, Casey," she said softly. "Besides that you seem to have forgotten your manners."

"Okay," Casey said. "What is it?"

"I called the insurance company about getting pre-approval for your father's physical therapy."

"He's not out of bed yet, is he?" Casey asked.

"No, he's not," her mother sighed. "I'm planning ahead."

"Well, tell me what's going on."

Her mother set aside the pie and began to slice up the kuchen. Domestic tasks usually settled her nerves, but it didn't seem to be working. Casey could see that her mother was making an effort to keep her hands steady.

"It looks like they will only pay a fraction of the amount, and he's going to need months of physical therapy to make an optimum recovery."

"If they deny the claim, we can file an appeal."

Her mother shook her head. "Yes, we can, but how do we pay for the therapy in the meantime?"

Casey thought it over, not sure how to answer that. "Have you talked this over with Dad?"

"No. Absolutely not. And I don't want you to bring it up. This is between you and me, Casey. Mark's too young and as for Johnny—well, I don't feel I can confide in him about money matters."

Between you and me. Even though the issue was troublesome, Casey liked knowing that her mother was turning to her to help solve the problem, and not Flint McAllister.

"We'll figure something out when the time comes. I guess we could sell some land—"

"No." Her mother straightened up and set aside the knife. "That's the last thing your father would want, and we're not going to do it."

"Mom, what do you want me to do? There aren't any jobs out here in the sticks, so leaving the ranch is not an option."

"I just don't know, honey." Her mother looked at her sadly. "But we have to make sure everything goes smoothly from now on. Try to get along with Flint. Maybe that's all you can do right now."

Casey blew out a frustrated breath. "Okay. I'll try. The one thing I want more than anything is to have Dad come home for Christmas and see that we're doing okay. Maybe even better than okay."

"Well, then, we can agree on that," her mother said.

Chapter Four

Casey had made a concentrated effort to monopolize Smitty and the conversation later that evening. She had deliberately steered the subject toward people and places that were known only to them, thus ignoring Flint McAllister. But Smitty had either been obtuse or stubborn, because he had continually switched it back to ranching. Casey had sat back in fuming silence while they discussed seed bulls, irrigation, the skyrocketing cost of feed grains, and the weather predicted for the winter. Heavy snow would cause the usual problems, but without it, there would be a high likelihood of drought.

And Flint had given her no opportunity to ask permission to use the Smiths' plane. One politely worded question was all it had taken, and Smitty had volunteered almost ecstatically. Afterward, when Smitty and Casey had been left alone by the discreet Mr. McAllister, she'd gotten on Smitty's case about it.

"The way you acted when you told him he could have the plane anytime he wanted it was positively disgusting," Casey had declared. "I could almost see you having a plaque made that says 'Flint McAllister sat here.'"

"Oh, Casey," Smitty had moaned in exasperation, "why do you keep on making mountains out of molehills? Our plane has been at your disposal ever since yours went on the blink. McAllister didn't know that, since you obviously didn't tell him. All I did was say he could use ours if he needed it."

Casey snorted at Smitty's statement. It had become apparent that she was alone in her stand against Flint McAllister. In one day she had seen the defection of her younger brother. She was quite sure that her mother had fallen under the charm of Flint's rugged good looks. And now Smitty had joined the throng of admirers.

Two fleecy white clouds drifted above the Cessna aircraft while Casey stole a glance at the man seated in the passenger seat. She immediately looked into a pair of gray eyes that had been watching her grow more sullen as each of her thoughts had grown more depressing. They had been flying for more than an hour now.

"What else did you want to see?" she asked, refusing to be disgruntled by the fact that he had been staring at her.

"Let's take another run past that pasture in the south section. Make it a little lower this time."

Casey nodded her compliance and expertly put the plane in a sideslip before completing her turn and leveling out eight hundred feet above the ground. Flying was one of her loves. There was exhilaration in feeling the plane respond to her lightest touch, as quickly as a well-trained reining horse. Plus there was a sensation of being detached from the world. In a small plane, there was a serenity that couldn't be duplicated on the ground.

"You're an excellent pilot," Flint told her.

"I know," Casey answered calmly and without conceit.

"Your father told me you're almost indispensable. And he doesn't strike me as the kind of man who would say that if he didn't believe it."

"No, I don't think he would," Casey agreed, feeling a warm glow of pride at the high compliment from her father. "There's the mesa," she pointed out, crabbing into the wind to hold a straight course. "The pasture's just on the other side."

"He seemed to think you could run the ranch quite efficiently by yourself," Flint continued, now gazing out his window at the Sand Hills below.

"I could." There was determination in the lift of her chin as she met his brief glance squarely. "I thought you wanted to inspect the ranch?"

"Partly."

"And what else?" she persevered.

"I wanted to get to know you better, Cassandra." His voice was nonchalant, but there was a seriousness in his expression that told Casey being with her was the main objective of the trip as far as he was concerned. "I had the distinct impression that if I tried to corner you at the ranch you would have managed to escape just as you did yesterday." He glanced briefly around the interior of the plane. "You must admit that you can hardly walk away from me here."

Casey's lips tightened and she forgot her promise

to her mother to be nice to him. "Let's get this straight, Mr. McAllister. I didn't want you here on this ranch. It wasn't my idea, and it wasn't really my father's. You're here because the bank wanted a *man* in charge." There was a loaded emphasis on the word "man." "To be totally honest, I didn't like you very much before I met you, and now that I have—"

"You still don't," he finished for her. "Your actions make your feelings pretty damn clear. But I'm here. And as they say in war, I'm here for the duration."

"Tough luck for both of us."

"If that's going to be your attitude, we're going to be in for a rough month and a half." Flint eyed her questioningly. "Or you can accept the fact that I'm merely a temporary stand-in for your father."

You could never fill his shoes, Casey thought.

"It's really up to you, Cassandra. You can treat me as an outsider or a fellow rancher, much like your neighbors, the Smiths. In either case, I'd like to remind you of that old Indian saying, 'Don't judge a man until you've walked ten miles in his moccasins.'"

Her hands clenched the controls. "Wow. That's deep." She railed inwardly at his ten-cent philosophizing. Part of her could recognize the truth of his statement, but she still resented the need for any conversation with him.

"As you say, we're both going to have to make the best of a bad situation," she agreed through gritted teeth and a tight smile. "Should I head the plane back to the ranch?"

Flint nodded, his keen gaze missing none of the emotion she was imparting.

"And another thing," Casey added. "From now on you either call me 'Hey, you' or Casey, but don't you ever call me Cassandra again. I hate that name."

The doctor had assured them that John Gilmore was progressing very well. And Casey had to admit that he was in excellent spirits. After Sunday morning church, Flint had volunteered to drive Casey, her mother, and Mark down to Scottsbluff, and if Mrs. Gilmore had no objections, he would drive on into Ogallala to visit his parents and pick the Gilmores up that same evening after visiting hours at the hospital ended. Her mother had quickly fallen in with the plan.

There was more color in her father's cheeks, Casey decided as they walked into the room. His dark eyes sparkled brightly as he grasped his wife's hand and drew her down to lightly brush her lips in greeting. The whispered exchanges of "I missed you" brought an immediate feeling of family warmth to Casey, but it didn't stop her from glancing at Flint McAllister to see if he had heard the exchange. He had accompanied them all to the room as a matter of courtesy and to look in on John Gilmore.

The solemnity of his expression assured Casey that he had overheard. Against her will, she had to appreciate the fact that he was remaining in the background until the family had a chance to exchange hellos, even though he must have been impatient to greet John Gilmore so he could leave to see his own family.

"You're looking much better, Mr. Gilmore." Flint firmly shook the hand extended to him.

It irked Casey to hear her father addressed so

respectfully, even though she knew it was irrational to feel that way. She would have much preferred that Flint adopt a superior attitude, one that wouldn't have earned the look of approval in her father's eyes.

"I'm feeling much better," he acknowledged. "And the name is John, Flint."

"I'm on my way to visit my parents." Flint smiled after nodding his acceptance of a more familiar attitude between them. "I wanted to let you know everything's running smoothly at the ranch, except for a few long faces over your absence."

His glance around the family served as a further explanation of his words, although Casey felt that his gaze rested a little longer on her than the others. But she refused to feel guilty.

"I appreciate your stopping by. I know you must be anxious to be on your way"—John Gilmore smiled broadly—"so I won't keep you with endless questions. I'll save them for Casey." Her father winked at her.

But Casey had difficulty meeting Flint's gaze and the dubious look in his gray eyes at her being able to give him an unbiased account.

With a casual statement that he'd be back about eight, Flint left. The promised questions from her father didn't come, because Flint had no more than left when the Smiths arrived.

"I've been trying to make up my mind why Casey wore a dress today." Her father laughed heartily as he shook Smitty's hand. "At first I thought it was for me. Then I decided it was for McAllister. Now you've turned up, Smitty, and I'm thoroughly confused."

Casey colored slightly in anger as she glanced

down at the maroon flowered dress she was wearing. It was styled after the dresses worn in the forties with a wide rounded collar and short sleeves that nearly reached her elbow, only the skirt was much shorter than the original version. The style was cute, but not the color, which was too dull.

"I wore the dress to church this morning, Dad," Casey stated. "You know how Reverend Carver frowns on pants."

"Oh, that's the reason. Is he still that old-fashioned?" But the twinkle in his eyes teased her outrageously. Casey was furious with herself for failing to respond with the same humor. But even in jest, it was disgusting for her father to think that she might have worn a dress to impress Flint McAllister. She was the only one who took more than passing notice of the remark and the subject was dropped fast, much to Casey's relief.

Her father was very well known and liked, so Sundays brought him an abundance of visitors. There was a constant shuffling of people in the room to conform to the hospital's limit on the number of visitors at a time. The only one who was excluded from the shifting was Lucille Gilmore. And John Gilmore's hand kept his wife firmly by his side throughout.

Just as the Smiths began to take their leave late in the afternoon, Johnny Gilmore arrived. Smitty immediately took advantage of the situation and cadged a ride home with Casey so that he could spend some time with Johnny. The three—Casey, Johnny and Smitty—ended up going to dinner together for old times' sake and for a thorough catching up on present news.

"Tell me about this new man," Johnny urged

nearly halfway through their meal. "Dad's filled me in on his background, but what's he really like?"

"He certainly isn't the ogre that Casey painted him up to be." Smitty cast a disparaging glance across the table to her before turning back to Johnny. "Flint's really a terrific guy. I've been over there several times this week. I swear to God, Johnny, I don't think there's any new technique in ranching today that he can't intelligently discuss the pros and cons about. But he's not pushy or showy with his knowledge, just matter-of-fact. McAllister never talks down to you, either." Smitty paused, eyeing Casey hesitantly before he continued. "He's not totally business, though. You get the impression that he's been around socially, if you know what I mean."

"Is he good-looking?" Johnny asked with a knowing smile and teasing glance at his sister.

"If you like that type," Casey answered in a suitably bored voice.

"Don't you believe her." Smitty laughed. "He's one of those lean, rugged dudes that looks like he just got off a motorcycle or a horse. You can bet he has any number of girls just waiting for him to crook his finger."

"You're disgusting!" Casey exclaimed angrily. "The next thing you know you'll be bragging about your conquests. I can believe that Flint McAllister wouldn't have much respect for a woman's reputation, but you two should."

"What did we do to earn that outburst?" Johnny looked at her with considerable amusement.

"Don't mind her." Smitty shook his head. "All you have to do is mention that guy's name and she loses her temper. The first time she saw him she was speeding down the highway and had a blowout. He read her the riot act. Her hair's been up ever since."

"That has nothing to do with it!" Casey protested weakly as she threw her napkin on the table. She fumbled in her purse, finally extracting some bills that she passed to Smitty. "I'm going back up to see Dad. Here's the money for my dinner. You two can stay here as long as you like!"

Flint arrived promptly at eight to take them all home. He made no comment about Smitty riding home with them, just nodding a hello as he held the back door of the SUV open for Smitty, Casey, and Mark. Then he helped Mrs. Gilmore into the front seat beside him before sliding behind the wheel himself. Casey's mother immediately engaged him in a conversation about his visit with his parents, their voices not loud enough to include the three in the backseat. That suited Casey just fine.

Somehow she had been seated beside the window directly behind the driver with Smitty in the middle and Mark on the other side. Smitty was strangely silent, Casey thought. Mark pulled his iPod out of his pocket, turned it on low volume, and leaned back against the door, holding an earbud in with his finger to hear better. She gazed out the window at the orange sun hovering over the horizon. She felt discontented and couldn't figure out why. Her eyes roved back to the man in front of her, examining the brown hair curling near the collar of his blue suit coat. She felt Smitty's arm slide around to settle on her shoulders. It was a warm, comfortable feeling to have his arm around her and she turned, a slow pleasant smile lighting her face.

Good ol' Smitty, Casey thought, taking his hand that

rested on her shoulder and bringing it to her lips where she brushed the tips of his fingers. For some reason probably only known to her subconscious mind, her gaze turned to the rearview mirror above the front dash. Dark, angry thunderclouds from Flint's reflection met her gaze. She was stunned by the expression she saw. Almost immediately her mother said something undecipherable to him and the look in his eyes was quickly veiled as he turned to answer her. The disapproval of his look at the innocent caress brought an equally potent reaction from Casey as she rebelliously snuggled closer to Smitty. Several minutes later she peeped through her lashes, her head resting comfortably on Smitty's shoulder. His eyes, as they briefly met hers, were a lighter shade of gray and remarkably indifferent.

The warmth of Smitty's arms and the darkness of the coming night finally lulled Casey into a state of semisleep. Not until the steady rhythm of the car slackened its pace did she become aware of her surroundings.

"Did you want me to run you on home, Smitty?" Flint half turned in the seat.

"I'll . . . I'll drive him on home from the house." Casey stifled a yawn while straightening in her seat.

"It's after ten now. We were going to get an early start in the morning to get started on some repairs around here. Gotta batten down for winter. Sooner or later it's going to get here." His tone sounded casual enough, but there was just enough doubt in it to upset Casey.

"Don't worry. I've stayed out later than this and still got up at the crack of dawn." The disguised criticism woke Casey completely.

"Suit yourself," he said.

They had made the turn on to the graveled lane to the ranch house. In minutes the SUV was halted beneath the yard light. The good nights were said speedily as Casey kissed her mother, spared Mark a cheery wish for a nice night, and smiled stiffly at Flint before she slid behind the driver's seat so recently vacated by him.

"See that she drives carefully." Flint raised a one-finger salute to Smitty. His dismissive gaze rested briefly on Casey.

Three-quarters of an hour later she was back. Except for the front porch light, the house looked dark. As quietly as she could, Casey crept into the house. There was a sliver of light showing beneath the office door now serving as Flint's bedroom and working quarters. One of the floorboards under the linoleum creaked loudly as she attempted to sneak past. Immediately the room was bathed in light, except where Flint's silhouette blocked it.

"You didn't have to wait up for me." She tried to sound casual, but that wasn't the reason her cheeks flooded with a red stain. It was the way his eyes studied her face so thoroughly, as if Smitty's kisses had been marked on her lips with indelible ink.

"I didn't." The muscles in his jaws twitched. "Okay, that's not true. Yes, I sort of did. I've seen the way you drive. Besides, I had paperwork to catch up on."

"Your concern is touching. But hey, guess what—you're not my dad or my big brother. And I'm a big girl." His unwelcome attention to her made her uneasy.

"Sorry. Didn't mean to make you feel like you weren't."

She lingered in the doorway, despite her annoyance with him, glancing at the spreadsheet on the computer monitor. "Can't read that from here. How are we doing? Everything adding up okay?"

"Yeah. Someone's been doing a good job of keeping current on the data entry."

"That would be me."

He only nodded. "Doesn't surprise me. You're good at a lot of things, evidently."

Casey couldn't figure out whether his remark was sincere, or just another pat on the head.

"So long as we stay in the black and don't miss a payment to the bank, we'll manage." Then she thought of what her mother had said about the possible difficulties with her father's medical insurance. Those forms were in a password-protected file, along with the rest of the family's personal information.

So long as Flint McAllister stuck to the costs of feed, maintenance, and repair work, and kept his nose out of the Gilmores' personal lives, hers in particular, she just might be able to deal with the man from Ogallala.

She almost wanted to confide in him. Strike that, she thought, annoyed with herself.

"So," he asked casually. "Got your Christmas shopping done?"

With what money? she wanted to reply. He came from a rich family and he probably thought everyone headed for Neiman Marcus and snapped up the latest in gem-encrusted whatevers for presents. But all she said was, "No."

"I figured you'd be heading for Omaha and the big malls to take care of that."

She shook her head. "I'm going to be knitting socks for everyone this year."

He looked a little baffled. "Okay, I'm willing to believe it, but—"

She folded her arms across her chest and gave him a belligerent glare. "But what?"

"You really don't look that domestic. It's hard to imagine you with knitting needles, clicking away in a corner by the fire."

"I just learned," she lied. Actually, Casey couldn't knit to save her life. Her first attempts were still up in the attic, a couple of cast-on rows that were meant to be scarves attached to snarled skeins of yarn that she'd abandoned. "We were planning to keep Christmas low-key this year."

"Oh. Why is that?"

"Well, we're not sure that my dad's going to be home in time—" She stopped herself when she saw the look of sympathy in his eyes.

"He will be, Casey."

She was alarmed by the teary feeling that his quiet reassurance evoked in her. "How do you know? You're not his doctor."

"Obviously." The one wry word didn't sound superior, just kind. "But John Gilmore has a fighting spirit." He looked at her warmly. "Which you have inherited."

Casey was at a loss for words, but not for long. "Think so? Then it's probably best if you stay out of my way, and I'll stay out of yours."

"Huh? Do you mind if I ask where that came from? I don't think I did anything to piss you off, if you'll pardon my French."

"Guess what," she snapped. "I've heard bad words before. And I can cuss a blue streak if I want to."

"I don't doubt it." There was a smile playing around the corners of his mouth. "I guess I got to see you on good behavior at the hospital and the church."

She gave him a curt nod, wondering why he had the ability to annoy her so easily. She reminded herself again of her mother's words. *Try to get along with him, Casey.* She was trying. Oh, how she was trying.

But it was hard to see him in her dad's chair, in charge.

"You still haven't said what I did to make you angry."

"And I'm not going to," she replied immediately.

Flint shook his head in a mixture of annoyance and exasperation. "Okay. Don't." He gave her one last, long, searching look before he half turned to glance at the monitor. The spreadsheet was gone, replaced by a screensaver of a flying cow. "Was that your idea?"

"Yes."

"Funny," he said. "Well, I have work to do. See you around the ranch, kid."

Casey left in a huff and stomped up the stairs as she heard him close the door to her dad's study.

Chapter Five

The day had been sunny but freezing all the same. Casey didn't think it had climbed over thirty-two degrees Fahrenheit until almost midday. She sighed heavily, wondering if it was the chilliness or the futility of her own anger that had sapped her self-confidence. She turned the leather band on her wrist to look at her watch. If it was any consolation, it was only four o'clock, and they were getting through the tedious process of preparing for winter's blasts. She rubbed the back of her neck, stiff with the tension that had been building up for three days.

In previous years she had enjoyed the time between fall and winter, hard work and all. Pumpkin season had come and gone, and so had Thanksgiving. In another week, they could drive out to the Christmas tree farm and cut their own.

The scents and smells of the season were her favorites, from mulled cider on the back of the stove for whoever wanted a cup, to her mother's spice-rich goodies. As far as Casey was concerned, there wasn't a more pleasing aroma than the smell of a fire in the hearth on the wind somewhere. But this December— her lips pressed firmly together—this December she hadn't had time for such small pleasures.

All because of Flint McAllister, who had gone from fake-friendly to what he really was: an autocrat. Every order he had given had grated her nerves until they were raw. It didn't matter what she had been doing, she had felt his eyes watching her, ready to pounce on the slightest showing of ineptitude. But she had shown him. She had been up and about before anyone else, stayed later in the fields and outbuildings than anyone else, and every aching muscle in her body could attest to it. Now all she wanted to do was get away. Her legs were weary as she climbed the front porch steps.

"Mom!" She pushed open the screen door into the kitchen.

"Right here, dear." Lucille Gilmore turned from the stove to her daughter. "Are you all done? You certainly look exhausted."

"Would you throw some food in a bag for me? I'm going down to the pond." Casey tried to put lightness in her voice, only to have the frayed edges show. That was her thinking place. Even if it was mostly frozen over, she could still summon up how it looked in warm weather and take herself away from the bleakness of an early winter with no real snow yet. In summer, the pond was lush, surrounded by rustling cottonwoods. She'd loved their big, heart-shaped leaves, which she'd thought of using for valentines to boys she'd had secret crushes on. In fall, the changing colors of the greenery around the pond had stirred her soul.

Her mother studied her thoughtfully. "Yes, of course I will." More gently, "You still haven't reconciled yourself to Flint yet, have you?"

Casey glanced guiltily at her mother. Parents had no right to be able to read their children's minds so well. Instead of replying, she announced that she was going up to her room to change.

When she returned downstairs there was a paper bag sitting on the table and a thermos of cocoa beside it. A tight smile curved Casey's lips at her mother's undemanding thoughtfulness. She hurried out the door to her already saddled horse, carrying the food and hot drink and a pad to put on the cold ground, just in case her saddle blanket wasn't enough.

Later, along the sandy shoreline of the small pond, Casey set up her camp, her horse tethered in the grass nearby. The stones from previous fires were still gathered in their protective circle around the darkened ashes. Dry twigs and branches from the cottonwood trees lay alongside. In a few minutes she had a small fire started and was sitting on her saddle blanket, her knees drawn up close to her chest so her chin could rest on them. Her eyes burned with bitter tears of unshed frustration. She couldn't admire the hawk circling in the brilliant blue sky, looking for a rabbit to fatten up on before his long migration south.

She wasn't going to give in to these childish tears, Casey vowed. Even as she sniffed back a sob, she swore anew that Flint McAllister was not going to get under her skin. But it wasn't really a matter of him so much as it was that she felt she was standing alone against him.

With a groan of irritation, Casey heard the sound of a horse approaching. *If Mark's followed me here,* she thought, *I'll brain him! He should be out trailing after his hero.* She rubbed her eyes quickly to wipe away the water that had gathered.

"Catch anything?" It wasn't Mark. It was Flint.

Inside her there was an explosion of emotion she didn't understand as she bounded to her feet.

"No. It's November. Most critters that swim or hop are down in the mud trying to stay warm."

"Sounds like fun," he said dryly.

"How come you followed me?" Casey asked. She hadn't expected to see him and didn't want to.

"I saw the smoke from your fire. I had no idea you were out here, so the first thing that occurred to me was that there might have been a grass fire started." The tightly controlled voice should have warned Casey, but it didn't. And neither did the muscle twitching along the side of his jaw. "It happens, you know. We haven't had snow yet."

"I'm aware of the danger, believe me. When you saw it wasn't a grass fire, you could have ridden home again." Her whole body trembled suddenly. Whether it was from the cold feeling of standing up after being curled into a nice, warm, sulky ball, or his presence, she couldn't say.

She was conscious of him striding toward her, but not until he got close did she see the anger in his face. His eyes resembled the hard, gray stone of his namesake and looked equally capable of throwing off sparks.

She met his challenging look. But she didn't know how to answer his unexpected question.

"Do you see that?"

Casey's eyes followed his pointing finger, unwillingly obeying the uncompromising voice. She stared blankly at the thistlelike plant at her feet and, at its top, a withered blossom that had once been white.

"That?" She stared again at the flower that except for its whiteness resembled a crumpled poppy.

"Go and pick the blossom for me," Flint ordered.

"Are you crazy?" She stared at him unbelievingly. "It's practically dead. I'm not going to put it in my buttonhole for decoration."

"I wasn't going to ask you to. Just making a point, Casey."

"So what? That's only a prickle poppy. There's thorns all over the stem." Casey didn't like the hard line of his jaw or the feeling that the lean, muscular body towering above her was barely held in check, but she didn't back down from her belligerent stand.

"And I've had to put up with your thorns for ten days, my little prickle poppy called Casey. I didn't ask for this job any more than you asked for your father to be injured. But I'm here and I'm going to stay here."

Flint hadn't stepped back. But it wasn't his proximity that was causing the shiver of fear. It was the quiet way he was talking.

"And I'm counting the days until you're gone, too," she retorted, her voice cracking ever so slightly.

"Your father may have taught you plenty about ranching, but it's obvious that he never bothered to teach you any manners." He made a gesture of disgust as he turned away.

"Don't you speak that way about my father!"

Casey reached out to detain him. The tears that had been burning her eyes now began to cloud her vision. "He's the best dad in the world. I'd do anything for him and he'd do anything for me."

"That's where you're wrong, Casey." Flint stared at her with uncomfortable coldness. "You're too selfish to do anything for him."

"That's a lie!" Her vehement denial ended in a gasp at his audacity.

"Is it? You can't even bring yourself to be civil to me, let alone friendly. If your father had a choice, he would have been just as satisfied having you run the ranch. But we both know he didn't. You don't hear him complaining. You're the sore loser, Casey, and nobody likes a sore loser."

She couldn't meet his gaze. Her eyes stared unseeingly at his scuffed boots. She tried valiantly to argue with herself that what he was saying was untrue. She felt about the size of a sand flea and just about as useful.

What if he was right? Worse, what if he told her father about her behavior?

She didn't understand her reaction to Flint herself, though. Chalk it up to the high expectations that tended to ruin the supposedly happy holidays. There was no getting around the fact that she was just overwhelmed.

Her little brother would probably characterize her as a spoiled, selfish, ungrateful brat who didn't deserve or appreciate the things she had. The sound of creaking saddle leather brought her trembling chin up as Casey saw Flint astride his horse, reining him in the direction of the ranch house.

"Flint." Her voice was weak, but he heard it. He

stopped his horse and looked back at her. Pride was an enormous lump in her throat, but somehow Casey swallowed it and walked slowly toward him. She didn't wipe the tears from her cheeks as she tilted her head to look up to him.

"I'm so . . . sorry . . . for the way I've acted."

Before she even completed the sentence, she had lowered her head to stare at the ground. She waited for him to throw her apology back in her face, to tell her that it was too late to make amends. Instead a hand was outstretched toward her.

"Maybe we won't ever be friends, Casey," Flint said, holding the hand she had placed in his gently. "But let's not be enemies. Christmas isn't far off. I hope I'll be gone by then, but if not, I don't want to be exchanging killer glares under the mistletoe."

That stopped her thoughts from going in circles. Damn right. He wasn't going to be exchanging *anything* under the mistletoe with her, she thought. She nodded, withdrawing her hand from his in embarrassment. A finger lifted her protesting chin until Casey was forced to look into his face. He was smiling that devastating smile that had always been reserved for others. She caught her breath at the potency of his charm.

"That was a hard thing you just did, admitting you were wrong, especially to me. Your father is a stubborn man or he wouldn't be a rancher, but he's fair and honest, too. I didn't believe his daughter could be any different, only a bit more bullheaded, perhaps."

Casey wondered why she had never noticed the twinkle in his eyes or the rugged, forthright lines in his face. A blush of red that wasn't from the nip in the air appeared on her cheeks as she realized she had been staring and liking what she saw. She stepped back hesitantly, not knowing anything more to say and feeling ridiculously shy.

From a near hilltop came a shrill whinny, answered immediately by Flint's horse. Casey wiped the tears off her cheeks, her glance turning toward the first sound. She smiled widely as she saw the white horse tossing his head a hundred yards from them.

"I haven't seen that horse around the ranch," Flint said.

"That's my horse, Mercury." Casey lifted her fingers to her mouth and whistled. A glow of pride lit her eyes as she watched the horse trot toward them, his stride long and swinging, his nose raised to catch the scent of the stranger, and his tail almost unnaturally erect above his rump. His white coat shimmered with health. Not until he had stopped in front of Casey was his age obvious. She rubbed his neck fondly while the horse nuzzled the pockets of her warm jacket. She laughed a little, extracting the cubes of sugar and offering them to him.

"He's nearly seventeen years old. You can hardly tell it, can you?" Casey glanced at Flint for his affirmation. "He was my first real horse, the first one that didn't have to be urged to get out of a trot." She hugged the horse's neck affectionately. "He was as fast as the wind. That's why I named him Mercury, after the Roman god with wings on his feet."

Casey glanced hesitantly at Flint, wondering if he thought her childish and silly. But he seemed to be studying her with interest and not amusement.

"I used to be a tomboy," she went on.

"Used to be?" He laughed, but it was a gentle laugh, one that she could join.

"Uh-huh. I liked to pretend that Mercury was an Indian pony. I was forever riding him without a saddle or bridle, guiding him with my knees. Most of the time it worked." She grinned.

"He looks in great shape for his age."

"His teeth are beginning to wear down a lot." A sad note crept into her voice. "Dad said this spring when we wormed him that by the time next summer is over, Mercury probably won't have any teeth left. They'll all be worn to the gum. He likes to run free," she declared fervently, a frown creasing her forehead. "I hate to see the day come when Mercury is reduced to eating mash instead of the pasture grass."

The white horse nuzzled her pockets once more in search of any sugar Casey might have overlooked. Deciding there was none, he turned away, trotting out toward the hills from which he had just come.

"It has to happen sometime." There was no prophecy in Flint's words, only fact. But Casey sensed the understanding he communicated.

"Yes, I know. He's led a . . . full life."

Even as she sighed the last words, she smiled. Living on a ranch had taught her that the cycle of life was never-ending; no one could halt it. She had learned to accept the things that weren't in her power to change, although it didn't make them any easier.

It was a new experience for her to be talking so easily to him, one that Casey found unsettling and yet immensely enjoyable. For these few brief moments

Flint had made her feel important. Perhaps that was why when he left, she felt just a little bit lonely.

Casey took the porch steps two at a time, humming a Trace Adkins song. She didn't realize right away that it was "Ladies Love Country Boys," but it made her smile when she did.

Yeah, Flint was one and then some. Not that she would define herself as a lady, though. She sang the raucous chorus under her breath so her mother wouldn't hear, grateful for her buoyant spirits. Finally accepting Flint as a fellow rancher whose interest, like hers, lay in what was best for the ranch had made the difference. Casey found a new enjoyment in working side by side with him, which filled her with a previously unknown satisfaction. She also found a certain admiration growing for Flint, one that she still tried to hide, but it was becoming increasingly apparent. Just as she opened the kitchen door, Casey heard Mark exclaiming, "No! No!"

He was standing in front of the table, a paper held in his hands as he shook his head vigorously. A disgruntled face turned to Casey at the sound of her footsteps.

"How could my own mother do this to me!" Mark's voice squeaked.

"What are you talking about?" Casey reached for the paper that he extended to her, while from the corner of her eye she saw Flint step into the room.

"Mrs. Grassick stopped in around noon," Flint explained even as Casey read the note left for them. "She offered to take your mother into Scottsbluff to the hospital to visit your father. She left that note explaining why she wouldn't be here for supper this evening."

"There's no way I'm going to eat my sister's cooking!" Mark flopped into a kitchen chair. "I put up with it for an entire week when Mom stayed with Dad. It's a miracle I didn't die of ptomaine poisoning."

"Mark!"

Flint shot her loudmouth brother a look that effectively said what he was thinking. *Shut up—and grow up.* Casey couldn't agree more.

But she couldn't stop the embarrassed flush from coloring her face as she glanced at Flint's amused expression. She also couldn't help noticing how his flannel shirt made his brawny chest look, well, pettable, and how good the rest of him looked in faded jeans.

"I'm telling you, Flint, you've never met a worse cook in your life than Casey." She longed to reach over and jam her fist in Mark's mouth, anything to stop his humiliating words from tumbling out. "One time she tried to make some instant Jell-O out of a box. She had to go and put too much water in it and we had to drink it!"

"I think we'd better change the subject, Mark," Flint said, his laughing eyes flicking over Casey's face, "before you're forced to defend yourself. I'd already decided that rather than have your sister slave over a hot stove after she's worked so hard all day, we would all go into Fort Robinson and have a meal out tonight."

"Awesome!" Mark whooped. "Is that okay with you, Casey?"

For the first time in her life, Casey wished she could cook as well as her mother. After Mark's obnoxious statements, she yearned to whip up something tasty and wow them both, even if the happy homemaker gene had skipped her. Instead she nodded stiffly. Mumbling quickly that she wanted to change, she escaped from the room before she lost her temper and said something breathtakingly bad to her brother. Even Flint was shockable, and her temper was a force to be reckoned with.

He only thought he'd seen her at her worst.

During the entire journey to Fort Robinson, Casey was unbearably self-conscious. She tried to convince herself that it didn't really matter whether she could cook or not, but her mind was stuck on the point.

She realized it did matter what Flint thought of her. Not even when the rolling Sand Hills gave way to the more spectacular scenery of the Pine Ridge region around Fort Robinson State Park did Casey's feeling of inadequacy abate. She found as she accepted Flint's hand when he helped her out of the car that she was uncomfortable. Flannel shirt and jeans . . . oh yeah. This close they looked even better on that male body.

Casey found herself wishing that she had taken more care in choosing her own outfit. The low-rise jeans and ruffled checked blouse did look nice, but she felt like a gauche country bumpkin all the same. Too bad she didn't look as good as Flint did, she sighed silently. At least she had forsaken her cowboy boots for her lone pair of pretty shoes.

As Mark led the way toward the one-time soldiers' barracks that had been turned into a lodge and dining room for tourists, he immediately began informing Flint about the fort's history.

"That big white building there used to be the post headquarters, but they use it for a museum now. This was a pretty famous fort, not just during the settling of the West, but during the world wars, too."

Casey knew that Mark had become enthralled with the history of Fort Robinson over the years, and it really didn't matter to him whether Flint was interested or not. He was going to hear about it anyway.

"On the other side of the highway as we came in," Mark continued, "is where Chief Crazy Horse—you know, the one who was with Sitting Bull at Custer's Last Stand—was killed resisting soldiers who were trying to take him into a cell. This is also where the Cheyenne Indians came, led by Dull Knife, when they fled their reservation in Oklahoma. When they refused to return to Oklahoma and were starved in an attempt to force them to make the long trek back in the dead of winter, they fought their way out of the fort. Of course, most people know all that stuff anyway." Mark made a deprecating gesture with his hand.

"How do you turn him off?" Flint laughed toward Casey as he held open the large door into the lodge.

"You don't. You wait for him to run out of gas." Her glance at the sheepish expression on her brother's face was teasing. Getting even was fun.

"Well, it was a pretty famous place," Mark defended himself while his long legs carried him into the lobby.

The trio had barely entered the dining room and seated themselves at a table when Mark was set upon by two blond-haired boys.

"Hey, Mark, we were just talking about you." The taller of the two thumped Mark soundly on the back.

"Kevin, Kyle!" Mark laughed as he tried to dodge a matching blow from the other one. "What are you doing here?"

"We convinced Dad to take us to a movie since Mom deserted us in favor of going to Scottsbluff." Casey had difficulty trying to figure out which one of the twin sons of Mrs. Grassick was speaking.

"She took my mom along, leaving me at the mercy of my sister's cooking. Flint rescued me." Mark gave them a goofy smile, in love with his own limited sense of humor.

"After you finish eating—or better yet, come and eat with us." The short one grabbed Mark's arm to pull him along and emphasize his invitation. "Dad's sitting right over there. We just ordered. Then you can come to the show with us later on tonight."

Mark glanced questioningly at Casey, the eagerness to join them lighting up his eyes.

"Go ahead," she nodded. "As long as Mr. Grassick doesn't mind running you home."

"He won't mind," the taller of the twins assured her.

The silence that followed the departure of the boisterous twins lasted through the first part of their meal. Despite her earlier annoyance with her brother, Casey found herself wishing he was with them, anything to ease this silence that was making her so uncomfortable.

"You're very quiet tonight," Flint finally observed, his gray eyes studying the sudden flush in her cheeks. "I hope Mark's teasing hasn't upset you. Brothers are like that, you know."

"Of course it didn't. Why, he teases me like that all the time." The brief hesitation in her denial made it difficult for her to meet his gaze. "Besides, it's a well-known fact that I can't boil water."

"Can Smitty cook?"

"Smitty? How should I know?" This time her puzzled eyes met his squarely. "What has that got to do with it, anyway?"

"From all I've heard, it's an accepted fact that you two are going to be married. It would be convenient if one of you could cook." One corner of his mouth slanted upward in obvious mockery.

"How quaint!" Casey retorted. "If we were planning to get married, which we're not, it wouldn't be any of your business whether or not one of us can cook." Suddenly she couldn't bear any teasing about her lack of culinary skill. It was an anger brought on by her own vulnerability that flamed through her words. "Tell me how you rate your girlfriends on their cooking."

"They all know their way around a microwave." Flint's eyes crinkled into an audacious smile, though the rest of his expression was completely sober.

There was no doubt he was making fun of her short temper now, which only angered Casey further.

"No doubt a big he-man like you only attracts the feminine type." The smile on her face clashed with the fire in her dark eyes. "The ones with long hair and frilly white gowns. And of course, you have such broad shoulders for them to lean on."

"I think you're turning into a prickle poppy again."

"Well, if I am, it's your fault." Most of her anger subsided under the irresistible warmth of his smile.

"It's interesting to watch you when you get angry.

Your eyes really glow and you blush like crazy. Great combination."

That was the first compliment that Casey had ever received from Flint, and it had a disturbing effect on her pulse. She lowered her gaze to her empty plate, wishing she were a sophisticated chick who could shrug off such an idle compliment with a witty remark.

"Let's take a walk around the fort before going back to the ranch," Flint suggested, rising from the table and coming around to pull out Casey's chair.

She was too aware of her new reaction to him to do more than nod agreement. Waiting discreetly to one side as he paid for the evening meal, Casey noticed the glance of admiration the girl at the desk gave him. She couldn't help wondering what it would be like if they were on a real date together. Casey immediately tried to banish the thought, telling herself that a man like Flint would never be even slightly interested in a countrified girl like her. Still, it was an exciting thought that wouldn't completely go away.

"Should we walk around the parade ground first?" Flint asked as they stopped on the wide veranda of the lodge. At Casey's agreement, they descended the steps and walked toward the large oval surrounded by buildings.

There was little activity around the oval. Only at a distance were the sounds of cars and tourists audible. At the near end of the parade ground was the flagpole, the stars-and-stripes lifting gently in the wind.

As they walked slowly past the building housing the fire station, Casey spoke. "It's easy to imagine this side of the ground lined with cavalry barracks. Sometimes I can close my eyes and hear the call to 'boots and saddles.'"

"Mark was right about Fort Robinson. It's been an important post for over a hundred years." Their pace slowed as they rounded the oval near the commanding officer's quarters. Casey paused a moment.

"In a way, I hope a lot of people don't discover this place," she mused. "I don't really mind tourists coming to visit it and taking horseback rides along the trails once ridden by Red Cloud and Crazy Horse. I just don't want it becoming all commercialized. So much of the flavor of the old fort is still here that I wouldn't like it to change."

"You're right. Some places can't be exploited for their monetary value, but should remain unchanged so that future generations can appreciate life as it was once upon a time." Flint glanced down at Casey, a smile curving his mouth. "And that is as solemn as I'm going to get! It's a beautiful evening, an inspiring place, and most of the time, enjoyable company. I refuse to get into discussions of the meaner side of the human race."

His hand rested on the back of her waistline with remarkable nonchalance, considering the havoc it wrought with her stomach, now turned upside down. Flint changed the subject, but Casey couldn't really concentrate on anything of any depth. She was too totally aware of him as a man.

He looked up at the darkening sky, holding out his hand to catch a flake or two of snow.

"Look at that," he said. "Here it comes at last."

Casey looked into his palm. The warmth of his skin

had melted the snow instantly. There were drops of water where the flakes had rested so briefly.

"I heard we were only going to get flurries."

He smiled at her. "Good. That brings me to Plan B. Now that your brother's ditched us—"

Casey's mind began to spin with a few interesting possibilities. They could go back to the ranch, light a fire, and snuggle up on the sofa. He didn't look like the kind of guy who was going to ask her for a heated game of Scrabble as foreplay, that was for sure. Or . . . they could . . .

He saved her the trouble of driving herself crazy.

"Let's go dancing. The Midnight Rodeo is about thirty miles from here."

"Uh—okay. I guess I should tell Mark, though."

Flint took her hand in his. She could feel her insides melting faster than those pretty little snowflakes. "Just text him. He won't care."

Casey gulped and nodded. She pulled out her cell phone and keyed in a message. Gone 2 Mdnt Rodeo 2 dance w/ Flint—have fun w/ yr frnds, k?

Flint leaned over and looked at the tiny screen. He shook his head and took the phone out of her hand, pressing the delete key. He handed it back. The first part of the message read a little differently. Gone dancing w/ Flint. No mention of where.

"You don't want your baby brother to show up, do you?" Flint asked. "If he needs you, he'll call you, right?"

"I'm not sure my father would agree with this." Casey gave him a slow smile. "Or my mother, for that matter."

Flint shook his head. "You're entitled to go out

on a date. Mark doesn't need or want your constant supervision."

She snorted. "He sure doesn't want it. But I'm tougher on him than my mom or dad."

"Why?"

Casey shot him a look. "I told you I used to be a tomboy."

"Yup. I remember."

She hesitated. "Well, I used to be a bit of a hell-raiser, too."

"No kidding." He didn't sound in the least surprised. "I happen to like hell-raisers, especially when they act like perfect ladies in church."

She swatted him. "Shut up. I shouldn't have told you that."

"Too late now." He grinned.

"Yeah. Okay, well, I have a pretty good idea of the kind of trouble a bunch of crazy boys can get into."

Flint squeezed her hand. "You can't hover over your kid brother like that, and he hasn't done anything yet."

She groaned. "I feel like he will, the second I'm not looking at him."

He guided her to his SUV and brushed the light accumulation of snow off the door before he opened it for her. Casey got in, not feeling like a princess on her way to a ball. "I'm not dressed up enough."

He flicked aside her jacket and allowed himself a very masculine once-over. "You're one pretty cowgirl, ruffles and all. And the jeans . . . mmm. I can see more of you in them than I can in a skirt."

"Flint!" She was secretly pleased by the outrageous

compliment. And it was nice to know that he liked what he saw.

She checked her phone to see if Mark had responded to her text. The screen was blank, except for the time. 9:30. The Midnight Rodeo would be just opening up. It didn't really get going until around 12:00.

Flint pulled out the seat belt and handed it to her. "Buckle up, beautiful."

She blushed and swept the belt across her midsection as he closed the door and went around to his side.

The drive was uneventful, and the snow wasn't sticking to the highway. She watched it hit the windshield and be brushed aside by the wipers.

He turned on the radio to get a weather report and nodded to her when it was confirmed that the flurries would soon blow through their area. "Good. I don't want to end up in a ditch. I have four-wheel drive on this thing, but SUVs aren't all they're cracked up to be for bad-weather driving."

"Really." Casey knew that, but she didn't mind listening to automotive talk. There wasn't a man on earth who didn't like to show off his knowledge of cars, and explain how they handled. It was a guy thing.

"Now, my other vehicle is a monster truck."

"Uh-huh."

He looked over at her. "I mean it."

"Okay, okay, I believe you."

He looked over at her. "You don't understand. But I can't whip out a picture of this baby when I'm driving."

"So describe it," she said indulgently.

"It's a decommissioned army transport vehicle. Reconditioned and rebuilt. By me."

"You like to get your hands that dirty?" She wouldn't have expected that of a rich man's son.

"Sure. My dad and I restored a couple of muscle cars just for fun. But the Beast is different. You'll see."

"You should bring it out to the Anchor Bar. There's a few jobs where a truck like that would come in handy."

"It's great for offroad driving. Winch and steel cable in the front, too."

Casey laughed at his pride in it. "Okay, then, definitely drive it down when you get a chance. My brother is going to want to get behind the wheel."

"Nothing doing. You can drive it if you want to." Casey was pleased, studying his profile as he looked straight ahead at the road in front of them. The line down the center was dusted with whirling light snow, but they still had good traction.

He pulled into the huge parking lot of the Midnight Rodeo fifteen minutes later. The slots close in were filled, and she knew that the outlying parking spaces would be completely filled in another hour.

Flint escorted her inside, checking their coats first and coming up beside her while she was being carded.

The ancient cowboy whose job it was peered at her photo on the license, and at her again, so carefully that Casey blushed again.

"Just makin' sure you're twenty-one, miss," he said, his voice a friendly rasp. "You don't look it. You're a whole lot prettier than that there picture, too."

Flint took out his wallet and paid the entry fee,

then turned the driver's license in the plastic sleeve so that the old cowboy could see it. The man glanced at it and winked at Flint. "You're a lucky feller," he said.

"I know," Flint replied. His hand on the small of her back moved Casey forward into the main hall of the Midnight Rodeo.

She hadn't been here for a while, and she'd forgotten how big it was. Or maybe just being out with Flint was making her feel a little nervous. But the long oval of the dance floor was nearly the size of a high-school running track. A few couples were already boot-scootin' to the music coming over the sound system.

Casey felt a happy tingle in her feet and wished she'd worn her cowboy boots instead of trying to impress Flint with her best shoes.

Oh, well. They'd have to do. If she danced quickly, she wouldn't get her toes stepped on.

"How about here?"

He stopped in front of a high table with bar stools gathered around, one of at least fifty around the dance floor.

"Fine with me."

She accepted his hand to help her up and settled in, resting her elbows on the table, and looked around. The dance hall's staff had gone all out with the Christmas decorations.

Big, fat, colored lights were strung from pillar to pillar, and the stage where the live band would play was framed with dark green metallic garlands that shimmered with the thumping beat of the music coming from the speakers.

Someone had made angels out of white glitter

paper and feathered wings, with sweet faces and miniature straw cowboy hats pushed back over their long, cottony tresses.

"Honkytonk angels," she said with a laugh, nodding to the one nearest their table. "Wow. Those are really pretty."

"Like the man at the door said, you're a whole lot prettier, Casey."

Casey looked down at the table, studying the patterned laminate like there was a message in it. She traced a fingertip along a swirl, wishing the waitress would come over.

"I'm glad you're my honkytonk angel tonight," he said softly.

She looked up, ready to dismiss that corny compliment with the scorn it deserved. But the look in his dark eyes stopped her. "Whatever," was all she said.

The waitress stopped by. "What can I get for y'all?" she asked cheerfully.

"Beer and nachos to start?" Flint asked Casey.

"Sure."

The waitress named the draft beers and the house specialties with machine-gun speed, smiling all the while. Flint did the ordering and they made small talk until the waitress came back with two longneck brews, a slice of lemon jammed into each one, and their snack.

"Let me know when you want more," she said, and walked away. Casey glanced at the short denim skirt the waitress wore, noting the ruffles on it. Good. She liked going to a place where ruffles were still cool.

Flint raised his bottle and she raised hers, and

they clinked as their eyes met. "Here's to the Anchor Bar," he said, "the home of the famous Casey Gilmore."

"I'll drink to that," she replied, "but I'm not famous and I never will be."

He took a long swig. "No telling. You could be."

"No. I don't have a college degree, I don't know what I want to do, and I don't come from a famous family or anything—" She stopped herself, not wanting to sound like she was that impressed by him.

They chatted through an entire bowl of nachos dripping with cheese, and another two longnecked beers. She was feeling pretty good when she slid off the stool and told him she was heading for the ladies'.

Once inside, she brushed her hair and freshened her makeup. No doubt in her mind that he was going to ask her to dance. The place was filling up. She was lucky to get a place at the mirror in here.

Casey took a look around at the other girls—no one she knew. Too bad, she thought, as she put a dab of colored gloss on her lips. She almost wanted someone she knew to see her with Flint McAllister.

Well, maybe not if she was going to dance with a beer buzz on. But then she didn't have to lead. With those big shoulders and firm grip, she'd bet Flint McAllister was going to do a fine job of that.

He didn't disappoint her. Lost in the whirling crowd of dancers, he'd two-stepped and swung his way into more than one female heart besides hers.

The live band had arrived and played one rousing number after another.

They were performing a slow ballad now, just to give people a break and give couples a chance to get close.

Mmm. Casey was an inch away from resting her head on Flint's flannel shirt. Getting hot, he'd unbuttoned just one button and she could see the faint sheen of male sweat on his skin.

Two beers weren't enough to make her particularly tipsy, but she wouldn't have minded just touching her tongue to that spot to get a taste of him. Salty. Male. Hers . . . at least for this one night.

His muscular arms went around her and they swayed as they danced, moving with the other couples in flowing rhythm that never stopped.

How easy it would be—her thoughts drifted with the music—*to fall in love*. No, she told herself, feeling sensually relaxed. That wasn't what she was actually thinking, those were the words of the song the band was playing.

He'd molded her pliant body to his hard length and he was most definitely doing a fine job of leading. Flint McAllister was an excellent dancer. She looked up dreamily into his eyes. The passion she saw in his nearly made her stop in her tracks, but he continued to move with her, gently masterful.

Then his lips parted. They came down over hers and he kissed her as they danced, right in front of every soul in the place and all the honkytonk angels looking down from the walls.

Casey surrendered to him then and there. Secretly.

Chapter Six

Casey had learned a lot about Flint since that night. She'd found the time to talk with him, put it that way. He told her about his parents and grandparents, his three brothers and one baby sister. For a time it had seemed they were growing closer. At least Casey felt that way. She was okay with the relationship, if it could be called that, being temporary. After all, he was older and a whole lot richer, and she wasn't in his league. She knew that. And she hadn't let him get as far as she had a feeling he wanted to go. Flint was a gentleman about it.

Or maybe he was just biding his time.

Hmm. She was aware that Smitty wasn't happy about that. She and Flint had gone out dancing again, and one night a disgruntled Smitty was waiting for Casey, not hiding his disapproval of her going out with Flint. For the first time Casey had found herself resenting Smitty's possessive attitude.

Flint didn't take a stand, which baffled her.

To make matters worse, Flint had taken Smitty's sense of entitlement to Casey's company as fact and silently withdrew to his office. The evening that had been so pleasant ended on a sour note—at least for Casey and Smitty; she wasn't sure that Flint really cared one way or another.

She tried to force herself to accept the fact that she was probably no more than a diversion to him. What she had found hard to figure out in the three days since that night was what Flint meant to her.

That was the main reason Casey had ridden out to Yucca Meadow alone today. She wanted time to rationalize her thoughts and put the recent events in their proper perspective. Checking for stray cattle was a secondary motive. They still hadn't had what she thought of as real snow, but she didn't want to have to borrow Smitty's plane to drop hay for the stragglers who would get caught in it.

She nudged Tally, her buckskin gelding, to the top of a small bluff, halting him a few feet from the sheer drop to gaze at the panorama of rolling hills. But the struggles of a small red-brown critter below captured her attention. The breeze carried a weak and plaintive bawl.

Her horse pricked its ears. She turned him toward the more sloping side of the bluff and let him pick his own way down to the calf, born late in the year and vulnerable for just that reason. All the while her eyes scanned the surrounding hills looking for its mother. Casey knew of nothing more dangerous than a cow protecting her offspring. Strangely enough, there wasn't another animal in sight. There was one possible explanation—the calf had come from a first-year cow whose maternal instincts hadn't fully developed.

A hundred feet from the calf Casey halted her horse. A rusted strand of barbed wire had become twisted around its feet. The white stockings were stained with bright red blood. Two coyotes appeared mysteriously on a nearby hill. Casey knew she didn't have much time to waste. The darkened sand near the calf's legs and the lack of any further struggle on his part told her clearly that the little guy had lost a lot of blood. All she could do was free him from the wire and transport him back to the ranch house over the saddle of her horse.

The calf was too weak to resist as Casey dismounted and approached him, the wire cutters from her saddlebag in her hand. She knew she had nothing to fear from the coyotes since the presence of a human would keep them at a distance. Large, pain-filled brown eyes stared up at Casey as she quickly began snipping the barbed strands and gently unwrapping them from the calf's legs. She was careful to avoid the rusted prongs while silently wishing for the heavy leather gloves she had left on the kitchen counter. At last the calf was free, but he was too weak to do anything about it.

Oh, man. Born late and without a lick of sense. Casey struggled to maneuver the heavy calf into her arms. He was like a dead weight when she finally managed to rise to her feet. Yet somewhere the calf found strength to emit one more frightened bawl. She had taken one step toward her horse, still standing where she had left him about fifty feet away, the reins dragging the ground, when she saw the buckskin's head turn toward the hill to Casey's left. The quick glance she cast occurred at the same time that a questioning bellow rang from the hill.

Casey's heart sank to her boot tops as she recognized the cow trotting purposefully down the

hill. There was only one cow in the whole Anchor
Bar herd with long, twisting horns like that, a
throwback to a distant strain of Texas longhorns
that her father had used some years back when he
was doing experimental breeding. Krazy Kow, Mark
had dubbed her. Even as Casey measured the distance between herself and her horse, she knew she
didn't stand a chance of making it carrying the calf.

Yet, illogically, Casey hurried toward her horse,
the calf still in her arms. Mingling with the sound
of the cow's hooves striding through the grass and
sand came other sounds of creaking saddle leather
and horse's hooves. From the corner of her eye,
her heart leaping from fear into her throat, Casey
saw spots—Flint's Appaloosa was charging down
the hill toward the cow. A rope snaked out from
Flint's hand, a wide loop settling perfectly over the
spreading horns, jerking the cow off her course
toward Casey.

"The pickup and trailer are over by the west
gate!" Flint shouted, his mount twisting and strain-
ing to keep the bucking and bellowing cow under
control.

Casey didn't waste any time slinging the calf over
her saddle, mounting, and riding away. When she
reached the pickup, she hurriedly fixed a place for
the calf in the rear, lowered him gently into it, and
loaded her buckskin into the trailer. She had barely
finished when Flint came galloping over the hill to
join her.

His turbulent gray eyes rolled over her swiftly, the
stormy sensuality in his gaze doing nothing to improve the trembling that had weakened her knees.
He sent his horse up the trailer ramp with a slap on

the rump, locked the door in place, and turned back to Casey.

"I'll . . . I'll ride in the back with the calf." Her voice rushed in to save her from the tempest that seemed to be brewing.

Flint crawled into the cab of the truck, slamming the door hard. The truck jumped into gear as it jolted its way over the rough road back to the ranch house.

"It'll be all right," Casey soothed, arranging the calf so that it lay partly on her lap. But she was trying more to comfort herself than the calf.

Sam Wolver, with his uncanny perception, met them at the main gate. He hopped into the rear bed of the pickup with Casey and began examining the wicked wounds on the calf's legs almost before the pickup ground to a halt. When Sam lifted the calf out of the truck, Casey hopped out to follow him. She wanted to be anywhere as long as it wasn't facing those unsettling gray eyes.

"Casey! I want to talk to you." Flint's voice was calm, but completely uncompromising.

"But—the calf—" She motioned helplessly toward Sam, who was walking swiftly away.

"Sam can take care of it."

"Listen, Flint McAllister." The best defense was a good offense, Casey decided, drawing a deep breath as she plunged in. "I can see you're gearing up for a big lecture, but you can forget it. Right now I'm only concerned about that calf. We can't afford to lose any of our stock."

"Now you listen, Casey Gilmore!" His hand shot out and jerked her back just as she was turning away. "Didn't you learn anything from your father's accident? Even he let someone know where he was going. If Sam hadn't seen you ride out that way, I would never have known where you were. Whatever prompted you to try to take that injured calf away from his mother alone?"

"In the first place, that calf was badly hurt." Her temper was slowly mounting and fighting back her initial trepidation. "And in the second place, that cow was nowhere in sight when I first got there. For all I knew it could have been a first-year calf. And in the third place"—Casey wrenched her arm away from him—"you don't have any right to boss me around!" Especially not the way he'd been romancing her. The sudden switch in his mood unsettled her completely.

"No?" There was a breath of amusement in his voice and face at her sudden flare of temper.

"Don't give me any crap, Flint!" It frustrated her that he should find amusement in her anger.

"That's not the kind of language for a lady to use."

"I'm not a lady. I'm a prickle poppy, remember?" She tilted her head back to gaze defiantly at the gray eyes under the mocking, lifted brows.

"Not when you're in my arms."

She looked at him with astonishment. Those paper angels should have told her this was coming. But then you weren't supposed to trust honkytonk angels. She should listen to the songs. Or figure it out for herself. "Just because you took me out to the Midnight Rodeo a couple of times means absolutely nothing, Flint."

"Oh, yeah?" he murmured.

In one lithe, fluid movement he captured her waist and drew her to him as his mouth settled possessively over hers. In angry resistance, her hands moved to his chest to push him away. Then the incredible warmth of his kiss swept through her, removing all thought of resistance, replacing it with an irresistible desire to respond. Casey felt her fingers curl into his shirt and the hard, muscular chest beneath it. A pulsating weakness spread through her body and she wanted to savor every moment of it. Part of her was shocked by the almost total physical response his kiss was generating.

When his lips slowly lifted from hers, Casey was left in a state of loss. She tried to swallow, to hold back the rising flood of breathlessness. His catalytic kiss had set off a fire, the flame of which was reflected in her eyes.

"I'd bet you've never kissed Smitty like that before." The words spoken by Flint's husky voice were like a pitcher of cold water to Casey.

"Why . . . why do you say that?"

"Because if you had, you'd either be married to him or in his bed. The first I know isn't true. And those innocent eyes of yours tell me that the second isn't true either."

Casey stared up at his sure eyes, feeling the shame that he should be able to know so completely about her. Oh, why did she have to react so wantonly to him? Her mind sobbed even as her eyes drank in the attractiveness of his face.

"You're lucky Smitty wasn't here to see what you just did," she retaliated.

"It takes two, Casey." Flint's gaze lazily rested on her still warm lips, softly swollen from his kiss. "I don't think anyone could believe that kiss was against your will."

She was impotent with frustration. The war of her conflicting emotions couldn't decide whether to melt into his arms or slap his face. So Casey did neither. She turned on her heel and escaped, his low, throaty laugh of triumph dogging her.

It would never do, Casey scolded herself, to get seriously attached to Flint McAllister; worse yet to fall in love with him. That was exactly what was going to happen if she didn't watch her step. Sound advice, she decided even as she stared at him seated just a little in front of her in the family living room. Her throat tightened as she studied the strong, chiseled lines of his profile and the way his auburn-brown hair waved away from his forehead with careless perfection. Inevitably her eyes were drawn to the sensuous curve of his mouth. Funny how a man you didn't want to admit got to you could rock the very foundation of your existence.

"What do you think of the idea, Casey?" The knowing gray eyes turned toward her.

"I'm . . . sorry," she stammered. She had been concentrating so much on him that she didn't remember any words being spoken. "I didn't hear what you were saying."

His smile mocked her openly while his gaze moved over her flushed cheeks. "Your mother was just talking about the old-fashioned barn dance the Gordons are having Friday night. She said she wasn't going because John wasn't here. I suggested that she should go, that we could all go as a family."

"I really don't think I'd better." Lucille Gilmore looked up from the pile of socks in her lap. "You three can go by all means, but I wouldn't feel right going without John."

"Mom, you know you'd enjoy it." Casey shook her gaze free from Flint's hypnotic face. "Besides, how many of those dances have you been to where Dad sat out every dance? He hates them, but he never begrudged your going."

"The people who will be there are your friends and neighbors," Flint inserted. "No one will think unkindly of you accompanying your children, even if John is in the hospital."

"I'm sure they won't," Casey's mother agreed hesitantly. "But . . ."

"No buts. It's settled. We're all going," Flint said firmly. "We won't take no for an answer, will we, Casey?"

She couldn't stop the tingle of pleasure at the coupling of her desires with his. Nor could she hold back the glow she knew was in her eyes as she agreed with him.

"You haven't made any arrangements to go to the dance with Smitty, have you, Casey? Because if you have . . ." Her mother spoke.

An uncomfortable twinge of conscience poked her as Casey tried to recall truthfully whether Smitty had mentioned it. "I don't think so." The convincing tone was more for herself than for her mother. She accompanied the statement with a shy shrug of her shoulders. "He's become . . . too sure of himself lately, anyway."

Lucille smiled at her, pleased at the suddenly feminine tactics her daughter seemed to be using. "All right, I'll go."

"Speak of the devil," Mark piped up. "Here comes Smitty now."

Casey twisted from her chair, aware of the thoughtful gray eyes watching her. "I'll go to the door," she offered unnecessarily, since Smitty came and went in their house as if it were his own.

"Hi, gorgeous," Smitty greeted her on the porch steps.

"Hi, yourself." She wished her sudden attack of nervousness would pass and that her smile would appear less forced than it was.

"You look a little pale. Are you feeling okay?"

"I'm fine." But her supposedly assuring laugh was jerky and unnatural.

Smitty's eyes narrowed on her face, not liking at all what he was thinking. "I stopped to ask about Friday night." He didn't like the color that washed over her face either. "You are going with me, right?"

"To the Gordons'?" Casey stalled. "We were just talking about it." She tried to smile into his questioning brown eyes. "Actually, Flint and I just talked Mom into going along. She didn't want to because of Dad being in the hospital."

"Flint and you?" His gaze was diamond sharp. "Does that mean you're going with him?"

"We're going as a family, Mark, Mother, myself, and . . . and Flint." Why did she feel so guilty? It wasn't as if she had promised Smitty she'd go with him.

"Good old Flint's a part of the family now, is he?" There was no mistaking the sarcasm Smitty was directing at her now. "What am I? An old shoe you've thrown away?"

"You know you're welcome to come with us." Hurt dignity lifted her chin.

"No, thanks. Two's company, three's a crowd and all that."

"Donald Smith! You have no right to talk to me like that!" Casey flared. "You don't own me! And just because I don't go to some party with you, there's no reason for you to get so sarcastic."

Gah. She really hated the way she sounded. It was a toss-up as to which of them was acting more childish. Maybe everyone was feeling the tension of the holidays. The season had been a lot easier when they were real kids.

They hadn't had to worry about a thing then.

"I don't mind you turning me down for your family, Casey," Smitty was saying. "I just object to you turning me down for Flint McAllister. Johnny warned me about him, but I didn't think . . . Oh, what's the use?"

"It isn't because of him at all." Her voice was low and trembling.

"Isn't it? It's written all over your face." Smitty stepped closer to her, his hands moving toward her only to fall at his side in despair. "I've been too damn patient about the situation, I can see that. Casey, he isn't that interested. He's been all over the world. What could he possibly see in a country girl like you?"

She wanted to put her hands over her ears and block out his hurtful words. Everything Smitty was saying was true, things she had already told herself. Worse, she had let Flint know that she was susceptible to his charms. What frightened her was how close she was from falling over the brink and tumbling into a love that would only bring her heartache.

Chapter Seven

Casey was glad she was sitting in the backseat of the car and her mother was in front with Flint. Her tingling senses were all too aware of the confined space. The magnetic force that emanated from him was just as powerful as it had been all week, drawing her to him even when she wanted to stay away. Only the sensible side of her wanted to stay away while the wild, reckless side urged her ever closer. She felt like the child playing with matches who became fascinated by the flame. Her fear wasn't in getting burnt, but in being consumed by the fire.

Thinking about the evening ahead, Casey could not suppress a tide of exhilaration from sweeping over her. She knew at some point during the night that Flint would ask her to dance. She remembered the sensual warmth of his hands on her waist and the feel of his muscular body pressed against hers. No matter how hard she tried to deny that she shouldn't put herself in a vulnerable position, Casey knew she was going to accept him and thrill to every wonderful, rapturous moment of it.

The many petticoats under her red-gold skirt rustled as she shifted position. It hadn't been easy stuffing a traditional square-dance dress under her warm coat, and the ruffles and whatnot were trying to make a break for freedom. Flint glanced over his shoulder at her. Under his smoky gaze, the last vestige of resistance melted away and Casey smiled at him.

"We're almost there," he said, as if needing to explain why he had turned to her.

Holiday decorations and lights were strung from pole to pole under the tent in the Gordons' back garden, but they'd taken the country Christmas theme a step further and added handsome painted cowboys with denim wings to keep their paper honkytonk angels company. Enormous sheets of plywood were stretched over the lawn to provide a dance floor, and electric heaters warmed the space. A hay wagon bordered one side, serving as a platform for a local group of musicians. The combination of guitars, fiddles, accordion, and drums filled the night air with a bouncing, lively tune as Casey and Mark followed Flint and her mother from their car to the party area. Jim Kingston was at the microphone, his foot stomping to the beat of the drums while he called out to the dancers on the floor.

"Honor your partner, honor your corners. Now, an allemande left with the old left hand. On to the next with a right and left grand!"

On the outside of the dance floor, hands clapped automatically to the tune while bright, multicolored skirts whirled around the two squares. Flubbed directions were laughed off and dancers were pushed in the proper direction by more experienced dancers.

Casey felt her toe tapping unconsciously. Her gaze strayed to Flint, who immediately smiled back.

"You like to dance." It was more a statement than a question.

"My one feminine characteristic." The festive atmosphere made her more bold than she had been and her brown eyes glittered up at him with laughter.

Her mother had been ensnared by Mrs. Gordon, and Mark had spotted Kevin and Kyle Grassick on the far side of the floor. Casey was left standing beside Flint, a situation she found interesting, if a little dangerous.

"Was Smitty upset that you didn't come to the party with him?" Flint's question was unexpected.

"Yes," she answered simply. She liked the way his eyes moved over her face, their smoky depths fanning the kindled fire inside her. "He blames you."

His gaze held her prisoner, frightening her a little with its intensity and exciting her at the same time. For a moment Casey felt overwhelmed not just by his superior height but also by his nearly unlimited power over her to arouse her hidden desire for him.

"Let me guess. He warned you about me." Flint spoke quietly, all the while studying her intently. "He told you I was more worldly and more experienced than you. That I could hurt you."

She nodded.

"It's true, Casey."

She blinked her eyes to hide the ache inside, before smiling broadly.

"So what?" she said airily. "A woman's entitled to

a dangerous interlude or two. After all, a man sows his wild oats before he finally settles down."

His appreciative laughter was wicked, almost spellbinding.

"You're right about that." The hand that touched her back sent a warm sensation up her spine as Flint swept her onto the dance floor.

Not even the glowering look from Smitty on the sidelines of the dance floor could change the bubbling happiness inside her. Other men held her as she danced to the commands of the caller, but they were ghosts, shadowy beings that held none of Casey's attention.

The square ended amidst laughter and happy voices. Flint's hand retained its hold on Casey's, his smiling eyes glanced at her flushed cheeks. Other people, but mostly men, recognized him and walked over to say hello. Flint accepted their deferential attention while Casey marveled silently at his upright bearing that still managed to convey midwestern friendliness. A gigantic swell of pride filled her heart as ranchers' daughters glanced down at her hand held so securely by Flint.

Brenda Fairlie, whom Casey hadn't seen since their high school days, was not the type to step back willingly from such a handsome man. She was tall and willowy. She walked toward Casey and Flint with a sulky-looking Smitty in tow. Brenda had always seemed to be filled with her own self-importance even in high school—an attitude that had kept Casey from attempting to make friends with her. Now, after almost three years of college, she still tried to convey an aura of even greater superiority.

"Casey, I've been meaning to stop by and see you."

Casey was forced to submit to a pretend-affectionate hug. "But you know how it is when you're home for only a few short weeks. You just can't see everyone. I was so glad when I heard the Gordons were having this party. It gives me a chance to see everyone." Brenda fluttered her mascara'ed eyelashes at Flint. "You must be the new boss man from Ogallala. Smitty's been telling me about you, Mr. McAllister."

There was the barest flicker of concern in Casey's eyes as she watched Flint's amused glance sweep over Brenda's slender but shapely figure.

"My name's Brenda Fairlie." She introduced herself swiftly before Casey had an opportunity to do so. "Casey and I went to school together. Of course, my parents sent me to college right away, so we haven't been very close since then."

She still manages to monopolize a conversation and get her little comments in, Casey thought, hating the way Brenda was playing up to Flint.

Flint smiled. A mysterious humor lit his eyes. His hand tightened its hold on Casey's. "If you'll excuse us, I promised Casey the first polka."

Before a word of objection could be raised, he had Casey in his arms and on the dance floor. The look in his eyes plainly said, "This is our night." That was all it took for Casey to feel lifted higher. The thought that he had chosen her instead of someone as beautiful as Brenda, who seemed much more his type, made her head swim. It was great to be this goofy. Her feet didn't seem to touch the floor, time was suspended, and the top of the world was below her feet. Casey wasn't even conscious of the music because the melody seemed to be coming from inside.

The firm pressure of his arm around her waist

had a warmth that brought a healthy glow of color to her cheeks. And his eyes held a promise that sent shivers of joy all through her. He whirled her through an intricate series of steps that she had never done before. But they stayed in sync and Casey never missed a move.

When the last note from the accordion faded away, they were on the far side of the floor, separated from the other guests. Casey was breathless, but from exhilaration and not exertion. The hand that had remained around her waist after the music stopped pushed her gently toward the darkness. Wanting to savor this moment of enchantment, she willingly succumbed to its pressure. Yet she couldn't meet his gaze for fear he would see how much more this moment meant to her than to him. A fence loomed before them and Casey raced to it.

"Do you always sweep a girl off her feet like that?" The slight laughter that accompanied her question revealed her nervousness as she leaned against the whitewashed fence, her hands gripping the boards. Still giddy, she felt as if only by holding on tightly could she keep her feet on the ground.

"It's the best way to keep them from stepping on my feet." Flint smiled. His eyes captured hers for an instant before he looked away, in the grip of an emotion he wasn't going to name. Through a gap in the tent, Casey looked away too, at the dark blue heavens filled with twinkling stars.

"I imagine you have a lot of them—girlfriends, I mean." She glanced at him over her shoulder and silently wished his face wasn't in the shadows so she could see what he was thinking.

"Oh, they stand in line," he teased, leaning against the fence post so he could study her face.

"I'm sure moms are always parading their daughters before you," Casey retorted, following his lead, teasing too. "Bet you've heard that you're the hottest cowboy in the territory."

"Are you contemplating throwing your hat in the ring with the others?"

"Me? I wouldn't dare." It was difficult to laugh when he was looking at her again. "I'm just a simple country girl. Yee-haw and all that."

"You don't have much competition."

Casey felt an absurd thrill as she gazed into his eyes and listened to the seductive quality of his voice.

"Those dark eyes—and the passion in them . . . oh, baby. All I want to do—all any man would want to do—is run his hands through your hair. Just to start." As if to prove his point, he reached out and ran his fingers through the curls before cupping the back of her head. She held her breath, her eyes closing briefly at the exquisite pleasure the intimate caress gave. "You are so very, very kissable." Her heart fluttered wildly. "And what's more—"

Flint didn't finish the sentence. He drew her slowly into his arms instead. She melted willingly against him, her back arching as his hold tightened around her waist. He kissed her with a thoroughness that left her weak and trembling.

"You're shaking," Flint drawled.

"Am I?"

"You know you are." He rubbed her arms, exciting still more uncontrollable sensations. Casey was almost frightened of the response he was capable of arousing because she couldn't control it. It was useless arguing the point when she knew her face revealed her feelings all too clearly to him.

"I've never had an affair before." Her voice was husky. "Just fooled around, I guess you'd call it. Never with anyone like you."

"What a pity." Flint sighed. His eyes roamed intimately over her face, not bothering to mask the satisfaction on his own when he saw the radiant glow there.

"What is?" she asked breathlessly.

"You're twenty-one. Now that everyone calls it hooking up, an affair sounds almost old-fashioned." He rubbed her cheek with the back of his hand. Casey felt like nuzzling against it like a purring kitten.

"It sounds wonderful," she whispered. "And romantic."

He sighed. "It's supposed to be."

"Then that's what I want."

"No." He kissed her on the forehead.

Anyplace his lips touched her skin left a tingling sensation. Oh, God, was he ever hard to resist. A man like Flint McAllister made the rest seem like awkward, bumbling boys.

"What do you mean, no?" she asked with soft indignation.

"Sorry. I forgot how much you hate to be told what to do."

"Thanks for remembering, Flint."

He took a deep breath and continued. "I mean, no to an affair. I've been thinking about what's been happening between us, thinking a lot. You may not know it, but you're not the type for an affair, Casey, and you're sure as hell not interested in just fooling around, either. You're a one-man woman, and that's rare these days."

She stood very still in his arms. His tender rejection stabbed at her heart.

"Do you always think you know women so well?" Casey lashed out in hurt anger.

A finger lifted her chin with gentleness. His head was cocked slightly to one side as he studied her wounded eyes.

"I've been wrong before. But I'd be very disappointed if I were wrong about you." He moved away from her, holding out his hand for hers as he did so. "We'll be missed at the party. I wouldn't want to get Smitty any more angry than I already have."

"Oh, we can't have that," Casey retorted sarcastically, refusing to take his hand.

"Prickle poppy," Flint whispered in her ear as he followed closely behind her when she move hurriedly toward the lighted area.

In spite of herself, she did smile slightly, mollified by his teasing voice but sore about him ending their little game of love even though she tried to convince herself it was for the best. The yearning emptiness was still inside her, aching to be filled. A wistful voice inside asked why she couldn't have spent a few more minutes in his arms.

"Ah, Smitty." Flint's voice echoed clearly through the music. "We were just talking about you."

"I can just bet you were." Smitty glared at Casey. "I've been looking for you."

"Have you?" she retorted defiantly. "What happened to gorgeous Brenda? I'm surprised you were able to tear yourself away from her."

"Excuse me, Casey." And Flint slipped away. She couldn't help staring after him.

"Oh, boy, is he setting you up for the kill!" Smitty exclaimed as he looked at the forlorn expression on her face.

"Would you like to dance with me? Because if you don't, you can just leave!" What a relief it was to turn her frustrated anger on someone other than herself.

That evening haunted Casey for days. Except for that one incident with Smitty, Flint had been exceptionally attentive the rest of the evening, but only in a crowd. Never again did he try to be with her alone, not in the days that followed. Casey felt he was trying to shut her out of his life.

If only she were actually sophisticated and capable of carrying off an affair with aplomb, she thought. Then she laughed bitterly. How could such an idea even cross her mind? Flint had been correct when he said she wasn't the type. That didn't compensate for the fact that an affair would be the only romance that Flint would offer. His worldliness and wealth excluded her from entering any race where the prize was marriage.

Casey tossed a pebble in the water. The pond that was her favorite place to think, where he'd come upon her unawares, was partly frozen, but the pebble sailed out over the part that hadn't. Feeling depressed, she watched the waves circling out from where the stone hit. A glance from Flint could send the same ripples through her body, but with a more violent reaction. The physical and emotional demands of her body had suddenly come of age. It was becoming apparent that her love for Flint couldn't be denied any more than her desire could. And her love for him grew daily.

She tried desperately to ignore what loomed ahead. It was such a short time until her father would be home for Christmas and Flint would be leaving. Once she had looked forward to that day. Now she could feel just a small amount of the hollowness his departure would bring. It was a void that yawned ahead of her. If the thought could make her so sad while he was still here, what would it be like when he had really gone?

A hailstone stung her arm as the ground suddenly vibrated around her. Her gaze left the pond in front of her, turning upward to the sky. A jagged fork of lightning pierced through dark, rolling clouds.

Hell. She was in for it. Blizzards were sometimes preceded by weird weather, hiding thunder and lightning and hail in their snowy depths as the great storms raced swiftly over the plains. She might be caught in blinding snow in minutes. When Casey had ridden out to the small lake, she had noticed these same clouds hovering near the western horizon. Now they completely blackened the sky. A growl of thunder shook the ground again as another little hailstone hit her. She glanced toward the level area where her horse had been tied.

His head was up, his eyes rolling in fear at the golden white spears of lightning falling out of the snow-laden clouds. An enormous clap of thunder sent the horse crouching on all four legs before he seemed to explode away, breaking the loose tie that hadn't been enough to hold him. Casey leaped to her feet, shouting at the horse already racing away, his head held high and to one side to keep the trailing reins from entangling in his feet.

"Tally! Tally!" But her call was muffled by the onslaught of stinging sleet that the black clouds set free. Snow would be next. She had to get home.

In seconds she was freezing cold and compelled to keep moving. There was no use standing here staring after the fleeing horse, Casey thought, furious with herself for brooding like that and not noticing the oncoming storm threatening the prairie. She ran to the top of the hill, but the buckskin was nearly out of sight. In angry desperation she placed two fingers in her mouth and whistled shrilly for him. It was useless. The horse didn't even slow up for two strides. She glanced at the menacing clouds, grateful for the prevailing wind that helped her bolt toward the ranch house nearly seven miles away. If only she had stopped feeling sorry for herself long enough to look up to the sky, she wouldn't have been in this mess. At least she was wearing two pairs of thick wool socks and waterproof boots. Frostbite was a real possibility, no matter how fast she ran. She stuck her gloved hands into her pockets after she pulled up her collar and yanked the drawstring of her hood as tight as it would go, squinting against the mean sleet and hoping she wouldn't sprain her ankle in a prairie dog hole.

A questioning whinny halted her feet. The corners of her mouth curved upward in a hopeful smile. Maybe Tally had come back. But when she stared ahead of her, Casey saw a white horse making his way toward her.

"Mercury, how's the old boy today?" Her voice

was a soothing caress as the horse nuzzled her face.
"No sugar, feller."

Lightning flashed again, this time much closer as
the violent storm moved in with all its intensity.
Casey knew she didn't have much of a chance of
making it to the house before the full force of the
storm descended on her. But she hadn't ridden
Mercury for several years. It was a question of
whether she'd be able to control him and direct
him to the ranch with just knee signals. She had no
choice; she had to give it a try.

The white horse was startled when she pulled
herself onto his back. He moved restlessly beneath
her while Casey spoke to him in a soothing and reassuring voice before urging him forward. He
stepped out hesitantly, slowly accustoming himself
to the weight on his back that he hadn't felt for
years. But memories and habits were quickly re-
called. Soon Casey had him in an easy canter, the
aging white horse responding to the slightest pressure as when he was young and he and Casey were
inseparable.

Snow began to fall, intermixed with stinging pel-
lets on her exposed skin. The ground vibrated beneath the horse's hooves from the rolling thunder
while the sky alternated between lightness and
dark. Mercury lengthened his stride until he was at
a full gallop. It happened so gradually that Casey
wasn't even aware of it until she noticed the ground
racing past them at a faster speed.

She had no means to slacken his pace and it was
all she could do to grip his heaving sides with her
wet legs. Her heart was pounding in her throat as
they raced full speed over the Sand Hills. Casey

knew she should slow him down, that the pace was too much for a horse his age carrying her unaccustomed weight. But she, perhaps like the horse, was remembering other times when Mercury was younger and they had ridden like this over the prairie. She kept telling herself that he wasn't laboring too much, that his stride was just as effortless as it had always been.

Just as the thought crossed her mind, Casey felt a slight difference in the rhythm of his gait. Two strides before Mercury went down, Casey knew he was falling. She jumped free just as he somersaulted through the air, head over heels. A thick, withered yucca bush broke her fall although she lay on the ground with the wind knocked out of her. She mentally checked her body to make sure she had no broken bones. Then her dark eyes turned toward the inert white form a few feet away. The sleet-churned mud had marred the pure whiteness of Mercury's coat. She stumbled and crawled to the horse. Her eyes filled with tears as she kneeled beside the huge chest that had been gulping large quantities of air just moments before. Now it was still.

"Mercury?"

Her hand reached out to touch the white forelock. Her whole body was shaking with the realization that her horse was dead. Sobbing openly now, Casey gathered the white head onto her lap, the gazelle-soft eyes now shut in death.

"I'm so sorry." The shaking, whispering voice was barely audible as she buried her head in the horse's neck. Her dearest possession and friend was gone.

The lightning, the thunder, the storm, they didn't matter anymore.

She was barely conscious of the snow and sleet lessening, and finally ceasing altogether. Not until two hands gripped her shoulders was Casey's mind drawn from the horse in her arms. Her misty gaze looked up at the sympathetic gray eyes below the wet hat brim.

"Your buckskin came back to the ranch. I was worried," was all Flint said as he helped her rise. He pressed a willing Casey against his broad chest, where she sobbed anew.

"I . . . I . . . w-was riding Mercury. He came out of nowhere—like he knew I was in trouble . . . H-he started running and . . . and I cou-couldn't stop him." The stranglehold of grief on her throat made her explanation difficult, but the comforting circle of his arms made her want to talk. "Then he . . . he fell. He's dead, Flint." This time Casey looked into his face.

Flint smoothed the curls of brown hair away from her cheek. "Don't blame yourself, Casey. Isn't it better this way?" His smile was so gentle. "I bet he's still running on into heaven, free forever."

The poetic image brought more solace to Casey than any logical argument would have. She wondered why the snow had stopped, then decided to just take it as a gift from above. Remembering the way they had been racing over the hills before he had fallen made it an all the more cherished thought. She rested her head on his shoulder, the pain in her heart easing.

When his lips touched her hair, she couldn't help moving closer against him, snuggling into the comfortable warmth of his arms. She felt Flint's lips touch her forehead and the quivering sensation race clear down to her feet. Then they brushed the wetness of her eyelashes, the bridge of her nose, seeming to take time to touch each occasional freckle on her face. His hand caressed her shoulder as he softly whispered her name.

Her lashes fluttered open to gaze into the smoky fire of his eyes while she tilted her head upward to receive his kiss. Without conscious direction, her hand reached up and removed his hat just before his mouth claimed hers. Then the other hand joined the first, curling into the silkiness of his hair, drawing him closer to her. Waves of ecstasy washed through her, each one leaving her weaker and more pliable than the one before. The warm sensuality of his mouth took care of any resistance. At the increased demand in his kiss, her lips parted involuntarily, sadly welcoming the forgetfulness she needed. He could keep her from crying—she would but not here and not now. His arms were steel bands that pressed her tightly against him until every button on his jacket was driven through her thick clothes.

"We gotta get somewhere warm. I don't know how much longer the snow will hold off. Mercury was right. You are in trouble."

As if he couldn't control himself, Flint quickly pushed back her hood and buried his head in the curve of her neck, nibbling at the sensitive cord until Casey moaned. Rocked by sorrow but comforted by his body, by his nearness, she didn't want to do the right thing or the sane thing. Now Casey could feel the rapid beat of his heart through his touch, marking time with the erratic pace of hers. A strange quiver claimed her as she realized that she had aroused him as thoroughly as he had aroused her.

Only seconds had passed, but it felt like forever. Flint returned his lips once more to her mouth, roughly and possessively, as their physical desire mounted to an even higher pitch. But suddenly she experienced fear. Her lips became still beneath his mouth. Without being aware that she had reached any decision, she began struggling to free herself from the male body pressing down on her, whispering a pleading no. At first Flint ignored her, increasing the ardor and passion in his kiss until he almost took her breath away. Casey tried not to respond, but she did, although the fact that she was fighting it showed through.

In the next instant the heat of his body vanished and a heavy-breathing Flint was towering above her. Casey knew the flush of her passion was still on her face and her lips were swollen from his kisses. And the flame of desire still burned brightly in his eyes, too. He stared silently down at her for a moment, then turned away.

What was she doing, or about to do? Casey couldn't begin to define the emotions that claimed her, only dimly aware that she was in a state of shock. She opened her mouth to speak, but Flint silenced her.

"Don't apologize." Flint grasped her roughly by the shoulders, forcing her to look into his face. "If . . . never mind. We have to get back. You wouldn't have been able to stop me, Casey, and we both know it."

Anger was in his voice and face. Casey felt a certain

amount of humiliation at the fact that it was directed at himself and not at her. Plus she knew that another few minutes under the expertise of his lovemaking and she wasn't sure she would have tried to resist.

"Take my horse and ride back to the ranch," Flint ordered crisply. "Get a weather report on the radio and see if it's safe to send Sam out. He can help me bury Mercury."

Casey glanced at the white body, then up to the thinning gray clouds overhead. The blizzard, if that's what it was, had blown itself well to the west. She'd been under the far edge of the storm and now it had left her and Flint behind. But it was still dangerously cold, and the high winter winds must have left destruction and devastation in their wake.

At least—cold comfort—her old friend Mercury had found her. The horse had probably been as scared as she'd been. She glanced at Flint and the hard expression on his face. There was a quality in his eyes that was as unpredictable as a Nebraska storm, and it almost scared her.

"What about you, Flint?"

"I'll be all right," he said quietly.

In only a few hours, her world had shifted off center, as if everything she knew and held dear had been tumbled and blown inside out by emotions she didn't understand, and feelings that threatened to overwhelm her. A strange calm began to replace them, for which she was grateful.

Her gaze returned to the still shape of her fallen horse. *Poor Mercury*, she mused silently, *how lucky you are to be free.* Then she mounted Flint's Appaloosa and rode off.

Chapter Eight

Casey hadn't seen Flint for several days. He'd left a matter-of-fact note saying he was driving back to his family's spread to get the truck he'd mentioned, figuring they'd need it now that winter was upon them. Nice of him. If only she could stop thinking about him, she could manage to get through a day. The afternoon was unbearably cold. Looming gray clouds hung motionless in the sky and she could smell the snow that had been predicted.

Patches of frost still dotted the sandy earth. Just looking at them made Casey feel morose and irritable, a state of mind that she didn't want to get used to.

To hell with self-pity. She had to do something—and since the ranch repairs and preventive maintenance had been mostly completed under Flint, she was going to put on an apron and turn into a real girl. And attempt the Christmas baking that her mother was so proud of. Casey had no doubt that she would screw up royally, burn every single cookie, and send a lot of one-eyed gingerbread men out into the world with no icing pants on.

The relatives and friends who awaited Lucille Gilmore's yearly goodies would just have to accept what Casey provided, because her mother wasn't around to do it right. She'd returned to the hospital in Scottsbluff to help Casey's dad make the transition to a wheelchair, then to a walker.

And then, God willing, he'd walk in the front door on his own feet by Christmas Eve. Just thinking about her dad made Casey choke up. He wouldn't care what her gingerbread men looked like.

She lined up the bags of flour and sugar on the counter, thinking that they looked like fat soldiers. Her mother used an assembly-line technique, and so would Casey. She was starting late to get the fruitcake good and soused, but she would add a little extra to make up for lost time once she had the things baked.

Casey unscrewed the cap on the bottle of whiskey and poured some into a teaspoon, tasting it. Not bad, but it made her cough.

Mark came in and caught her at it. "Hitting the hooch, sis?"

"Yeah," she said, blowing her breath his way. Mark made a big show of waving away the alcoholic fumes. "Gotta do something to chase away the blues."

"Come off it. You don't drink."

"I have been known to have a few beers, Mark."

"I'm talking real drinking," he said. "Like Kyle and Kevin, in the rec room."

"Right. I don't even want to know. Just promise you won't ever get in a car with one of them at the wheel when it's party time."

"I wouldn't. I'm not that stupid, Casey."

"Glad to hear it."

He picked up a bag of colorful chunks of pre-served fruit and squeezed it.

"What are you doing?" she asked.

"Looking for the maraschino cherries. What else?"

"How old are you again, baby brother?"

"Fifteen going on sixteen. Like you don't know."

"That's old enough to leave a few cherries for other people to enjoy."

"They won't be missed. Nobody actually enjoys fruitcake," he said disgustedly.

"As I remember, you were the one who was so gung-ho about making it."

"Yeah, but that was two weeks ago."

She gave him a long-suffering look. "An eternity to a teenage boy, I know. Anyway, I've decided that making it is an important ritual and we're going to do it."

"You mean you're going to do it."

She grabbed the bag of fruit chunks back and set it down on the counter. The thin, clear wrapping split. "Look what you did. Now it's all mashed."

"Which is exactly what will happen anyway when you mix up the batter," he pointed out.

"True." She set up the large index card with her mother's handwritten recipe and began cracking eggs into a bowl. She creamed the butter she'd left out to soften with the sugar and spices and baking powder, threw in what seemed to be not enough flour for four cakes as specified by the recipe, and hoped for the best. Then she added the fruit.

The gloppy mess was almost impossible to stir. She left the spatula in it standing upright. "Come here. Show your strength. You're the man of the house now."

"I am?"

"Yes. Dad's not home yet and Flint's not around."

"You two fight or what?" her brother asked casually, washing his hands and taking over the task.

"No."

"I was thinking maybe that was why you have the blues." He was too tactful to mention Mercury and she knew it.

Casey dusted the flour from her hands with a dishtowel, then used it to wipe away a couple of unexpected tears. "Shoot. I got flour in my eyes." Which was an excellent reason to not have to explain much more to the uncomprehending Mark. "I'm fine. The holidays just kind of got to me this year. You know how it is."

He hummed as he stirred the fruitcake batter, doing a surprisingly good job of it. "Yeah, I guess so. But me and Kyle and Kevin saw you at the Midnight Rodeo with Flint, you know. We figured that's where you went that night, even though your text message didn't say."

"How'd you even get in? Don't tell me you three have fake IDs."

"Nah. Kyle knows a way to get up in the rafters. We just watch. It's really fun from above."

"Fun for you, I guess." She'd had no idea her brother and his buddy had been spying on her. Mark hadn't said one word about it until tonight.

"Yeah. You looked like he charmed you right out of your cowboy boots. I have a feeling you miss him."

"Thank you so much for sharing that insight," she said sweetly. "I don't. Not really."

"You sure?" Mark persisted. "Kyle thought you were, like, in love."

"I'm not."

"Good," he said, sticking the spatula into the batter just the way she'd done. "Because it's too weird to think about. Flint's a lot older than you."

"Excuse me? What right do you have to say something like that?" She glared at him, even though she was a little amused by his protectiveness toward her.

"Maybe you should stick to Smitty."

Casey pushed a straggling lock of hair back with hands that were free of flour. "That's my decision. Are you done with that?"

He peered into the bowl of batter. "You tell me."

She came over and looked. "I guess you are. I don't really know."

"Now what?"

"You get to grease the pans."

Mark groaned. "What if I don't want to?"

"We all have to do things we don't want to do, Marky boy." She peeled back the wax paper from a stick of butter and handed it to him like a lunchtime banana. "Hold it by the paper and it won't be so messy."

"Okay, okay."

He did a good job of greasing the pans too. She gave him a paper towel to wipe the trace of butter away. "Now scrape the goo into the pans." Casey put each one into the preheated oven as he filled it.

"Is that all there is to it?"

She looked again at the handwritten recipe on the

index card. "Bake one hour or until a straw comes out clean. Yeah, that's it."

"Like making mudpies," he said, giving her a goofy grin, pleased with himself.

"I hope they taste better than that," Casey replied.

"Mind if I hang out with you and do so more baking? What's next?"

She consulted her list. "The sugar cookie batter. That has to chill for a while before we roll it out, so the fruitcakes will be done by then."

"Do I get an apron?" he demanded.

"Frills or no frills?"

"I want a man apron and you know it," Mark said exasperatedly. "Like the one Dad uses to barbecue. Plain."

"Gotcha." Casey tried several drawers before she found one he would wear, feeling almost happy again. Sugar, butter, and a little company went a long way to making a girl feel better.

She hadn't even thought of Flint for a whole hour. She smiled at her brother, who looked at her suspiciously.

"What's that for?" Mark asked. "The smile, I mean."

Casey only shrugged. "For cheering me up. Thanks."

"Aw, shucks. Don't get used to it, sis." But his answering smile was for real.

They were done with baking just before midnight. Casey put her hands on her hips and surveyed the baking sheets loaded with treats.

"Not perfect, but pretty good," she said with satisfaction.

"Glad we're done with it. I don't ever want to see another Christmas cookie as long as I live," Mark said, untying his apron and flinging it on the counter.

"Put that in the wash," she said automatically.

"You sound like Mom," he grumbled.

"Just do it, okay?"

He wadded the apron into a ball and tossed it in the general direction of the laundry room that led off the kitchen.

"Mark!"

For a wonder, he picked it up and actually walked all the way to the washing machine, putting the apron in it and shutting the lid with a bang.

"There. I'm a good boy. Do I get everything on my Christmas list now?"

Casey looked at him curiously. "What do you want for Christmas, anyway?"

He named a couple of electronic gizmos and the latest version of a video game she knew he played with Kyle and Kevin.

"I'll see what I can do. You know that money is tight this year."

"Yeah," he sighed. "I wish I could get a job and help out."

"Like Mom and Dad would let you drop out of school. Forget it, Mark."

"I didn't mean drop out," he said. "I was thinking seasonal. You know, stocking shelves at Big Buy or something like that."

Casey gave him a sympathetic look. "Even jobs like that have a lot of applicants. People are having a tough time making ends meet in this economy, you know."

He went to the kitchen sink to wash up. "So I hear. I wanted to get Mom a dishwasher, but I don't think I can."

"A dishwasher? You were going to buy her a dishwasher?"

"Yeah," he said, drying his hands vigorously on a dishtowel. "I mean, you two are always slaving away. What's the point?"

Casey thought it over. "It's something we like to do together, believe it or not. Gives us a chance to talk, without it being a serious, sit-down occasion, if you know what I mean."

"I guess so." He tossed the dishtowel on the counter, caught her eye, and hung it up neatly so it would dry. "That better?"

She laughed. "Thanks for being thoughtful. And thanks for not making me into the Cleanliness Cop."

"You're welcome."

His voice was gruff and Casey suspected her younger brother was really missing his mother. She did a little quick thinking. "So," she said brightly, "what are we going to do with this mountain of goodies?"

"Dunno."

She eyed the plastic-wrapped trays and baking pans thoughtfully. "What do you say we drive down to the hospital and see Dad, and give it all away?"

"After all that work?" he asked incredulously.

"Beats gaining ten pounds," she retorted.

"Hey, you're always saying I'm too skinny, Casey." He lifted a corner of the wrap and took out a broken cookie, nibbling the edge. "Huh. It tastes good but the thrill is gone. Okay, you're on. Let's give them away."

"I'll call him and Mom and let them know we're coming."

"Okay, sis. Let me throw some clothes in a duffel and I'm good to go."

Mark was a typical teenaged nocturnal animal, but Casey wasn't. She held her hands up. "Whoa. It's after midnight. I'm not planning to show up in Scottsbluff before dawn. Let's get some sleep. I'll talk to Sam in the morning and make sure he can hire someone to help out while we're gone, and then we'll hit the road."

She was also going to call Flint, just so he didn't come back and find them both gone with no thought given as to running the ranch. She hoped he would miss her like crazy, and when she got back . . . Well. She wanted to go dancing again, wanted to find more ways to be alone with him, wanted to find out if they really had something.

She wanted *him*.

"You're, like, so responsible all of a sudden," Mark was saying.

"Is that a bad thing? Someone has to be while our parents aren't around."

He was giving her a look that could be defined as admiration. "You're pretty good at it, Casey."

"I try," was all she said. But his words of praise made her glow a little on the inside.

Her father had wheeled himself to a window and was gazing out, lost in thought, when Casey and

Mark arrived. They snuck up on him, although they were not exactly invisible to the nurses in their red Santa hats trimmed with white fake fur.

They set down the bags of treats and announced themselves. "Woo hoo! We're here! Merry Not Quite Christmas!"

Startled, John Gilmore turned away from the bleak landscape outside the hospital window. "Already?" he asked with astonishment. "Holy cow, you must have been speeding."

"Nah. Casey drives like an old lady. She won't go a mile over ninety on the interstate," Mark said, bending down to give his dad an awkward hug. The pompon on his Santa hat got caught on the wheelchair and the hat fell off in John's lap. The older man picked it up and put it on, beaming at his kids. "Ho ho ho! How do I look?"

"It suits you, Daddy." Her heart almost broke at the happy expression on his face.

"But does it match my hospital pajamas?" he asked her out of the side of his mouth.

"Sure does," Mark said. "Actually, I like those. Nice and baggy."

"You're welcome to them," her father said wryly. "See if you can charm one of the nurses into giving you a pair."

"Okay," her brother said absently. "Where's Mom?"

"Around here somewhere. Chatting with the orthopedist, would be my guess. She thinks he's cute."

Mark gave his father a puzzled look. The idea of his mother thinking any such thing seemed truly weird as far as a teenaged boy was concerned.

"How's your hip?" he asked, looking for a safer topic.

John Gilmore lifted his hands in an expressive shrug. "Hurts. The doc says I'm on the mend, though."

"That's great," Casey said warmly.

"At least I'm out of that crazy ropes-and-pulleys contraption."

"Are you doing physical therapy now?" she asked.

"Yup. I can walk pretty well between the parallel bars."

His son gave him a light punch on an arm that still had plenty of old-fashioned farmer muscle on it. "Good upper-body strength. Wish I had your biceps, Dad."

The older man sat up straighter in his chair. "I got those the hard way."

"Beats a gym rat workout," his son said loyally.

"You know, you're right," his father grinned. "When I get back to the Anchor Bar, you and I can start a body-building program together and get in shape. Bale tons of hay, lift a few cows—there's nothing to it."

"Okay," Mark said. "If I ever get into a fight, I'll win."

"You'll be fighting off the girls, son." The older man winked at Casey.

Mark turned scarlet when he noticed a pretty young nurse in scrubs listening in and smiling. "I guess," he mumbled.

Casey turned around when she heard the click of a woman's shoes behind them. "Mom!"

Lucille Gilmore opened her arms and her daughter rushed into them for a hug.

"It's good to see you, honey," she whispered. "You look so cute in that hat. Reminds me of when you were a little girl. You used to put one just like that on to wait for Santa. You always fell asleep, though."

Casey straightened it on her head when her mother let go, and Mark took a turn.

"Did you get taller while I was gone?" his mother asked him.

"It hasn't been that long," he said.

"I could swear you've grown an inch."

Casey picked up one of the bags and spread the handles apart to show her mother what was inside. "We did the baking yesterday."

"For heaven's sake!" her mother exclaimed. "Did you find my recipes?"

"Yes, we did. Right in the tin box on the low shelf in the cabinet."

"My goodness. One of these days I'm going to hand that over to you and retire from the kitchen."

"Never," Casey said.

"I mean it," Lucille insisted. She peered into the bag. "Looks like you did a fine job."

"We broke some and we burned some, but eventually we got the hang of it." Casey patted Mark on the shoulder. "You should see this kid do the stirring. He mixed up the fruitcake batter. I didn't have the muscle."

Her mother laughed. "It is pretty thick. Sounds like you did it right."

"We made four fruitcakes," Casey said. "They're soaking in whiskey right now."

"Sign me up for a soaking too," her father joked. "The painkillers I get around here don't work too well."

She saw him shift in his wheelchair. It was obvious he wasn't joking about the last part but he was too tough to complain. "You bet, Dad. Anyway, we're saving the fruitcakes to send out."

"Did you find the list inside the tin box?" her mother asked. "The names with stars by them are the ones who get fruitcake."

Casey hesitated. She'd seen way more than four stars on the list. "I don't think we made enough."

"Not a problem," her father said. "I've been telling Lucille for years that pretty much everybody hates fruitcake but she doesn't listen."

Lucille gave her husband a mock glare. "They expect it all the same. And Casey, I never send out whole ones. Just nice big chunks wrapped up with a pretty bow. A little fruitcake goes a long way."

"You're telling me," her father laughed.

"All right," Mark spoke up. "Enough on that subject. Casey thought we should share the cookies around here. We made, like, ten tons." He reached into the bag and pulled out a wrapped stack of thin brown slabs. "I did the gingerbread dudes."

"I'll try one of those." Her father motioned the pretty young nurse over. "Pamela? Do you think I could get a cup of coffee to go with a gingerbread dude?"

She giggled. "Sure. Can I have one too?"

Mark nodded and began to unwrap the stack.

"Be right back," the nurse said. "How about you, Mrs. Gilmore?"

"Goodness, you don't have to get me coffee, Pamela."

The nurse smiled. "I'm on break. Might as well spend it with friends, right?"

"This is my daughter, Casey, and my son, Mark. I don't think you've met either of them yet."

"No, I haven't. Hello. I'm Pamela, but I guess you know that." She tipped her head and gave a self-deprecating smile, then went off. Casey looked after her. "Nice people on staff here," she murmured.

"Yes, but I still want to get home," her father said. He held the gingerbread that Mark gave him in his strong hands, looking it over. "I have to say, son, that this here dude looks pretty tasty. I'm proud of you for helping your sister in the kitchen."

"Uh, it was fun," Mark mumbled. "I like baking better than I like cleaning up all the bowls and stuff, though."

"That's a fact," his mother sighed. "Casey's always helped me with that, but she's not going to be around forever."

Mark and Casey exchanged a look, silently telling each other not to mention the dishwasher on the Christmas wish list.

"Where's she going?" her brother asked, more as a distraction than anything.

Her mother hemmed and hawed a little. "Well, you know. Girls get married eventually."

Mark fixed a stare on Casey. "Is that true?"

She was not at all sure what to say. "Generally speaking, yes—I mean, I guess so. Specifically, no. I'm not marrying anybody at the moment."

Her younger brother relaxed visibly. "Okay then."

Casey realized that her father was picking up the undercurrents of the supposedly idle conversation. There was an interested look on his face.

"Be sure and tell us when you do," he said, joking again.

"Of course, Dad."

Pamela came back with four coffees and packets of sugar and creamer arranged on a brown plastic tray. "Here you go, happy family."

Casey was touched by the caring gesture. "Thanks so much," she said, taking the tray.

"Here," Mark said, handing the nurse one of his gingerbread creations.

"Thanks," she said, nibbling at it. "See you soon, Mr. Gilmore. Nice to meet you all." And off she went again. Mark shot his father a mortified look and didn't say anything.

Lucille took a bite and her face lit up. "Perfect. Just gingery enough, Mark."

"Thanks, Mom."

"Tell you what. I'll walk around and introduce you to the people I know, and you can hand out cookies."

Casey saw her brother begin to cringe, but he straightened up and said, "Sure. Glad to."

Now how about that, she thought. She wasn't going to embarrass him even more with the praise he deserved. But it was nice to see a little Christmas spirit shining through. "Go for it, Mark," she said.

"I bet Casey and Dad would like to talk for a little while, too," Lucille went on. "Then you'll get your chance, Mark."

Mark just nodded, obviously not wanting to admit to anything babyish like missing his parents. Casey admired her mother's way of making it easy for them to be a family again.

She looked after the two of them as they went

down the hall, realizing how hard it must be for her mother to go back and forth between home and hospital at this time of the year.

Spending hours in the kitchen working with her mother's kitchenware and following her routines had made Casey really think about how deep her family's roots were at the ranch. They might not have much money, but there was more than enough love to go around.

She turned to her father. The gingerbread dude had been devoured and he was sipping his coffee, looking at her thoughtfully.

"Sit down, Casey."

She laughed a little self-consciously and dragged over a lightweight plastic chair. "I haven't been doing too much of that lately."

"So what have you been doing?" He gestured at the cup of coffee. "Drink that. Slow down."

She sat and took the cup from him. "Doesn't it have caffeine in it?"

Her father made a funny face. "We're talking hospital coffee. It's not very strong, but it's hot. Better than nothing."

"It was nice of the nurse to bring some for all of us."

John Gilmore nodded. "I've gotten to be a familiar face on the ward. You stay here long enough, you get an unexpected cup of coffee once in a while. It's kinda like watering a plant, I think."

"Dad, you're terrible," she laughed.

"If you have a sense of humor, you recover faster."

She patted his hand. "It's going to happen. You're coming home for Christmas."

"Looks like you and Mark are holding down the fort."

She nodded, waiting for what she knew he was going to ask next.

"So how are things working out with Flint Mc-Allister?"

"He's really capable."

Her dad gave her a shrewd look. "I know that. Does he drive you crazy, Casey?"

"N-no," she stammered. "Not at all. He does exactly what you wanted him to do—he runs the ranch. Sam doesn't seem to mind answering to him."

John Gilmore sighed. "Good old Sam. He just goes with the flow, no matter what, and hardly says a word."

"He hasn't changed. Just looks a little older and a little tireder, that's all."

The second the reply was out of her mouth, she regretted it. Her dad didn't need a reminder of the passing of time, not when he was stuck in a hospital where the hours and days dragged so slowly.

He didn't get to see the last hawk of the year circling in the dramatic sky of winter, or ride over his land, feeling fully alive inside despite the bitter weather. No, John Gilmore could only look up at fluorescent light fixtures and move about as fast as a wheelchair could go down a tiled corridor, waiting and hoping for his strength to return.

"Tell me about physical therapy," she began. "How's that going?"

"Oh, right. We got sidetracked by cookie therapy." He gave her an affectionate smile. "Really well, Casey girl. I just keep at it and don't let myself get discouraged."

"That's great. Did the orthopedist give you a release date?"

"Late December was all he would say. He's not sure that I'll be entirely healed by then." His lips tightened and there was a glimmer of moisture in his steady gaze.

"You could come home in this," Casey said, touching the wheelchair. "We could make a bedroom for you downstairs." Then she remembered Flint taking over the daybed in her dad's office.

"Your mom said she'd set up everything for Flint."

"We wouldn't need him around if you came home," she said quickly.

Her father drummed his fingers on the armrests. "Well, I wouldn't mind if he would be willing to stay on for another week if I did. You know, in case any problems cropped up."

"Oh. Do you want me to ask him?"

He studied her for a long moment. "No, I'll do it, if it comes to that. But the jury's out on this damned hip of mine."

"I understand."

John moved his hands to the wheels and rolled himself a little way forward. "I don't want to think about it anymore. Let's go find your mother and Mark."

"Okay," she said, getting up and putting their empty cups into a trash container. "Lead the way."

It was good to see him relatively independent and out of that contraption, as he called it.

"I am officially refusing to talk about myself," he said as they left the area and headed down the hall.

"I want to hear more about the Anchor Bar. Got the Christmas tree up yet?" he asked.

"No." Last year he'd gone out with Sam and picked the exactly right one from some Christmas tree farm. Wouldn't say where it was. This year, with just her and her brother and maybe Mom, it might not be worth taking the trouble.

"Not waiting for me, I hope."

Casey couldn't hold back the tears. "Of course we're waiting for you," she burst out. "Nothing is the same without you there."

He stopped the wheels from rolling and took her hand, squeezing it hard. "Aw, Casey. I'm sorry you have to be the strong one for your mother and for Mark. It's getting to you, isn't it?"

"Yes," she whispered.

"I knew Flint could handle the day-to-day business of running the place," he sighed. "But that's not all there is to it."

"He does his best," Casey said. "He really looks out for me, Dad. The other day, when I was out and a storm kicked up, he—he came looking for me."

Her father looked immediately alarmed. "What the hell happened?"

"My horse showed up at the ranch without me, so Flint rode out to find me."

"When was that?"

She counted the days backward and named the exact date.

"I remember that storm. It took out a few windows in an upper ward when it blew through here."

"It was fierce. I was just glad that it didn't stick around."

"So you got back okay."

"Yes." She didn't want to inform him that Mercury had found her before Flint had or that her beloved old horse had died underneath her.

"There's something you're not telling me, Casey," he said in a level voice. "What is it?"

"Mercury was f-frightened by the storm. He came galloping out first—I was so surprised to see him. It was like I'd shouted into all that wind and he'd heard and come for me. I rode him partway home without a saddle or anything."

John Gilmore nodded sadly. "I think I can guess what happened."

"He was running all out and he suddenly died, Dad. Just like that. Not long after that Flint found me. He said that—that Mercury just kept running into heaven. It was so strange . . ." She was crying openly now, and another visitor gave her a sympathetic look.

"Come in here," her father said, leading the way to the informal chapel set up in a quiet room.

She followed, looking around, grateful that they were alone.

He stopped by a polished beechwood bench and motioned to her to sit down, then enfolded her hands in his.

John Gilmore's hands felt as strong as Flint's, she noted with faint surprise. But then they were both ranchers, toughened by the work they'd done for years. Strong men who knew how to be gentle.

"You need to cry," her dad said softly. "This is the right place. And I'm here."

With that reassurance, she allowed herself to grieve for what really had passed away from her young life. Despite what he'd suffered through himself, her father radiated masculine strength that seemed to flow from him to her. She'd never needed it more.

In a little while, she quieted and wiped away her tears. "Mom will know," she gulped.

"Of course. She's your mother. But that doesn't mean she's going to ask a lot of upsetting questions. Trust her to read between the lines, Casey."

"Okay."

"Sometimes you don't give your mother enough credit. She's been my rock, you know."

"Oh, Daddy." She didn't want to let her emotions get the better of her again, but there didn't seem to be any help for it. "I hope—I wish—that someday when I get married—"

He held up a hand. "Not yet, right?"

"N-no," she sniffled. "Anyway, I want what you and Mom have. The real deal. True love."

"You will, honey."

She just looked at him. "How do you know that?"

"I just do. You're born to be a one-man woman, and when you find that one man, you'll know."

Casey's eyes widened. Flint had said nearly the same thing.

"But true love takes work and commitment and time." He brushed away the last tear that trickled down her cheek. "And you're young yet. It'll happen."

She nodded, not ready to confess how happy she'd been in Flint's arms. She wouldn't even tell her mother about how his passionate kisses made her feel, or the wild joy she'd found in his embrace. It was all too confusing and too new, and her father's full recovery had to come first.

"I'm glad you believe in me, Daddy," was all she said.

He nodded. "Why wouldn't I? Now take a couple more minutes to calm down before we find your mother. I'll get you a Kleenex from over there—" He indicated the box set on a side table and rotated his chair.

"I can get it," she said, half rising.

John Gilmore was already wheeling away. "You stay put. Fetching you a tissue to blow your nose in is about all I can do for you right now. Give me a chance to be a hero, okay?"

He came back with the whole box and put it in her lap. Casey gave him a wan look. "Thanks. I guess I've been overdoing it, huh?"

"Sounds like you have." He smiled understandingly, and her sadness dissolved in the warmth of it.

They caught up with her mother and brother about half an hour later. Mark had made a few new friends: a couple of little kids were trailing after him and Lucille, along with a hospital-trained visiting dog in a red Santa jacket with a black belt, and its handler. Pamela, the nurse who'd brought them all coffee, was with them too.

The group was chatting animatedly as they stopped by the door of a patient room.

"Hello," she heard her brother say to whoever was inside. "We're making the rounds. Mind if we come in?"

"Want a Christmas cookie?" Pamela chirped. "How about a wet nose where you least expect it?"

Casey smiled at her father when someone in the room guffawed and said, "Bring on the nose!"

"That's Mel Daniels," her father said. "He's become a buddy of mine by now. He cracked a vertebra and they stuck him in a body cast. You should hear us. We sound like a couple of cranky old geezers, but we have a great time."

"Introduce me," she said.

When they got to the door of the room, they couldn't even see Mel. The dog's handler, a middle-aged woman with a kind face, had brought the dog, a retriever mix, to the side of the bed. The kids, both boys, were petting it and Mel was roaring with laughter.

Mark had already handed over a gingerbread dude, and the dog was gazing at it with longing.

"Will you look at the costume on that damned dog—" Mel guffawed again. "Sorry, pooch. You can't have my cookie," he told the dog, who sat politely at a hand signal from the woman. "I gotta have a few pleasures." The man in the bed took a bite of the treat. "Mmm."

"How are you doing today, Mel?" her mother asked him.

"Lousy. But it's nice to see everybody."

The little boys kept on patting the dog, who panted happily, content with lots of attention if he couldn't have a treat.

"So are you all going to sing carols or what?" Mel said when he finished munching and briskly brushed the crumbs from his hands. "There's enough people here."

"I don't see why not," John Gilmore said, rolling closer. "You kids know the words to 'Jingle Bells'?"

The two little boys looked at each and shrugged. "Dunno. We could fake it."

"Good enough."

"There you are, John." His wife turned around and motioned Casey into the group. "We were wondering what happened to you two."

Casey bent down to pat the dog, who basked in even more attention. "We weren't far away," she said.

John waved his hand to line up the impromptu chorus. "Little guys in front. All the pretty ladies in back of them. Mark, you stand on the left and I'll take the right."

Everybody moved where he directed, which left the confused dog, looking up at its laughing handler for instructions.

"Right in the middle, pal," Casey's father said to the dog. "Bark if you want to."

He rolled his chair to the right, counted to three, and the group burst into song.

Chapter Nine

Meanwhile, back at the ranch, Casey thought, in low spirits again. She'd driven over to the Smiths' to make arrangements to use their plane the following day to check fences in the far sections. Unfortunately, as far as Casey was concerned, the entire family was sitting around a roaring fire when she arrived at the Bar S, making merry.

She handed over a bag with the rest of the Christmas baking that they hadn't taken to the hospital, with the exception of the fruitcakes, which were still marinating in whiskey. Smitty's parents greeted her with their usual enthusiasm, insisting that she sit with them and have hot cider, but their son's moody silence was so marked that it was impossible for his parents not to notice. When he finally did speak, his sarcastic inquiries about "McAllister" had brought startled looks from his parents and questioning glances at Casey's unrevealing expression. Casey had tried her best to keep her replies civil, but occasionally her own short temper crept through. Mr. and Mrs. Smith had nervously laughed off some of the more pointed barbs exchanged between Casey and Smitty, trying to treat the animosity between the pair as a lovers' quarrel.

Yet it was when Mr. Smith had jokingly said to Smitty, "Well, it's Friday night. I suppose you're going to be taking the car tonight and going to the movies with Casey," that the barely disguised show of politeness had vanished.

"I'm sure Casey and McAllister have other plans for this evening," Smitty had retorted sharply. "But I will need the car." He had glanced at Casey triumphantly. "I thought I'd stop over to the Fairlie place and see Brenda."

Casey muttered the first excuse that popped into her head and left. It had become vastly immaterial whether or not the plane was to be borrowed the following day or not at all. Flint had come back, but he seemed to be a million miles away. Her overactive imagination went straight to the worst-case scenario. What if he'd decided to turn his back on her, treating her as if she were poison ivy that he shouldn't get close to? Now Smitty was deserting her as well for that ridiculous Brenda Fairlie. Casey was so mixed up that nothing seemed to make any sense anymore.

Part of the problem with Flint was her own making. She had difficulty meeting his eyes squarely. A mixture of shame and elation washed over her when he walked into a room where she was. She was so confused that she didn't know if she was supposed to ignore what had happened between them or what. But Flint's clipped words whenever he did speak to her had implied that was the direction she was to take.

In a fit of pique Casey slammed the heavy storm door shut behind her as she entered the kitchen. The room was strangely empty. At this time of the afternoon it was usual for her mother to be in the kitchen preparing the evening meal. She'd stayed on in Scottsbluff, and although Casey was miserable without her, she knew how blessed her father was to have his wife with him. She shrugged away her uneasiness and removed the pitcher of iced tea from the refrigerator. Mark's brief foray into baking didn't extend to other kinds of cooking. A glance at the stove told her that it wasn't on.

She had just poured herself a glass of tea and was raising it to her lips when she heard a sound from the doorway. She glanced back and saw Flint. He was rubbing the back of his neck in a gesture of tiredness and studying Casey with an abstracted thoughtfulness. There was a strained, hard look in his expression and weariness in his eyes. She stifled a desire to rush over and comfort him, choosing instead to keep her back to him.

"I've spent half the day looking for you." The sharp edge of his voice slashed her already frayed nerves. Luckily her back was to him and he couldn't see her flinch. "Won't you ever learn to let someone know where you're going?"

"I didn't think it mattered," Casey said just as sharply.

"The next time, don't think, just do as you're told." It hurt to have Flint speak to her as if she were a child. "By the way, your mother called from the hospital this morning—"

"Is Dad coming home?" There was nothing she

wanted more, even though such an event would mean Flint's eventual departure.

"No."

The decisive word forced Casey to swallow hard as she waited expectantly for an explanation. Flint studied her before continuing.

"He contracted a virus, something like flu, apparently. Your mother's been with him every minute since this morning because the doctor felt his condition was close to critical."

Her quick gasp for air didn't ease the sudden knotting of her stomach muscles. Casey didn't even notice his sympathetic glance.

"But he rallied. Your dad's a tough customer. Lucille called just a few minutes ago saying he had improved," he reassured her. "I've convinced her that right now her place is with your father, so she'll be staying in Scottsbluff until he's officially released from the hospital."

Flint crossed the room and poured himself a glass of tea while Casey stared at him silently. She was trying to adjust to the sudden news and the unusual tension that seemed to possess Flint. She had studied him so often that she could tell there was something more he wanted to say. He studied the tea in the glass before he bolted it down as if it were hard liquor. Then he turned his gray eyes to her.

"And I also called my sister this morning." He paused, examining Casey's face. "I've made arrangements for you to stay with her until your mother and father come home."

"What?" Casey was flabbergasted. "What are you talking about?"

There was just enough outrage in her question to

bring a tightening of Flint's jaw as he set the glass on the counter.

"Your mother and I talked it over. She agrees with me that you shouldn't stay here on the ranch with an unmarried man in the same house, namely me. She seems to be aware that you and I, are, uh—"

"We're not anything." Her mixed emotions where he was concerned suddenly got a whole lot clearer in her mind. She glared at Flint.

He cleared his throat. "Whatever you say. But I don't think I can keep a steady hand on the operation with you around to distract me."

"Distract you? That's blunt. Or maybe the right word is rude."

"It's the truth, Casey." He looked at her levelly. "The most important thing right now is that your father have absolutely nothing to worry about. You and I"—he hesitated—"that's going to take some figuring out."

"What do you think I am? A total innocent?"

He gave her an odd smile. "I guess I think . . . you don't want to be innocent. And that could land us both in a whole lot of interesting trouble. I may be repeating myself here, but your family doesn't need trouble."

"What about Mark? He's here."

"A fifteen-year-old boy isn't much of a chaperon."

"This is ridiculous. I can't imagine what got into my mother's head!"

"Maybe she has your best interests at heart." Flint attempted to reason with her. "If you don't mind my saying so."

She shook her head in disbelief. "Maybe she thinks you're God's gift to women, but I don't. Resisting you is not actually that difficult. If you don't mind *my* saying so."

Before the anger in Flint's eyes could be voiced, she rushed in, more calmly this time. "You can just call your sister back and tell her I'm not coming. My place is here at the ranch. There's too much work to be done for you to do it alone."

His hand slapped on the countertop and the sound made her jump. "Casey, I have something to say and you're going to have to listen!"

"Do I have a choice?" she asked in utter bewilderment.

"Of course you do, but—oh, hell. Can't you get it through your head that I don't want you here?"

It was as if his hand had knocked all the wind out of her as she stared blindly at the uncompromising gray eyes. Their cold hardness froze her as effectively as their fire had once burned her.

Casey turned away, her vision blurred with tears. She was certainly left in no doubt of his feelings toward her. If he had drawn her a picture it couldn't have been any plainer. He was tired of her. Well, Casey thought, gathering herself together, she had some pride left. "I'll go." The admission of defeat was hidden in her calm voice.

She heard Flint sigh behind her, but it wasn't a sigh of relief but of exasperation and irritation. His hands gripped her shoulders and turned her to face him. Casey rigidly controlled her muscles so they wouldn't react the way they wanted to and move into his arms and against his broad, inviting chest.

"I've handled this badly." Flint seemed to be choosing his words with care, trying to appear logical and in control. But the muscle at the side of his jaw was twitching.

"What I'm trying to get at is that there have been some things happening between us." His eyes bored into hers, willing her to make it easier.

But Casey remained stiff and unyielding, her gaze challenging. Her lack of cooperation angered him.

"If we were here alone . . ." He stopped. Casey raised her eyebrow in what she felt was mocking amusement. "To put it plainly, I think you've fallen in love with me," Flint stated. His forbidding expression brought a faint flush of humiliation to Casey. Why did her emotions have to be so transparent to him?

"What an ego you have"—Casey fought to keep her voice as cold and biting as she could and not let her trembling body take over—"it beats them all! Are you so used to women falling all over themselves to get near you that you expect it? With your arrogance, I suppose you think that one hot kiss and we all melt." She paused to take a deep breath. "Well, let me tell you one thing, Flint McAllister, this little gal isn't going to. I played along with you for a while because I wanted to find out what your game was. So don't bother to add me to your list of conquests."

"Are you telling me the truth? Because if you're not, I'll—" His fingers tightened on her shoulders. She stared up at him, not wanting him to get the real truth out of her.

"What do you think?" she retorted sarcastically. "If you'll just let go of me, I'll go and pack. It should be fun enlightening your sister about her big brother."

"Oh," Flint said hoarsely, releasing her abruptly. "So you're going to cooperate?"

"Do I really have a choice?" she asked, still baffled by his abrupt change of heart.

Nearly three hours later Flint and Casey arrived at the hospital. John Gilmore looked considerably weaker, but he still managed to joke that the hospital was going to do him in. Casey was surprised that she could appear so natural and relaxed in front of her parents. The happiness of their all too brief reunion had vanished with the renewed onset of ill health. She avoided any reference to Flint, who stood silently in the room. He had barely said five words to John Gilmore before moving to a wall where he could lean back and stare at Casey.

There was a moment when Casey had to meet her father's questioning eyes after her mother had mentioned that Casey was going to stay with Flint's sister. His mouth was covered with a disposable paper mask to avoid spreading whatever it was he had. The doctors had said it was an unusual type of viral pneumonia and they weren't taking any chances.

"Now how do you like that, Dad?" she'd said softly. "You always said there was a silver lining to every cloud. But now you've got some weird bug and I can't be with you."

"Yeah," he said tiredly, his voice muffled. "Can't win for losing, can we?"

"No." She wanted to cry.

He coughed and it took a while for him to get his

breath. "Be a good girl, Casey. Do what your mother says. She's in charge now."

A few minutes later, her mother cast an apprehensive glance at Casey, then over to Flint. Although her daughter seemed much the same, Flint was different somehow. But then Mrs. Gilmore didn't know him well at all. However, no mother would have been unaware of the undercurrents between her daughter and the man she'd spent so much time with in the last weeks. Perhaps, Lucille thought, she'd made a mistake agreeing with Flint's suggestion that Casey stay with his sister. It had seemed reasonable when they'd found out how sick her husband was, and leaving a grown man and a very young woman alone together when they were obviously attracted to each other just wasn't wise. Just as she was about to make an excuse to see her daughter alone and find out exactly what, if anything, was going on or had happened between Casey and Flint, one of the doctors stopped in for a late check on his patient.

Flint took the opportunity to recommend that he and Casey leave for the ranch. The strain of being a good soldier was getting to Casey again, so she agreed quickly. She paused long enough to assure her father that she would be back to see him as often as she could.

Her mom drove home in her own car, talking to Casey on her cell phone now and then, saying she was coming but not staying, to collect some things she said her husband needed for his prolonged stay.

Still upset by that—and thoroughly annoyed at

being pressured into staying at Flint's sister's house—Casey hadn't given much thought to getting ready to go herself. But she'd tidied up some before her mother's arrival.

Lucille Gilmore looked around the living room when she entered, seeming pleased.

"You've been taking care of things," she said. "Thanks, honey."

Casey nodded, accepting her mother's praise without comment.

"Now let me dash upstairs and find John's pants," her mother went on.

"Isn't Dad going to be wearing hospital gowns for a while?" Casey asked.

"Not any longer than he has to. He hates them. Says they make a man feel undignified the way they open in the back."

Casey thought that was funny and sad at the same time. "The last thing he needs to worry about is his dignity," she said.

"Well, sometimes that's the last thing a body has," her mother replied.

"Wait a minute—"

Her mother held up a hand. "Now, I didn't mean anything by that, Casey. He's not taking a turn for the worse. He just isn't happy about the situation he's in."

"I still don't see how clothes he can't wear are going to change that."

Her mother patted her daughter's shoulder. "It's all about hope. If the pants are there, then he knows he's going to walk out of that darn hospital wearing them. And besides—" She hesitated for a fraction of a second. "He likes me to look pretty for him. So I'm getting some nice clothes for myself."

Casey was silent.

"Does that sound silly?" her mother asked wistfully.

"No." Casey snapped out of the odd mood that had descended on her. "It sounds like you two really love each other."

"Of course we do," her mother said. "Don't ever doubt that, Casey."

"I don't," Casey said. "Go on and get the things. I want you to drive back before it's so late you get sleepy."

"Now who's the mom?" Lucille teased.

"Me? Hey, I'm not ready." She didn't frown when her mother pressed a light kiss to her cheek.

"Maybe you will be sooner than you think," her mother said mischievously.

Casey scowled. "Mo-om!"

"All right, sorry I said that." She gave her daughter a measured look. "I don't like leaving you on your own, you know."

Casey snorted. "Not a problem. Dad provided me with a babysitter. And now I have two, apparently."

"You'll like his sister. I hear she's a very nice girl. You could use a few new friends, Casey."

"Would it be okay with everyone if I chose my own?"

"Of course," her mother said absently. "Where is Flint, anyhow?"

"Out doing something. He's always fixing things or checking the fences or keeping an eye on the cattle and horses."

Lucille breathed a sigh of relief. "Good. Does he take you along?"

"Not often enough."

Her mother picked up on her mulish mood. "Then that's all the more reason you should have found ways to occupy yourself on your own."

"What did you want me to do? Yell at Mark for not cleaning up his room? Tell him to get off the computer once in a while?"

"Wouldn't hurt," her mother said in a mild voice. "You might want to get on it yourself. Catch up with your friends from high school and 4-H."

Casey shook her head. She hadn't felt like e-mailing anybody for weeks now, not since her dad's accident. Most of them had gone off to college or on to different lives in other states anyway. A few had joined the army or the air force.

Chatting with them online and looking at their happy pictures on Facebook just depressed her. Of course, no one ever put unhappy pictures online, so she couldn't be sure if their lives were actually perfect. But she didn't have much to announce in terms of news, and she assumed everybody who cared already knew about her dad.

"It's going to be a long winter," her mother added.

"Thanks for reminding me," Casey snapped and regretted it right away. "Sorry. You have enough to worry about without me. I'll find something to do."

"You could start a blog."

"Oh, right. The world is waiting breathlessly for daily dispatches from Nebraska. No, I have nothing to write about."

"You could post pictures, then."

"Sure. If I took nineteen thousand photos of

Nebraska in winter, they would all look exactly the same."

Casey disliked the tone of her voice. But what she was saying was true. She missed the blazing summers and the waving fields of wheat and corn. Just going into a cornfield when it had grown high enough to hide in was like entering another world, a game she'd often played with her brother.

But now the fields were cut down to faded stubble and there seemed to be less than nothing to see or do. Didn't matter. She would be soon be cooling her heels at Flint's sister's place in the middle of nowhere.

"Now, your grandmother would always start a quilt by November," Lucille said.

"Mom, please—"

"There's no reason you couldn't. You used to love to sew scraps together when you were a little girl."

"The last time I picked up a needle and thread, I sewed the material to my shirt. So no quilting for me."

"Okay, honey," her mother sighed. "But what about your photographs? You were taking wonderful pictures with that digital camera your dad gave you."

Casey shrugged.

"The ones of sunflowers were really beautiful."

Her mother didn't know when to stop, Casey thought crossly. Oh, well. Let her talk it out.

"It was awfully nice of Marci to let you hang the framed ones on the walls at her café. I bet you that one or two will sell."

"Not if people don't know who did them."

"Well, why wouldn't they know?" her mother asked, perplexed.

"Because I didn't have a business card to put up, and I told Marci they were just for show anyway, and not for sale."

"Why?" her mother persisted. "I thought they were very artistic. I don't think I ever saw a sunflower quite the way you do."

"They're just giant honking daisies, is all," Casey said impatiently.

"You're always so hard on yourself. There was something special about those photos, and I bet you could sell them. Maybe to a magazine."

"Mom," Casey said, steering her mother to the stairs. "Go get Dad's stuff. We'll talk about the photographs some other time."

"Okay. I can take a hint."

In a few minutes, she could hear her mother rummaging through the drawers in their bedroom, and wondered if she should get her dad a sweater for Christmas. So long as she didn't have to make it, she could. Then she wondered what her dad, or her mom, for that matter, wanted for Christmas. She would have to pick up a little money working at Marci's café.

If push came to shove, she could always give her parents a very nice photograph of sunflowers.

Restless, Casey headed down the road to Marchand, the nearest town to the Anchor Bar. In Nebraska terms, thirty miles away was near. She could see it for a while before she got to it. The road she was driving on went right into its one wide street,

less than half a mile long, which was anchored at
one end by a feed store that took up nearly an acre
and at the other by a sprawling gas station that
served big rigs passing through this less populous
part of the state. Beyond that were towering silos,
or Nebraska skyscrapers, as her father called them.
The town buildings looked small from where she
was, but she knew their every detail by heart.

They had fronts and sides of solid brick with
deep-set windows, and ornamental brick set in pat-
terns to frame them. No one in Nebraska went hog-
wild with decorations, but the men who'd built
Marchand had allowed for a little in the way of
something fancy and kept the severe winters in
mind as well. It was a typical prairie town, keeping
a low profile and looking, most of the time, like it
was trying not to be blown away.

It seemed timeless, as if nothing much had
changed since the early 1950s, not the old neon
signs or the storefronts.

And not much had.

But lately, with the boom in ethanol and the
increasing value of good farmland, the little town
had seen some improvements. There were new
streetlights, although done in an old-fashioned
style of painted cast iron, plantings, even a sculpture or two.

One, a bronze, life-size figure, commemorated a
local character, Hiram Nungesser. Before Casey's
time, but their hired hand Sam and her dad had
known old Hiram well back in the day.

He'd jaw the ear off anyone who had a minute to
listen, and he'd been sculptured in just that pose,
one skinny arm stretched out along the back of the

bench his statue sat on, about to tell one of his famous and never-ending yarns.

Sometimes out-of-towners driving through would wave to him before they realized he was a sculpture. And sometimes they stopped and read the plaque attached to the bench explaining who Hiram was, then sat down next to him to have their pictures taken.

She drove onto Main Street and found a parking spot about five doors down from her destination, the Café Girasole. Run by Marci Salvatore, it was about the only interesting place to hang out in the whole county.

Even the truckers had discovered Marci's place, lured there by the proximity to the interstate and the presence of old Mrs. Kreutzer in the kitchen.

Casey knew both women would see her enter. There was a round mirror strategically placed just outside the kitchen so they could keep track of what was going on in the main area.

The café wasn't exactly a restaurant and wasn't exactly a coffee place, but it managed to combine the best of both.

"Yoo hoo!" Marci called. She'd married and divorced a Chicago guy years ago and come back home to Nebraska after everything was settled. She wasn't any more Italian than Casey was, but she figured keeping her ex's name would be good for business.

"Get your fanny in here, Casey!" Mrs. Kreutzer added even more loudly.

Casey obeyed, laughing and ignoring the looks from the few customers in the café.

"I need help with these doughnuts," Mrs. Kreuzter said. "Put on an apron and hop to it."

"Yes, ma'am." Casey kissed the wrinkled cheek, pleasantly powdered with a light dusting of flour, and awaited her orders.

"Here's the paper towels." Marci handed her a roll. "And there's the cooling rack."

"Ready and waiting," Casey said.

Mrs. Kreutzer peered into a vat of bubbling oil, assessing the doneness of her prize-winning doughnuts, which had puffed up and now floated on the top.

She picked one up with a pair of tongs, dipped the sizzling circle of dough into a big bowl of cinnamon and sugar, and set it on the rack.

"Mmm," Casey said. "Smells heavenly."

"Just line 'em up nice and easy," Mrs. Kreuzter said. "And stand back. I gotta move quick."

The yeast-based dough was an old recipe, Casey knew, and Mrs. Kreutzer had been making them all her life. Almost faster than the eye could see, she took out and dipped doughnut after doughnut, leaving Casey to push them into neat rows with a wooden spoon.

As soon as one rack was filled, Marci took it away and set an empty one in its place. In a matter of minutes they had done over a hundred.

"There." Mrs. Kreutzer pushed a straggling lock of gray hair back under her hairnet. She grabbed a dishtowel and wiped the oil and flour from her hands. "I may not be beautiful but them doughnuts sure are." She sat down on a chair to take a breather.

"Here come the truckers," Marci sighed, glancing into the mirror.

Casey chuckled. "You've got them trained."

She helped Marci set out the doughnuts on cake stands, piling them in pyramids and taking them out to the café's main area. Sure enough, flannel-shirted guys in trucker caps and waist-length jackets were filing in.

Hellos were called all around and the men took their accustomed places.

"You want to take the coffee orders, hon?" Marci asked.

"Okay. But this apron is all covered in sugar and cinnamon."

"Believe me, they won't notice," Marci said. She gave Casey a pinch on the cheek.

"Hudson, Earl, Jim—what'll it be?" Casey found a pad and jotted down the orders. Most of the men she'd known since forever, or she knew their sons and daughters. There were orders for sandwiches mixed in with the coffees, and she wrote those down too.

She slid the pad over to Marci, who took it back into the kitchen, calling for Max, the young guy who worked as a line cook. He hadn't been in there at doughnut-making time, so Casey figured he'd just gotten in.

She got busy serving up coffee in thick mugs, making small talk and adding fresh doughnuts to the heavy, diner-style plates with blue stripes around their rims.

Plates that never broke, unlike Marci's collection of tag-sale plates and cups, which were proudly displayed on shelves against sunny, yellow-painted walls, along with a lot of knickknacks from the shop next door, which was sometimes open at the same time as the café and sometimes not.

Then Casey sat down to take a breather herself in her favorite part of the café. The walls were painted ruby red and the banquette seats were upholstered in vinyl to match. Marci didn't have her Christmas decorations up yet, Casey noticed. She'd give her friend and boss a hand with those as soon as Marci asked.

Her photographs looked good against the red, she thought, unwilling to praise herself much. But the giant sunflowers depicted in all stages of their growth were a natural for the café—Marci had thought so, anyway, because *girasole* meant sunflower in Italian.

She brought out a huge tray balanced on one arm and set down the truckers' orders, then flirted a little as Mrs. Kreutzer brought out another tray laden with sodas for those who didn't want coffee. Eventually she joined Casey at the banquette, waving her dishtowel at the older woman, who headed back into the kitchen.

"Whew," Marci said, "the pre-dinner rush in Marchand is getting more rushy."

"Rushy? Is that a word?"

"It is if I say it is."

"Word's getting around. Home baking and big sandwiches—you're a big success," Casey said. "Wish I could say the same."

"Oh! That reminds me," Marci said.

"What?"

"You could be successful too."

"Gee whiz," Casey said. "How? I don't have a blue-ribbon pig or a pony who does tricks."

Marci waved away the sarcasm. "A man came in today and was looking at your photographs. He asked if there was a way to contact you."

"I hope you said no."

"Casey, I asked for his business card."

She was interested despite her bad mood. "Really?"

Marci patted her pockets. "I have it here somewhere." She pulled out the little piece of paper and held it out to Casey. "Here it is. He's the editor of *Heartland Home* magazine—you know, based in Omaha. He said he buys photos from freelancers sometimes."

"No kidding." Casey looked at the name on the card. "Brad Heller, huh? But I'm not a freelancer. I'm just an amateur."

"No, you're better than that, if someone like him thinks so."

"I don't agree. And don't try to blind me with logic."

Marci laughed. "Okay, I won't, but call him, okay? Or e-mail him."

"Ah . . ." Casey hesitated, looking again at the card. *Heartland Home*. She'd seen it. There were a few dog-eared copies of it in the pile of magazines Marci kept for customers to peruse if they felt like reading. It featured photos of quaint houses and funny folks and back roads. She never would have imagined that her photographs could appear in a publication like that. "No, I don't think so."

"Why not?"

"There's a lot going on in my life right now,"

Casey said vaguely. "I don't think I'd make a good impression on the guy."

"Your photos did. He really liked that one in particular." Marci pointed at one of a sunflower past its prime, its immense head drooping on its thick, muscular-looking stem. A little bird clung to it, picking out seeds.

"Yeah, well. I still don't think so." Casey didn't know why she was so reluctant. "So why did he come in here?"

"He'd heard about Mrs. Kreutzer's doughnuts. He wanted to do an article on her."

"Wow. Did he talk to her?"

"Yes," Marci laughed. "She gave him a lot of sass but she wouldn't give him her recipe."

"That's classified."

"Sacred is more like it."

The two women chuckled at the thought of Mrs. Kreutzer giving an Omaha man hell.

"But I'll call this magazine guy soon," Casey promised Marci. "When Dad gets home and Christmas is over and things are more settled."

Marci looked mystified, but she didn't press the point further. "Okay. Don't lose that card."

"I won't."

They turned as the café door opened and a bunch of noisy teenage boys sauntered in.

"Next wave," Marci said, rising from the table. Casey moved to get up too, but her friend motioned her down. "Isn't that your brother with them?"

Casey looked and saw his lanky frame inside a sloppy hooded sweatshirt. His eyes were hidden by wraparound sunglasses. "Yes. Trying to look cool."

"He's coming over."

Casey groaned. "I'm not sure I want to share a table with him."

"Lighten up, Casey. He's a good kid."

It was a moot point, because Mark was only two steps away. He settled himself into the chair that Marci had vacated. "Hello, sis."

"Hello, yourself."

"You don't look thrilled to see me." He pushed his sunglasses up on his forehead. "How about we make eye contact?"

"Let me put it this way," she began. "I see a lot of you."

He wasn't even paying attention to her answer, just whiffing the aroma that was coming from the kitchen. "Hey, I smell doughnuts."

"You're right."

He got up and ambled back to join his friends, who were filling their mouths with hot, fresh, cinnamon-sugar doughnuts just about as fast as Marci could bring them out.

Casey sighed and settled back on the banquette, looking at her photos again. So an Omaha magazine editor liked them. That was something to think about.

She'd never seriously considered anyone who mattered liking the pictures she took. She'd only been fooling around with the camera when she'd first gotten it, trying to figure out everything it could do.

Sunflowers were her favorite flower, and her mom always planted them by the side of the house where it was brightest. Casey had recorded every stage, from the fat, green-yellow buds about to burst open, to the enormous flowers with tightly packed seeds forming a pinwheel pattern as they ripened, to the heavy, dry-petaled heads that pulled down the massive stalks before the whole plant collapsed.

She was lost in thought, admitting to herself that the composition of some of the photos was probably not too bad, when someone slid into the seat opposite hers.

Flint McAllister. Casey blinked at him, embarrassed to be caught contemplating her own work.

He turned around to examine the photos, smiling with appreciation. "Great photos," he said. "I could see why you were admiring them."

"Uh, I wasn't."

He looked a little surprised. "They really are good, though. I'd buy one or two if I knew who did them."

"Really?"

She winced. What a question to ask. Maybe she should just shut up and let him do the talking.

"Do you know who the photographer is?"

"No," she said quickly.

"Then maybe Marci does."

Casey shook her head. "I don't think so."

Flint gave her a doubtful look. "She must. This is her café. Someone didn't come in and hang a bunch of framed photos without asking her."

"Well, she's busy right now."

Flint looked around at the hustle and bustle of the teenagers, trying to out-talk each other with earbuds popped in and blaring music.

"She's got her work cut out for her," he said. "Hey, there's Mark."

Casey nodded, trying to think of a way to extricate

herself from this and somehow ask Marci not to tell him she'd taken the photographs. Nothing came to mind. As usual, Flint was just too distracting. "Yes, he already came over and said hi."

"I see." Flint studied her thoughtfully. "Do you mind if I sit here with you?"

"No, not really," Casey said. "After all, everyone from around here knows you're staying at the ranch and a few of them even know you personally. So it's no big deal if you talk to me, is it?"

"Guess not," he said wryly.

Casey stiffened. It was just too bad if he was expecting a response that would stoke his male ego. She wasn't excited to see him or anything. In fact, she felt awkward.

"Want a doughnut and coffee?" he asked, noticing that there was no plate or cup in front of her.

"No, thanks. I helped make them," Casey said. "You know how it is."

He crossed his arms on the table. "I think I can guess. But that delicious smell is getting to me. I may not be able to resist temptation much longer."

Casey thought, panicked, that she would have to speak to Marci before he did, just in case he made some remark about the photographs.

"How many would you like?" she asked in a rush.

"Two for starters," he said. "But don't get up."

His hand on her arm restrained her for a second but Casey shook it off. "No problem. I was going into the kitchen anyway."

"If you insist, then."

She could practically feel his gaze on her bottom as she rose and walked away, and she wished she'd worn a baggy pair of jeans instead of the tight ones.

Casey pushed through the double swinging doors that led to the kitchen and looked for Marci.

Mrs. Kreuzter waved the tongs at her. "There you are. I need some help."

"Sure," Casey said. Hot-out-of-the-fryer dough-nuts couldn't wait, and she didn't see Marci. She picked up her wooden spoon and pushed them into order on the rack and Mrs. Kreutzer dipped into the vat.

Marci came out from the back, carrying more dough in a big bowl. She set it down on the counter and headed out.

"Hold on," Casey exclaimed worriedly. "I have to talk to you."

"Go ahead."

Casey turned her face away from the old lady in the hairnet, making it clear that she didn't want to talk in front of her.

Marci stopped and helped, so Mrs. Kreutzer could sit down again. Then she steered Casey into the back area where she had come from.

"What's up? You look upset."

"I'm not," Casey said. "But Flint showed up. Do me a favor—"

"Okay." Marci sighed. "What is it?"

"Don't tell him I took those pictures."

Marci nodded. "First Brad Heller and now Flint—oh, I'm not even going to ask why. If you want to be all mysterious about some really good photos you happened to take, that's your problem."

"Thanks. I owe you."

"No, you don't. But I do think you're crazy, Casey." She amended that remark when she saw the look on her friend's face. "A little bit crazy. Not a lot."

"Thanks for that too."

"Oh, please," Marci laughed.

"Flint wants two doughnuts," Casey said, looking at Mrs. Kreutzer, who was resting.

"Do you want me to take them out to him on a silver platter or do you want to do the honors?"

"Tell him I'm busy in the kitchen," Casey said. "And behave yourself."

"I don't know," Marci mused. "He is good-looking. A little young for me, but nothing I can't handle."

"Hey," Casey began indignantly, then realized that she might sound possessive. "Never mind."

They heard a hammering on the wall that separated the Café Girasole from the shop next door.

"Sounds like Helen came in today," Marci said. "Why don't you dash over there if you don't want to sit with Flint?"

"Good idea. I have to start looking for Christmas presents for my mom and dad anyway."

"A perfect excuse," Marci said. "Now shoo. Out of here. And I promise not to flirt with Flint McAllister."

"I don't care if you do," Casey lied. She went out the back way of the café and into the back door of Helen's shop.

"Hello," Helen called absentmindedly. "Who's there?"

"Me, Casey Gilmore."

"Oh, hi, Casey. How come you came around the back? Are you avoiding someone?"

Good old Helen wasn't so absentminded as all that, Casey thought ruefully. "No, it just seemed quicker. I was making doughnuts with Mrs. Kreutzer and Marci."

"Aha." Helen sniffed the air. "I'd probably have

to close this shop if not for those little goodies. Did you bring me any?"

"No."

Helen raised a neatly plucked eyebrow. She didn't even have to ask.

"Be right back," Casey said.

She returned with four on a saucer. Helen took one off the top and munched it, looking at the piece of china carefully. "I think I sold this saucer to Marci."

"You probably did," Casey said.

The shopkeeper finished the doughnut. "Excellent," she said, brushing the crumbs from her smock top. "I'll have the others later. So to what do I owe the pleasure of your company, Miss Casey Gilmore?"

"I just wanted to look around. Maybe I'll find something one-of-a-kind for a Christmas present for my mom, maybe even my dad."

"Make yourself at home." Helen went to her antique rolltop desk and pulled various papers out of its nooks. "I have paperwork to do."

Casey nodded and walked around to see what was new. Everything was old, of course.

Helen sold things like china poodles that foretold the weather in shades of pink and purple, and china vases shaped like women's heads or sleeping fawns. There were farm artifacts, too, like old milk cans and stoneware jugs, and even a chicken feeder that had been scrubbed up and filled with cellophane-wrapped peppermints for anyone who was feeling peckish.

There were baskets heaped with doilies and cross-stitched dishtowels, and other handiwork lovingly completed by women who'd found a few moments to make pretty things in between their household chores and cooking.

All the items spoke to Casey somehow. She wandered on, picking up an old book for children, *Shoes and Ships and Sealing Wax*, with illustrations that were still vivid decades after it had been new. Then she ran a finger along an endless row of Nancy Drew mysteries, bound in blue buckram, from way back when the girl detective had been hot stuff herself.

She didn't see anything her mother would like. And there certainly wasn't anything that would interest her dad. The streetlamp outside made the antique Christmas ornaments that Helen had placed in the window gleam, and Casey went to look at them.

There were silverglass Santas and hand-painted baubles from Czechoslovakia, treasured for decades by farm families whose descendants had left the area long ago, scattering through the US like seeds on the wind. She picked up a funky little felt Snoopy ornament from the 1960s and touched his round black nose, then set the cartoon pup back down amidst a green metallic garland where he'd been placed.

As if making a gift suggestion, Helen had arranged sets of novelty salt-and-pepper shakers on a tiled tray. Casey looked them over, enjoying the funny pairs. But one figurine was solo.

"I like the salt shakers," she called to Helen, who was humming to herself at her desk. "But one fell or something—there's a little woman in a gingham dress and a bonnet standing on a cheese, but she's all alone."

"Yes," Helen said. "That's an Old MacDonald set. The farmer takes a wife, and all that. But she's lost her husband."

"Oh," Casey said. "That's too bad." Somehow the sight of the lonely little wife made her think of her mother, driving all the way back to the hospital in Scottsbluff by herself tonight, and Casey felt a rush of sudden, sentimental tears. How ridiculous of her to get all choked up about a salt-and-pepper set.

"It happens," Helen said, not looking up.

"Yes, it does," Casey agreed. Someone outside moved in front of the window and she recognized the man at once. Flint again.

She smiled at him, not really wanting to. She dismissed the idea that he was following her. The town of Marchand was so small that you couldn't take two steps without running into everyone you knew. No, he'd finished his doughnuts and left, and was heading for his car—she noticed where he'd parked it.

Flint gave her a nod and didn't enter the shop. Casey felt suddenly bereft. Nothing she could do about it. She had ditched him and she didn't feel like running into the street after him to offer an explanation.

If he wanted to ask her, she could come up with something then. Not wanting to leave home and go stay with his sister would be number one on her list.

She watched him walk off and then went back around to the Café Girasole.

A young guy who was already balding was sitting

at a table near the door she entered, and he looked up with a friendly but nervous grin.

Uh-oh. Elwood had found her. He was nice but nerdy. In fact, he was known as Nerdy Birdy Elwood. Sure enough, he had his *Field Guide to American Birds* open on the table and was checking a few species off his life list.

"Hello, Elwood," she said, trying to get by. Someone heading for the restroom blocked her path.

"Hey, sit down for a sec," he said. "Can I buy you a cup of coffee or something?"

"No, thanks." She looked up to see Marci bringing over Elwood's order, catching the be-nice-to-the-customer look her boss was giving her. "But I'll sit down. Just for a sec."

Casey eased into a chair as Elwood turned his list around for her to look at.

"Check it out," he said proudly, pointing to the entries he'd just made. "I added two new birds today. Don't see those often in Nebraska. Late migrants, I think."

"Maybe so," she said politely.

Casey loved birds, had taught her dad about helping them. She'd persuaded him to not chop down the two dead cottonwoods by the creek and to leave brushy areas for them to nest in, even talked him into fencing off a pristine pond so the cattle couldn't muddy it—but she didn't go as far as Elwood.

It wasn't that she didn't like him. He was nice. He just didn't thrill her. She sighed inwardly, listening to him talk about bobolinks.

Around here, there just weren't very many guys her age besides Smitty, and she'd known him for forever and a day. *Anyway,* a little voice in her mind whispered, *Flint makes guys your age look like little boys.*

She was still wildly attracted to the oh-so-virile scion of the McAllister clan, whether she wanted to be or not. Good thing he'd left the café, though. She wasn't up to dealing with him right now.

Elwood droned on. Casey waited for a pause to say politely that she was needed in the kitchen, and then rose.

"Want to go birdwatching with me?" he asked hopefully. "I have an extra pair of binoculars."

"Sure. In spring," she said. "And I have my own binoculars."

"Great. Okay. That's a date then."

He actually looked satisfied with her reply and Casey felt a little guilty. "See you around," she said, giving him a wave and heading back to a safer haven behind the double swinging doors.

Back in the kitchen, she distracted herself with a thousand little things that needed doing, until Marci shooed her out again. Casey took a peek and saw Elwood, head down, reading his field guide.

Good a time as any to make a break. She walked out, snagged her coat from the hook, and headed down the street to where she'd parked.

She did a double take when she saw the bronze statue of Hiram Nungesser on the bench. He had company—yes, someone from out of town.

Flint.

"Hey," he said.

Casey stopped. She couldn't just walk by him and get lost in the crowd. There wasn't one. They were the only two people out on the street. "Hey, yourself."

"Mind if I ask why you ditched me?"

"I didn't really."

"Yes, you did. Unless you find salt-and-pepper shakers more interesting than my company."

"Flint, I was looking for a Christmas present for my mom. She loves that funny old stuff."

"Oh."

Casey was nettled by his flat tone. "You don't get to decide everything about where I go and what I do, you know."

"I wouldn't want to." He glanced over at the bronze statue. "Who's the old guy?"

"Didn't you read the plaque?"

"No."

Casey thrust her hands into the pockets of her warm coat. Like practically everything else in the town, she knew it by heart. "Hiram Nungesser, a friend to all," she recited. "Storyteller and raconteur." She finished with the dates of his birth and death.

Flint looked at the statue again. "How about that. Howdy, Hiram."

"You must never have been in Marchand."

He shrugged like it was no big deal. "I've passed through a few times."

"Who told you I was here?"

Flint hesitated. "Sam Wolver thought you might have come this way."

Silent Sam had ratted her out. She would have to talk to him about that. No, she decided. There was no way Sam had meant to do her harm.

"Well, I'm going back to the Anchor Bar."

Flint got up. "What a coincidence. So am I. And then you and I are going to head out to Ogallala. When you're ready," he added when she made no reply.

Chapter Ten

Casey never realized the journey from the ranch to Ogallala could seem so long. Nor did she ever think that Flint could treat her the way he was, given the circumstances. Even the arch of his eyebrow when he turned in her direction, which was seldom, seemed to convey displeasure. As for herself, she didn't attempt to inject any warmth into the car. She huddled against the car door and stared out the window, trying to make believe that Flint wasn't there at all.

When they passed Chimney Rock, painted a fiery orange by the late setting sun, Casey felt the tears she'd held back for so long cloud in her eyes. Gazing at the inverted funnel formation of rock, a famous landmark on the way west, made her wonder what hardships were ahead of her. Her conversation with her father in the hospital chapel on the previous, much happier visit made her understand that her love for Flint was genuine. The sneaking feeling that he probably didn't want her was one that her pride would never let show.

The dark waters of Lake McConaughy blinked at them from behind the sandy bluffs that rimmed the Platte River Valley. Casey found herself wondering more and more about her final destination. She discovered that she knew very little about his sister, the woman she was going to stay with, other than her name, Gabrielle, her age, twenty-four, and her occupation, freelance writer. She longed to ask Flint questions, but each impulse to do so was pushed back. Feeling as she did for him, she had to be nuts to become involved with his family. How many endless days would stretch ahead where she would picture him with them? An ironic smile teased her lips as she remembered wanting to say to her father that this was going to be a vacation. That was far from the truth. It was going to be a test of her nerves. Right now she didn't think she could stand up under it.

Flint turned the SUV off the main road toward the lake and continued along a dirt road until he reached a group of lakefront cabins. In the waning purple of the evening light, Casey could make out the chalet-type cabin with a wide porch at the rear of the structure looking out over the shimmering waters. The angular design was a little too austere, which was probably the reason Casey shuddered when Flint pulled into its narrow drive. The affluence it represented intimidated her and made her more aware of her ordinary, just-plain-folks background.

The car rolled to a halt at almost the same pace that her heart slowed its beat. Flint turned off the engine. Casey waited expectantly for him to open the door and signal the end of the journey, but he didn't. In the dimness of their confines, she saw him turn toward her. The focus of his attention quickened her impulse. The distance between them seemed so small that with just the slightest effort she could be in his arms. It was surprising how cold she suddenly felt inside, and she remembered vividly the feel of his warm body against hers.

"You didn't have an easy time of it in the hospital." The compassion in his voice bothered Casey for reasons she didn't really understand. She didn't want his pity.

"My father's a lot worse off than I am," she said.

"That's true. Too many things have happened in a few short weeks, and the holidays are almost here." He paused for a beat. "Maybe staying in Ogallala will help you think things through. The pace is slower here—"

"Skip it," she answered bitterly. "I agreed to come here only to reassure my dad and my mom. If you really want to know, I feel like I've been put in a corner."

For a moment annoyance flared in his eyes before the gray calmness returned. "Common sense should make you admit that what I'm saying is right."

"Common sense told me that I shouldn't have been such a good sport about you coming to the Anchor Bar. The biggest mistake I ever made was not kicking up more of a fuss about it." As if she was making up for lost time, she kicked at the SUV door instead, using the blunt, scuffed toe of her roping boot to open it when she pressed down on the handle. She didn't do any damage, but she wanted to.

"You're acting childish," Flint warned, leaning closer. "Just talk to me. You don't have to kick my car."

"Conversation with you is pointless," Casey replied scathingly, unwilling to admit that she was slightly unnerved by being physically close to him. She pushed open her door and stepped out before he had a chance to stop her.

Her legs felt wobbly beneath her, but she managed to gaze haughtily at him as he slammed his car door shut and removed her suitcases from the back. The lack of expression in his face brought a lump to her throat. All she wanted was to be away from him, to indulge herself in the tears that she had fought all afternoon. She didn't want to give him the satisfaction of knowing he could make her cry. Flint signaled for her to precede him to the cabin. It was difficult to keep her back straight, her chin up, and her pace slow with his steady gaze on her back. Relief washed over her as the front door opened and she was bathed in the light.

"I was beginning to think you weren't coming!" the tall, dark-haired girl in the doorway called out in a happy, welcoming voice.

"He was abrupt, wasn't he?" Gabrielle, or Gabbie as she had insisted that Casey call her, commented after Flint had left. "Not very polite—not like him."

"I guess so," Casey willingly admitted, glad that his own sister, who could be considered an authority on the subject of all things McAllister, had noticed his cold indifference.

Flint had been almost rude, making only the

briefest of introductions before setting the suitcases down and stating that he had to leave to make it back to the ranch. Gabbie's offer for refreshments had been brushed aside. He'd left with only a curt nod to Casey that was supposed to serve as good-bye.

Although Casey was still uneasy, Gabbie's handshake had been warm and friendly. Even now she was obviously trying to establish some degree of comradeship between them. The trouble was that Casey had discovered that Flint's sudden departure had removed her protective armor. The rigidity and tenseness were gone and she was dangerously close to tears.

"Let me fix something for us to nibble on in the kitchen. And would you like a drink?"

"Yes, thanks. Whatever you have. I'm not picky."

"Why don't you go on into the living room and make yourself comfortable?" Gabbie suggested.

Casey glanced appreciatively at the tall girl with long, straight dark hair.

"Thanks, I will," she agreed.

The room was cozy and cheerful, but Casey wasn't in the mood to appreciate it. The walls were white with large, dark-stained beams giving it a rustic but elegant atmosphere.

A Christmas tree dominated one corner, imaginatively decorated with at least a hundred feathered birds that seemed almost real. They perched on raffia nests that held tiny glass eggs in jewel colors, and sparkling strands of green glass beads had been carefully arranged in symmetrical loops all around the tree.

Casey thought about the living room of the Anchor Bar's main house—she hadn't even moved the big armchair that stood where the Christmas tree always did, let alone gone out to buy one.

It seemed too weird to make a big fuss with no one but her and Mark to enjoy the result. Flint would head home before Christmas Eve, and her father wouldn't be home in time—it just wasn't possible. The chances of the Gilmores having a good old-fashioned family celebration were slim to none, she thought miserably.

An enormous white wicker chair offered its cocoonlike shelter to her, and Casey allowed herself to be lost in its bright cushions, which were decorated with holiday motifs. Her restless hand touched the large fern in the cedar pot beside her chair. Gabbie was big on natural decor. She joined her only a few minutes later, handing her a tall glass already gathering moisture on the outside.

"I'd better warn you. I put some vodka in that," Gabbie told her as Casey lifted the drink to her mouth.

The citrus tang of juice refreshed her dry throat, while the potent liquor relaxed her and chased away the hollow feeling inside.

"You looked like you needed a serious drink," Gabbie added.

"I did." Casey sighed. She stared at the glass, listening to the sound of the ice clinking against the side.

"How's your father?" Gabbie curled her long legs under her on the sofa.

"Much better. I guess the virus had burned itself out this morning. He had a high fever for a while, I heard. But he was able to talk when Flint—when I was there." Casey's mind was racing to think of anything to say, anything to keep from returning to those thoughts of Flint.

"Flint seemed really concerned when he called me that day." Gabbie's blue-green eyes studied Casey thoughtfully before returning to the large silver bracelet on her wrist. "He isn't the type to cry wolf without a reason."

Casey swallowed hard, but she couldn't get rid of the lump in her throat. Gabbie paused just long enough to give Casey an opportunity to comment if she wanted before she continued.

"Each time Flint's been back, he's told us quite a lot about your family. He admires your parents. You have two brothers, don't you?"

Casey nodded that she did.

"Flint thinks that Mark—he's the youngest, isn't he?—will make a fine rancher. Flint said he had a natural feel for the land."

Casey looked surprised. "I guess they worked together—my brother doesn't tell me everything." There was no escape from the subject of Flint, apparently. Tears welled in her eyes. In another moment they would be running down her cheeks. Casey jumped to her feet, placing the glass haphazardly on the glass coffee table.

"You'll have to excuse me." Casey fought for composure. She refused to cry in front of Flint's sister. "I know it's early yet, but I'd really like to"— she swallowed back a sob—"to turn in. The drive— my dad—I'm kind of overwhelmed lately."

"You don't have to make any excuses." Gabbie smiled, rising as well. "I understand."

She led Casey to a small bedroom in the rear of the cabin, showed her where the bathroom was, the empty drawers in the bureau, and the closet for her clothes before turning to leave.

"Stay in bed as late as you like. I write in the mornings, so just cover your head with a pillow when you hear me clicking away. Get some sleep, Casey. It'll do you good."

As the door closed behind the dark-haired young woman, Casey sank on to the single bed. She forced herself to remove her clothes before she leaned back on the bed and stared at the ceiling. Then it happened. The whole room disappeared, obscured by tears.

It took Casey nearly an hour the following morning to repair the ravages wrought by last night's storm of tears. Even carefully applied makeup didn't restore the lack of color in her cheeks and the dullness in her eyes. Shrugging that it didn't really matter what she looked like anymore, Casey pulled a pastel top over her head that looked about as washed out as her faded jeans. Just as she entered the living room, Gabbie walked out of the kitchen carrying a tray.

"Ta da! Breakfast," she announced, walking on past Casey. "I always indulge when I have a particularly bad morning at the computer. Any excuse to get me away from that monster! I made toasted muffins, jam and coffee—how does that sound to you?"

"Really good." Casey followed her. She couldn't help admiring the sea green kimono Gabbie was wearing and the way her long dark hair was piled on top of her head.

"Like the outfit?" Gabbie asked at Casey's careful study of her. "Most people expect writers to be slightly eccentric. I don't like to disappoint them."

"You look great. Not eccentric at all. I think the right word would be chic." Casey smiled as she pulled a chair away from the table. "What's it like being a writer?"

"It has its peaks and valleys. The valleys seem exceptionally deep when you're staring at a blank monitor. But it's the supreme ego trip when you see your name below a published article or quoted on a major blog, if—capital letters, IF—you don't let yourself get weighted down by rejections."

"What do they say? I hear that submissions are hardly ever read all the way through."

"Editors are pretty good at being vague. Um, let me think. Oh yeah. 'Thanks for the opportunity to consider your work and sorry to say no, but this just isn't right for us.'" She used a droning tone to make her point. "That's a popular one-line reply. I believe they just want to say 'What were you thinking?' and let it go at that. But usually they come up with some tactful reason."

"Got it."

"They'd better be tactful," Gabbie chuckled, "because they never know who's going to be famous someday."

Casey sipped carefully at the scalding cup of coffee, inhaling the aroma at the same time, then setting it down. "What kind of things do you write exactly?" she asked as she spread blackberry jam on a muffin.

"Short stories, magazine articles, on-line essays." Gabbie's hand waved, suggesting more. "The Great

American Novel is waltzing around in my head, but so far it hasn't danced itself onto paper." She leaned back in her chair, nibbled at her muffin, and gazed out at the partly frozen lake outside the glass door.

Casey studied Gabbie's aristocratic profile against the backdrop of blue sky. She could have been a model. It was startling to see how much she looked like Flint. Gabbie had the same strong cheekbones, straight nose, and high arched brows, although her jawline was more refined and feminine. She was strikingly beautiful in her own way. But now she was a constant reminder of Flint's unnerving handsomeness.

"Did you find the family resemblance?" A pair of blue-green eyes stared back into the pain-filled brown ones. Their knowing look was extremely difficult to meet.

"I . . . I don't know wh-what you mean," Casey stammered, trying to ignore Gabbie's direct gaze.

"All of us McAllisters look alike in some way or another. Flint and I have almost the same bone structure, although my hair is darker than his and I don't have those cute creases that give his mouth a permanent smile. You were bound to notice the resemblance sooner or later," Gabbie replied blandly.

Casey made an attempt to hide her confusion by picking up her coffee cup again as she admitted that she had.

Gabbie waited a beat and then spoke her mind. Too bluntly. "You look as if you've spent the night crying."

Casey couldn't stop the cup from clattering back to its saucer at Gabbie's pointed remark.

"I didn't get nicknamed Gabbie just because my first name is Gabrielle, and I didn't become a moderately successful writer by not observing the people around me. I'm not a subtle person and I'm not going to pretend to be one." Her eyes softened as she watched the conflicting emotions race across Casey's face. "I bet those tears last night were over my brother and not your father. Am I right?"

Casey stared at her aghast. How could Gabbie possibly know? How could she possibly guess? She opened her mouth to deny the charge, but instead an almost inaudible "yes" tumbled out.

"Do you want to tell me about it?" Gabbie coaxed her gently.

Casey raised her lowered head and gazed at her thoughtfully.

"I talk a lot, but I never betray a confidence, so you don't have to worry that I'll go carrying tales to Flint," Gabbie assured her. "If you'd rather not tell me, that's all right too."

The need to lighten her burden by talking was overwhelming. Besides, there was something about Gabbie, just as there had been about Flint, that told Casey she could trust her. But there was also a certain point beyond which Casey wasn't going to go. She held back the more intimate details, relating only the briefest of outlines to Gabbie, ending with, "He made it pretty clear he didn't want me."

The composure with which she retold the story surprised her. The words seemed to have come out of another person. Perhaps, she decided, she had cried out all her tears last night and no emotions remained.

"What an unfeeling brute!" A somewhat theatrical sigh puffed expressively from Gabbie's pink-tinted lips, but she did seem to mean what she said. "Even if he is my brother, that was a callous thing to do." The glimmering green of her dress was reflected in the gleam of her eye. "If Flint was so blind not to see what a gem he could have had, then he deserves whatever comes next."

"What are you talking about?" Casey was a little bit puzzled by Gabbie's cryptic remark.

"Just thinking out loud." Gabbie shrugged, rising from her chair. "I have to get back to work. You're welcome to walk along the shore if you like. It's freezing out but it's still gorgeous."

Minutes after Gabbie left, Casey heard the tapping of a computer keyboard. She sighed heavily, wishing she were back at the ranch where she could have at least busied herself with repair work or seeing to the horses. Now all she had to do was to gaze at the beauty of the lake, its icy surface stretching out like fingers to the edge of the water. Stuck in a winter wonderland, Casey was mostly conscious of her aching love for Flint. His face was unforgettable—she wished she could stop imagining it.

The jangling ring of the phone in the house startled her momentarily. She'd forgotten how loud and monotonous a land line could be, like an alarm clock ringing her out of a bad dream. Casey waited expectantly for Gabbie to answer it, but the distant tapping of the computer didn't even pause. At the fourth ring, Casey rose to her feet and walked back into the house. The white phone was sitting on an end table, still intermittently ringing. She glanced toward the room where Gabbie was working. Perhaps she didn't want anyone to know she was here, Casey thought. But Casey couldn't ignore the ringing and finally answered it.

"Hello," a male voice responded cheerfully, sending Casey's heartbeat racing at triple speed. "Is that you, Gabbie?"

For a moment the caressing deepness of the man's voice had reminded her of Flint. Her knees had nearly buckled beneath her as she sank onto the sofa adjoining the end table.

"No, no, it's not Gabbie." She had trouble finding her voice. "I'll get her for you."

She set the receiver down before the man could reply and hurried to the room where Gabbie was working. She tapped lightly on the open door.

"There's a phone call for you."

"Who is it?" Gabbie glanced up from her computer reluctantly.

"I didn't ask. It's a man."

"Woo hoo." Gabbie smiled broadly, leaving her desk to enter the living room. It was impossible for Casey not to listen to the one-sided conversation.

"Hello . . . I was working. You know how I am when I'm in front of that computer. It would take an explosion of dynamite beneath my chair . . . Oh, that was Casey Gilmore. You remember Flint telling us about her. She's going to be staying with me until her father's out of the hospital . . . I'm finishing up an article, so why don't we make it next weekend? That's a date, then. Bye now, love you."

Gabbie turned to Casey after replacing the receiver on the hook. Her eyes twinkled with laughter.

"You were right, it was a man," she said. "My dad. They're coming over next weekend. Mom and Dad are both outdoorsy, so it's just about impossible to keep them away from Big Mac for long, even in winter. Big Mac is what the locals call the lake," Gabbie explained. "An affectionate abbreviation of Lake McConaughy."

Casey's attempt at a smile barely lifted the corners of her mouth. She thought again of the unlikelihood of her father being released from the hospital next week. Wasn't it bad enough that she had to be staying with Flint's sister? Did she have to meet his parents, too?

If Gabbie noticed her lack of enthusiasm at the news, she didn't comment about it. She quickly excused herself and returned to the small den she used for her writing.

Chapter Eleven

A snail seemed to be powering the hands of the old-fashioned clock in the cabin. The slow ticking was driving her crazy, so much so that each day seemed to contain forty-eight hours for Casey. Forty-eight hours in which her unrequited love hung like a yoke around her shoulders, weighting her down until she felt that she could stand it no longer. Gabbie had done her best in the last four days to fill in Casey's hours. She worked only in the mornings and devoted the rest of her time to planning activities for herself and Casey.

Two afternoons she had driven with Casey to Scottsbluff so that Casey could see her father and not have to go alone. But those were strenuous, tension-filled hours during which Casey had to watch every word she spoke lest she give away the true state of her emotions. Her father had improved somewhat and was looking forward to returning home.

He kept on talking about Christmas, as in I'll-be-home-for-Christmas, but no one would say if that was going to happen. Not even the doctors wanted to contradict him.

Hope might be what was making him get better. For the first time Casey even had difficulty discussing the affairs of the ranch with her father. It seemed that all their sentences contained the word Flint. Now even that life was linked solidly with him.

The ever-perceptive Gabbie realized the problem and immediately tried to do something about it: distract her guest. The following afternoon she conducted Casey on a sightseeing tour of Ogallala, which was just ten miles from Lake McConaughy, taking her first to the mansion on the hill, decorated with wreaths and garlands for Christmas. Then Front Street, Boot Hill Cemetery, all the attractions that made Ogallala the "Cowboy Capital of Nebraska" were paraded before Casey.

Gabbie didn't try to pretend the friendly town was a booming metropolis, not with a population of about 5,000, or so said the sign. It was what it was. But the faded museum pictures of cowboys at the end of a long cattle drive had merely reminded her of Flint as Casey had so often seen him silhouetted against the sky, his farseeing eyes scanning the horizon. The loneliness of Boot Hill Cemetery struck a chord in the loneliness of her own heart.

Then Gabbie took her shopping, thrusting garment after garment at her and insisting she try them on, still trying to cheer Casey up. Some Casey took into a dressing room, knowing that retail therapy could be pretty effective. She bought one outfit, trying to don a new image at the same time, only to wonder afterward why she had bothered. Brightly colored cloth couldn't brighten her gloom.

They got in the car and drove for who knew how long and how far, to a mall and outlet area that had a boot store. For a minute, she really did cheer up when Gabbie stood by her to look in the window, their jacket collars turned up against the biting wind.

Casey pushed a lock of hair out of her mouth and pointed to the boots in the window. "Check those out." Part of a Christmas display, the pointy-toed cowboy boots were a jazzy green with scrolled cutouts showing red leather underneath. For a whimsical touch, someone had added spurs in the shape of snowflakes.

The boots looked handsewn and handtooled, but they obviously weren't meant to be worn and had been made just for show.

"Those are awesome, aren't they?" Gabbie said. "But I don't know what they would go with."

"Nothing," Casey laughed. "But boy, you'd get noticed in those."

"I wonder who made them," Gabbie said.

"Let's go inside and look."

"You're not going to buy them, are you, Casey?"

Casey shook her head. "I don't think they're for sale. And it's not like I need a new pair." Casey was grateful that Gabbie didn't comment on her scuffed roping boots.

But Gabbie must have noticed them. The next thing she said was, "Doesn't hurt to look."

"I guess not."

Just being with Gabbie had strengthened Casey's determination to distract herself from obsessing over Flint. The only trouble was, it was a major war. The battle came every time Flint's image drifted before her eyes. Restless and edgy, Casey found her only release in constant activity. That way she could tumble into bed at nights and be assured her exhaustion would bring instant sleep. But the heavy dreamless sleep, while it kept away the nightmares, always ended early in the morning and, just as this morning, a long day stretched mockingly out, daring her to fill it without him around to annoy her.

Yes, more retail therapy was definitely in order. They went in.

Gabbie led the way to a wall with no less than seven shelves that stretched the length of the entire store. The place stocked hundreds of styles and colors of boots, and the display was dazzling.

"Which ones do you like?" Gabbie inspected a pair in black suede with silver studs. "These are nice."

Casey picked up one of a pair of more traditional boots with carved leather tops, looked at the price tag on the bottom, and quickly put it back. "Nope, I don't need new ones."

Was it the wind through the bare cottonwood trees or her sighing so heavily, Casey wondered. Sometimes the two sounds blended so well that it seemed the earth was agreeing with her. Her watch said it was nearly nine o'clock, but the sun had yet to take the mean edge off the cold day. Casey's bundled-up walk along the shore had already taken her out of sight of the cabin where Gabbie was working. She climbed up on a rock and gazed out across the partly frozen lake.

She sat motionless on the rock for way too long,

imagining that the sun was warming her, then took it a step further and imagined herself being held in an even warmer embrace. It was strange how physical inactivity triggered memories of Flint. Her mind rekindled the fire of his embrace. She had only to close her eyes and feel his breath upon her face as he rained kisses on her. It was tender . . . and painful.

"It isn't fair," she muttered, rising quickly to her feet. A loose rock she hadn't seen made her stumble, but she righted herself, wondering if she'd twisted her ankle. It did hurt. Tentatively, she put her weight on it.

Now nature was conniving against her. Even the shadowy gray clouds on the horizon reminded her of the color of his eyes—a gray that could shift from the burnished brightness of old silver to the violent, turbulent shade of storm clouds and on to the metallic hardness of iron and steel.

"You okay?" someone called.

Casey looked up. A young guy, nice-looking, what she could see of him. He was as bundled up as she was.

"I think so," she said when he reached her.

"I'm Sean Sorenson," he introduced himself. They shook gloved hands, and Casey felt comforted by the strong grasp of his hands.

"Casey Gilmore," she offered.

"Visiting someone here? I don't think I've seen you around."

The friendly question made her hesitate. The only other people around were a little ways off. Okay, they *were* there and it was safe enough to pass the time of day with someone she didn't know. He really did seem nice.

"Uh-huh. Staying in a friend's cabin. It's pretty fancy," she amended her remark. "I don't know if cabin is the right word."

"Oh," Sean said, looking like he didn't want to pry too much. "Come for Christmas, huh?"

She only nodded. She hoped not, but there was a limit to how much explaining she was going to do at the moment.

"I'm visiting friends myself," he said. "I'm a med student at Creighton University in Omaha, and I work in Ogallala for the summer, at one of the resorts down the beach, servicing boats," he said. "Thought I'd see what Lake McConaughy looks like in winter."

"Huge and grim." She hoped she didn't sound too critical.

He didn't seem to disagree. "Yeah. But I wouldn't mind being out on it. Sailing is my one great love, next to medicine. What about you?"

Casey didn't want to answer but she did. "Ranching, I guess. My family has a ranch up north in the Sand Hills." She didn't want to talk about her photography. She'd only dabbled in it, anyway.

"That's a beautiful natural area. Unchanged and unspoiled."

She was pleased that he knew something about it. "Well, the bison don't roam free anymore, but you're right. The Sand Hills don't change."

"Are you anywhere near the Rowe Sanctuary, where the cranes go? I saw the video of them online, doing their mating dance. Those birds can boogie."

She nodded. "I know where it is."

"Ever go there?" He looked eager to know, not like he was trying to make a move on her.

Casey liked him more and more. "No. I always meant to, but you know how it is when you live right near a well-known place. People from all over the world get there before you ever do. Birdwatchers, nature lovers—nice folks."

"Yeah," he said. "I haven't been there either, that's why I was asking."

They exchanged smiles.

"Anyway, I'm not going anywhere lately," Casey continued. "My dad broke his hip a few weeks ago when he was thrown from a horse, and he's in the hospital in Scottsbluff."

"I'm sorry to hear that."

"He was doing okay, but he's had some setbacks. So he hired a man to take his place. Since Mom was in Scottsbluff with Dad, he thought it was best if I stayed here in Ogallala as opposed to remaining on the ranch alone with a bachelor."

"Sounds very proper and practically Victorian." Sean laughed. "Who are you staying with here?"

Casey hesitated. "Gabrielle McAllister. She's the sister of the man we hired."

"McAllister!" Sean whistled, studying Casey intently. "That's high-priced help, if you're referring to the local cattle baron family."

Her neck stiffened slightly. She didn't like the conversation and wished now that she hadn't responded to his question, or at least not truthfully. Then Casey checked her rising temper. Sean certainly didn't mean anything personal by his comment, and she was being childish again.

"My father wanted the best," she said finally.

"From all I've heard, he got it." Sean's eyes widened as he nodded his head in affirmation.

"What time is it getting to be?" Casey started walking. Her ankle twinged a little but she hadn't sprained it. "Gabbie will be expecting me pretty soon."

Sean pushed the cuff of his thick glove down to look at his watch. "Quarter to one."

Casey glanced at the lake one last time, then at him. She'd been awfully preoccupied but she'd promised to be back from the lake by noon. She knew for sure that Gabbie would be worried about her. She turned quickly back to Sean.

"Do you mind? I'd really like to leave now. I didn't realize it was so late." Casey walked faster to add emphasis to her request.

"No, not at all." Sean picked up his own pace. "Looks like your ankle's all right."

"Yes, I can walk on it."

In a little while they had come far along the shore from where Casey had met Sean. The sun had reached its zenith and hovered there. The lake was a sheet of glass where it hadn't frozen, shimmering under the brilliant rays in the cold, clear winter air.

"This is where I turn off."

"I'd like to see you again, Casey." His blue eyes roamed over her face in admiration.

It had been an unexpectedly pleasant interlude, but Casey wasn't sure she wanted to repeat it. "I don't know how long I'll be here," she stalled.

"I'll probably see you out walking again. We'll make a date, okay?" Sean suggested hopefully.

"Okay," she agreed nervously. "I really had better get going. I'll see you soon, I'm sure, Sean."

Casey remained long enough on the shore to wave a polite good-bye before scurrying toward Gabbie's place. As she drew even with the cottonwoods, there was a rustling of twigs and withered grass, followed by the crunching of rocks. She glanced apprehensively at the shadowy place, then stopped abruptly in her place as a tall, lean figure stepped out. It was as if an electric shock went through her. Casey's hand went to her chest to still the erratic hammering of her heart.

Chapter Twelve

"Who was that?" Eyes as gray as shadowy clefts of rock ice glared at Casey as Flint came forward. He wasn't an apparition. He was really standing there in front of her.

"How . . . how did you get here?" Breathlessly she drew her scattered thoughts together and tried to still the trembling in her voice. "What are you doing here?"

"Keeping track of irresponsible females."

"Give me a break," she said crossly, even though it occurred to her that he might be teasing. But he didn't sound like it. "I agreed to stay with your sister. I'm not under house arrest." He must have seen her with Sean and thought the worst. Well, the hell with that. She hadn't done anything wrong. All the same, her eyes were held captive by his until the very intensity of his gaze forced her to look away.

"Granted, but—"

"I'd better get back to the cabin," Casey murmured, turning away from him toward the cabin. "Gabbie will be getting worried."

"Now you're talking." Flint covered the distance between them before Casey could even begin to move away. "What do you think I'm here for? Of course my sister's worried. She's responsible for you and as far as she knows, you went for a walk and disappeared."

She didn't reply. She was fighting the desire to be in his arms, to turn her face up to his and evoke the physical response she knew she was capable of creating. All she wanted to do was put her arms around him and have him hold her and never let her go. She swallowed hard to gain control, to force her body to obey her mind and not her heart.

"I know I'm late," Casey asserted calmly. "I was sitting by the lake, just thinking. I lost track of time."

"So did that guy have a watch?"

"Yes. His name is Sean Sorenson. He thought I'd turned my ankle when I got up, so he came over and introduced himself."

"How gallant," Flint said. "But you seem to be walking just fine."

Surprising even her, Casey's temper exploded with white-hot intensity as her hand lashed out and connected with his cheek. The stinging of her hand didn't really tell her what she had done. It was the red mark on Flint's cheek that showed her. His reaction was just as swift. Before she could struggle, he had both of her hands pinned behind her back at the same time. "Do you want to try that again?" There was a bold light of challenge in his eyes. "It's probably not a good idea."

"Yeah!" Her voice was incredibly husky. "Stand still!"

"No. But maybe you have your reasons," he mocked. "Care to share?"

He let her go and stepped back.

"No!" Her brown eyes snapped fiercely at him. "You talked my parents into parking me here in Ogallala, but that doesn't mean you get to treat me like a child."

"I'm not trying to—"

"Flint, I'm twenty-one. Even though my dad asked you to stay at the ranch, all I want you to do is stay out of my life." She was even more surprised by her own resolution. Maybe it was because she'd chatted—not that it was going to be anything more—with a guy who was around her own age. Sean hadn't done anything more than ask to see her again, but he'd been easygoing with her in a way that seemed difficult for Flint. Damn him. It was impossible to ask him to stay out of her heart.

"I'm looking forward to the day I can wash my hands of you, don't worry. Right now all I want to do is deliver you safely back to Gabbie." Flint reached out and grasped her wrist, dragging her behind him through the trees where the chrome of his car winked in the clear winter air.

He guided her none too gently toward the passenger side and then climbed behind the wheel on the other. He glanced at her once as if to make sure she wasn't trying to escape. Casey sat stiffly against the door, determinedly keeping her gaze riveted to the outside. Flint inserted the key in the ignition, then paused before starting the car. She could feel his eyes on her, but she refused to meet them.

"Casey, I want you to promise me something," Flint said.

She turned her belligerent gaze on him. "Don't you get tired of bossing people around?"

"I want you to promise that you won't go off like that again without telling Gabbie where you're going." Flint didn't seem to register her jab, although his eyes did narrow.

"Why don't you make it an order?" A bittersweet smile matched the glare in her eyes. "After all, you are the big boss man." She spat out the words.

"We could trade insults all day," Flint drawled. He was trying to keep his temper under control and Casey was trying desperately to rile him. "All I want from you is your word that you won't send Gabbie off on another wild goose chase like this, worrying herself sick for hours. I'm asking for her sake, not my own."

"What?" Casey echoed. A frown creased her forehead. "Why should she be looking for me? She always works in the morning, or at least she does since I've been here. So I got in the habit of wandering down to the lake."

"Casey, I called this morning and wanted to talk to you. Why I called doesn't matter right now. She went down to the lake to look for you and couldn't find a trace, except for your footprints in the sand. Then they disappeared."

"The reason why isn't very dramatic. I climbed up and sat on a rock. Mystery solved."

"Well, my sister has an overactive imagination. She was afraid you'd drowned. At least she didn't panic. Instead of calling the rescue unit and have them drag the lake for your body, she called me back and got me up here. It saved us a lot of embarrassment since you were out all morning with your Scandinavian boyfriend."

"He's as American as you are. And he's not my boyfriend," Casey retorted savagely, still stunned by the news that she had been the object of a search.

"It's none of my business what he is," Flint answered just as sharply, "whether he's your cousin, boyfriend, or lover!"

He didn't give her an opportunity to reply, immediately turning the ignition and gunning the motor so that any words Casey might have said would've been drowned out by the noise. She bit her lip tightly to keep the tears back until the pain made her aware of what she was doing. Weird as it was, she would've preferred Gabbie calling the rescue squad and enduring that and the explanations that followed, rather than face this inquisition with Flint.

Gabbie was waiting when they returned, her bright blue-green eyes taking in the tension between the two. If Casey had been less wrapped up in her own emotions, she might have noted that there was a remarkable lack of anxiety on Gabbie's face.

"Casey, are you all right?" Gabbie rushed forward to embrace her lightly. "You gave us a scare. Where were you?"

"I went for a walk because I wanted to think." Casey spoke up before Flint could put in a sarcastic remark. "I'm afraid I didn't keep track of the time."

"No doubt she was thrilled with the company she was keeping." Flint glared at her briefly.

"Company?" Gabbie echoed, looking to Casey for an explanation.

Casey gritted her teeth and explained, aware of

the piercing gaze of the gray eyes. "I met this guy who works at one of the resorts here in summer. We talked about, oh, sandhill cranes and bison and what I was doing here. Nothing more thrilling than that."

An incredibly uncomfortable silence followed her words. The crushing lack of sound seemed to have been ordered by Flint so that he could make a point of impressing her with her own foolishness.

"Gabbie, would you get us something cold to drink?" Flint's gaze never strayed from Casey.

Gabbie raised a dark eyebrow at Casey before gliding quietly away.

"Stop making a federal case out of it," Casey muttered. His implied criticism of her was unbearable. He would never believe how supremely innocent the morning had been. "Sean was a nice, outdoorsy guy who was out for a walk, just like me."

Flint came closer. "Whatever you say. I can't really argue."

"What's the matter?" Casey taunted, fire darting out of her brown eyes as she stared defiantly into his. "Why are you jumping to conclusions? Are you regretting not getting me into bed when you had the chance?"

She could feel the incredible tenseness in his body transferring itself from his grip on her shoulders to her. His gaze fastened on her trembling lips and a coursing flood of heat raced through her body. Her lips parted in anticipation of his kiss, wanting, desiring it with every part of her body. She could see the answering flash of desire in his eyes. Flint had started to draw her toward him when his sister returned.

"Whoops! Bad timing. I'll go get some Christmas cookies," Gabbie called out at the sight of the couple. She turned around swiftly to go back to where she came from.

"Don't bother," Flint said, releasing Casey and walking swiftly toward his sister. "You didn't interrupt a thing."

"My mistake." Gabbie smiled widely. "I thought I had."

Casey breathed a little more slowly, needing time to gain control of herself and her emotions. The silence at the table could have been cut with a knife and served in generous portions. Instead she was going to get milk and cookies.

The scraping of Flint's chair brought her tear-bright gaze upward. She was imprisoned by the defeated look on his face. For a moment, she could have sworn that his eyes were pleading with her and she swallowed hard.

"I'll skip the goodies, okay? I have to get back to the ranch," Flint said. "Think you could walk me to the car, Casey?"

Somehow she managed to stand while Gabbie made small talk with her brother. How she wished Gabbie would have gone with her. Then Flint wouldn't have been able to subject her to any more of his barbed remarks. Flint waited with cold politeness for Casey to precede him. She felt stiff all over, and the irritated expression on his face told her he noticed it. "I'm sorry you bothered," Casey said once they reached the pickup truck. "But I really don't need you hovering over me."

"I promised your parents." Flint sighed heavily, his gaze roaming over her intense face. "They're expecting me to keep an eye on you, along with everything else." He opened the door and swung up himself up into the cab, then stared at her with disconcerting blandness. "You can talk to whoever you want to."

"Thanks," Casey answered calmly. She had no intention or desire of meeting Sean.

"I actually have a feeling you aren't planning to see him again." One corner of his mouth lifted with mocking amusement as he studied her face. "But you wouldn't want to give me the satisfaction of knowing that."

Score one for Flint, Casey said silently while she cocked her head to one side in a gesture of defiance. "I might have a date with him tonight for all you know."

"Yeah?" Flint's mouth twitched and his eyes glittered humorously. "Somehow I just don't think you do."

Casey crossed her arms over her chest and hummed under her breath rather than speak to that.

"Is that a Christmas carol?" he asked.

She hadn't realized that it was, in fact. "I guess so."

"Getting into the spirit?"

Casey shot him a glare. "Not exactly. No tree, no time, and I'm stuck out here with your sister, who happens to be very nice, even though I think she must be baffled as to why she's expected to babysit me."

"Have her take you shopping. Gabbie is a mall rat."

"She did. We looked at cowboy boots."

"See anything you like?"

"I didn't see anything I could afford, Flint."

He looked at her thoughtfully. "Got it."

"Actually, you don't get it at all, Mr. McAllister. I've walked you to your truck. It's time you left." His total sureness that he was right irked her beyond words.

"You're still the same prickle poppy. Trying to lodge your thorns into anybody who comes too close to you, aren't you, Casey?"

"Only when it's the wrong person." She turned on her heel and retreated toward the cabin, the sound of the truck's tires moving over gravel interspersed with muted laughter from the driver, following her.

Unsettled by the argument even though a night had passed, Flint got comfortable on his sister's sofa. Thinking that maybe he didn't deserve to be comfortable, he got up again and poured himself a shot of whiskey in a chunky glass. No ice. No water. He sipped his drink and stared at the Christmas tree without really seeing it. It occurred to him that Casey hadn't mentioned getting a tree for the Anchor Bar before he'd brought her to Ogallala.

Maybe he should have thought of it. Sure, she was capable of doing just about anything around a ranch that a man could do, but maybe she didn't want to do something that emotionally loaded. Not on her own.

Of course, she had Mark to turn to, but by Flint's guess, the Gilmore kids got along best when they weren't together too much. But Casey wasn't a kid. He took a swig of the whiskey. No, she was a gorgeous, grown-up woman of twenty-one. He winced. That age just didn't sound grown-up.

Good thing she'd gone to bed. Helped him think.

He got up, glass in hand, and looked out the window at the view of the frozen lake. Then he happened to notice the natural theme his sister had chosen for her tree. Birds in nests. Unusual. And nice.

He wondered what Casey would put on her tree. It would probably be the first one she'd do all on her own, if she decided to have one, what with her mother spending so much time at the Scottsbluff hospital. He'd seen her looking wistfully at the ornaments in that store next to the Café Girasole. She'd hang traditional ornaments, of course— every family had those, and by the time the kids were grown up, usually by the thousand.

But Casey being Casey, she was bound to add something unique and really her. Again he felt a pang of guilt for not giving the matter serious consideration before now. Could he make it up to her by buying her a present she really wanted and wasn't expecting?

Hell, he had no idea what to get. Maybe Gabbie could help him out there. He heard her come into the room and turned around.

"I really like your Christmas tree, sis."

"I try," Gabbie said airily. "I like to do something different every year."

"The birds are great. Did Casey like it?"

His sister looked at him curiously. "She seemed to."

"It was nice of you to ask her to stay here."

She nodded. "Once you explained what was going on and how Mr. Gilmore felt, it made sense to me. And it's not as if it's permanent."

"Well, no. Does she seem homesick to you?"

Gabbie nodded again. "She doesn't say so, but I would guess that she is. She's never been away from the ranch for long, has she?"

"Not as far as I know."

She came to stand next to the Christmas tree, adjusting the position of a nest. "Oops. We're about to lose these eggs."

With amusement, Flint watched her rearrange the fake eggs. "You're a mama hen."

"As if."

"Don't you want kids?"

"Someday, yes," she admitted. "But a husband would be nice, don't you think?"

"Of course," he said indignantly. "There aren't going to be any shotgun weddings in the McAllister clan."

"Stop talking like a hick," she teased him.

"Was I?"

Gabbie patted his shoulder. "Yes."

He gave her a baffled look. "Is it possible to embarrass you even when we're not out in public? I didn't think that was possible."

His sister laughed. "You knew exactly what I was talking about. It's one thing to be from Nebraska, it's another thing to act like you grew up in a barn and ate hay for breakfast."

"That all-natural cereal you have kinda tastes like that," he grumbled.

"Sorry. I'll lay in a stock of bacon and eggs if you're going to stay much longer."

Flint lifted his shoulders in a resigned shrug. "Can't. Have to be getting back to the Anchor Bar. Right now it's just me and Sam, the world's gnarliest cowpoke. He's a hard worker, though, even if he doesn't say much."

"What about Casey's brother?"

"Mark? He comes and goes. I guess he thinks I'm not really keeping an eye on him, but I sure as hell try to."

"When it comes to teenagers, you'd better. I remember the trouble you used to get into."

"Don't remind me," Flint sighed. "I tried to redefine the term 'bad to the bone' every Saturday night."

"Dad used to be angry with you just about all the time," she said. "C'mon, let's sit down." She chose an armchair and settled into it, tucking her slippered feet under her in a cozy way.

Flint went back to where he had been sitting on the sofa and leaned back with a huge sigh. "So what do you think?"

"About what?"

"Me and Casey." He kept his voice very low, just in case she could hear. "Think I stand a chance with her?"

"Huh?" She collected herself. "I mean, I did know there was something—but not what. Um, I really couldn't say."

Flint groaned and turned his head from side to side, easing the tension in his neck. "She's so smart and capable for her age, but I still feel like a cradle robber."

"She's twenty-one. You're off the hook."

He came up for air. "I'm older than her friends."

"Not so much so that people would talk."

Flint gave a huge sigh. "They always do. No matter what."

Gabbie opened a drawer in a side table, and took out a pen and a legal pad.

"Always prepared, aren't you?" he said.

"Yup. I'm the Flying Freelancer. I like to take notes."

He scowled at her. "I don't want to be interviewed."

"I'm not going to," she said. "Let's make a list, though. Pros and cons of you and Casey."

He gestured toward the fireplace. "Just so long as you burn it before she accidentally sees it."

"Of course." Gabbie twirled the pen in her fingers. "Begin with the positive things."

"From my point of view or hers?" He gave his sister a suspicious look. "Are you going to play this game with Casey too?"

Gabbie chuckled. "No. She doesn't like to talk that much. Seems to me that she'd rather be outdoors most of the time."

"Well, so would I. That's on the pro list as far as I'm concerned."

His sister wrote it down while he slouched deeper in the cushions, trying to think.

"More pros: she's super-smart. And anything I can do, she can do at least as well. Sometimes better."

"Hey," his sister prodded him with the pen, "I know you want to impress me by saying the right things, but let's keep it real."

Flint blew out his breath. "Okay, okay. She's sexy too. And cute as can be—ah, lay off, Gabbie, I feel weird talking like this to you."

Gabbie giggled. "I swear never to reveal a word." She wrote it all down. "Cons?"

Flint looked like he hated to even think of any. "Hmm. Hard to say. I mean, I'm not talking about her personality when it comes to cons."

"I understand."

"But here goes," Flint said. "She hasn't been to college, hasn't traveled, isn't sure what she wants to do."

"What do you think she wants to do?"

Flint grabbed a pillow, threw it into the air to stall for time, then tossed it at his sister. "Do you really believe she'd even tell me?"

"I don't know," Gabbie said, catching the pillow and setting it aside. "You two have spent a fair amount of time together. You must have a clue."

Flint thought it over. "She's a talented photographer, but making a living at it is probably the last thing on her mind. She did the ones on the walls in that little café in Marchand, but she didn't want to tell me that."

"I haven't seen them."

"It's a series of sunflowers. In bud. Full-blown. Dying. They're unusual images. Really strong composition. They looked professional to me."

"Wait a minute. Do you mean the Café Girasole?"

"That's the place."

Gabbie looked excited. "I did an article about it for *Heartland Home* magazine when it opened a couple of years ago. Took me a minute to remember that it was in Marchand."

"Well, there isn't much to remember about a town that small. Blink and you'll miss it."

"I described it as charming."

"The café is. I mean, that's not a word I throw around a lot, but it is."

"I remember the owner, Marci," his sister mused. "She'd had a place like it in Chicago, but she wasn't sure she could make a go of it in rural Nebraska."

"I would say she succeeded beyond her wildest

dreams. The place was packed. Mixed bag—truckers, college-age kids, some of Mark's friends, a few of Casey's—"

"I got the feeling that most of the people Casey knew in high school had moved away."

"Yeah, except for that Smitty kid from the ranch next door to the Gilmores," he said in a low voice.

"How old is he?"

"Smitty? I don't know. Around Casey's age, I guess. Maybe a little older."

"Not serious competition, is he?"

Flint glared at her and grabbed another pillow, brandishing it at her. "How many pillows do I have to throw at you?"

"Do your worst, brother dear. I think you've got it bad for Casey Gilmore."

"You're right," he sighed. "And as the song says, that ain't good."

"Oh, not necessarily," Gabbie said, making a note on her pad. "It all depends on how it turns out."

"There's no telling."

Gabbie tapped her pencil against her ankle while she thought for a moment. "Let's get back to those photos on the wall. How did you find out she'd taken them if she didn't want to tell you she had?"

"Her brother has a big mouth. He was there too."

"Oh. I assumed you'd asked her directly."

"Jesus, no. She's prickly. And she's private about what she does on her own time. Just yesterday I got my head handed to me for asking about that guy she ran into at the lake here." He was quiet for a few seconds and didn't look too happy.

"So you interrogated her brother."

"That's a pretty strong word, Gabbie," he

protested. "Actually, Mark mentioned it on his own because he happens to be proud of her."

"Isn't that nice."

"Are you trying to make a point about you and me?" Flint asked.

"No. I assume you're proud of me," she said smugly. "And you get to see the family name in print. The glory rubs off."

Flint snorted. "Rest assured I brag about you every chance I get, okay? What kind of brother do you think I am?"

"The good kind," she said diplomatically.

"Anyway, after Mark went back to his pals, I got a few more details about the photos out of Marci. She paid to have them framed but she couldn't talk Casey into putting up contact info in case a customer wanted to buy one."

"Hmm."

"They're good friends, though Marci's easily fifteen years older. She wants Casey to figure out what she loves to do, and she thinks photography could be it." He sat up straight, remembering something else. "Hey, apparently some guy from *Heartland Home* magazine thought they were good too. He left a business card but Marci said Casey didn't want to contact him yet."

"Give her time," Gabbie said. "What was the guy's name?"

"Brad something."

"Brad Heller?"

"Yeah, that was it."

"I know him," Gabbie said slowly. "At least I think I do. Thick blond hair, blue eyes, tall, athletic?"

"I couldn't say. Marci didn't describe him and I

didn't meet him," Flint said, looking irritated by her description. "And I don't think I want to."

"Well, it's up to Casey. If she wants to connect with him, she will."

Flint had a stormy look in his eyes, as if the thought bothered him. A lot.

"Anyway," he went on, "I bought some of her photos. Marci and I agreed on a price, and she's going to surprise Casey with a check drawn on the café account the next time she comes in. Marci figures she acted as an agent."

"For a mystery buyer. You."

"Something like that."

Gabbie shook her head. "That scheme could backfire if Casey thinks you did it just to make her feel good."

"It wasn't a scheme, she doesn't have to know I did it right this red-hot second, and I really wanted the photos."

"Even so."

Flint shifted uncomfortably on the sofa, not wanting to look at his nosy sister. He was waiting for a question that was sure to come.

"Exactly what red-hot second did you plan to tell her that you bought the photos?"

"None of your business, Gabbie," he mumbled.

"Speak up."

"The answer is when I'm good and ready!" he burst out. "Or when she is! Whatever comes first." His tone softened even though he gave Gabbie a hard look.

"Got it."

"She's unsure of herself, and she's got so much to handle right now." He sighed. "I can't help thinking that a whole lot of attention from me isn't going to help either problem. But the more I looked at those photos, the more I thought that tourists driving through would snap them up."

"They're photos. More can be printed."

Flint frowned. "I didn't buy them all. Just the ones I liked. Thought it would give her a thrill, maybe a little bit of an ego boost. And it'll put cash in her pocket. I think she's feeling the lack of that too, and she's not the type to ask her parents for it."

"On all levels, I think I get it," Gabbie said, setting aside her pad and pencil and getting up. She stretched out the stiffness from sitting for so long, bending to the left and then to the right with her hands over her head like a ballerina.

"Good. Then we can stop talking about it."

"Um, I didn't say *that*—"

"Gabbie!" Frustrated by her persistence, her brother almost howled her name.

"I just think it's best to be direct. Tell her how you feel. You might be surprised to find out that she likes it."

"No way. Feelings are dynamite. I'm not lighting that fuse."

Gabbie walked around the room, still stretching. "Then give her something nice for Christmas."

"Like what? We're not at the diamond stage," he blurted out. "Forget I said that, Gabbie. Right now. I mean it. You never heard the d-word come out of my stupid mouth."

She stared at him for at least half a minute. "Whatever," Gabbie said after a while. "Anyway, Casey may not be a diamond kind of girl. She's a rancher's daughter."

Flint looked fixedly at his boots.

"I know something you could give her that would make her happy," Gabbie said, inspired. "Get your jacket. Let's go shopping."

"Noo-ooo." He drew out the word as if his sister were suggesting he submit to some weird torture. "Not shopping. Not with you. Please, anything but that."

"It'll be over with before you know it."

"I hate shopping."

She came over, took his hands, and made him get up. "I know. Mom always used to do it for you. She spoiled you rotten."

"She said the housekeeper did that." He got to his feet and stretched too, but like a guy, not a ballerina.

"Sally used to make you throw your dirty clothes outside your bedroom door before she would throw the clean ones in."

"I remember. Pretty good system."

His sister chucked him under the chin. "It worked. Poking meat through the bars at supper-time also worked. I don't know how parents can afford to feed teenage boys."

Flint growled. "Speaking of that, can we stop for a burger on the way?"

"Of course," Gabbie said. "I could go for one myself. With fries."

Chapter Thirteen

"And this is my father, Lucas McAllister." Gabbie wrapped her arm affectionately around the older man who bore such an uncanny resemblance to Flint.

Casey had difficulty looking at him, but she didn't want to be rude. The incredibly charming smile was the same, one corner of his mouth lifting higher than the other, but his hair had been darker, now showing a distinguished touch of gray at the temples with fine silver threads in the rest. He was still an imposing man and attractive.

"How do you do, Casey Gilmore." His hand clasped hers warmly, the resonant timbre of his voice chasing away some of her nervousness. She gazed hesitantly into his eyes, basking in the warm glow that looked back. "We've been looking forward to meeting you."

Lucas McAllister glanced affectionately at the slender, auburn-haired woman at his side. Jade green eyes smiled welcomingly at Casey, enhanced by the laughter lines that edged them. She couldn't help smiling back.

"We've heard so much about you, Casey, that you seem part of the family." The older woman's smile was genuine. It lifted some of the dread that Casey had been feeling.

"That's very kind of you, Mrs. McAllister," Casey returned.

Her last phone call to her dad hadn't prepared for the meeting. He sounded a little better, but his request that she meet the McAllisters struck her as odd. Casey suspected she was being set up in some way.

But she wasn't going to argue—she just couldn't. It wasn't such a big deal to play along, at least until her dad made it home and got better, and her mother got a chance to take a breath and get back to her own life.

Then Casey would argue with them. The self-mocking thought made her smile. In truth, she felt like she'd gotten beyond that stage of her life in a hurry. She'd wanted to do more than she'd been allowed to do: Flint McAllister had taken over.

She'd hoped that Flint's parents would be cold, snobbish people so that her feelings for him wouldn't extend to them. Now that she had actually met them, their openhearted friendliness was disarming. Unless she missed her guess, they were drawing her into the circle of their love.

"Call me Meg," Flint's mother insisted, squeezing Casey's hand affectionately. "We're not a very formal family."

"You two go park yourselves by the Christmas tree," Gabbie said to her parents. "You have to see what I did this year."

"Oh, all right," her mother laughed. "It's always different."

She had to assure her mother that she didn't need her help before the pair finally made their exit, leaving Gabbie alone with Casey. She turned her radiant face toward her. "I'm biased, I guess, but I think I've got the greatest parents."

"They seem really nice," Casey acknowledged, looking after the retreating pair. Their warmth reminded her of her own family, whom she missed terribly.

Gabbie sighed, her eyes rounding as she followed Casey's gaze. "My father could turn the heart of any woman. Is it any wonder with four brothers and a father who looks like that, the men I meet seldom measure up? I'll probably be doomed to spinsterhood."

"I doubt it." Casey laughed, looking back at Flint's dark-haired sister.

But from Casey's point of view it wasn't a laughable observation. Not when she had a feeling she was always going to compare the men she might meet with Flint. Just her luck: was she one of those women who only loved once in their lifetime? And she didn't even know him well enough to be sure . . . but her heart didn't care about that.

Knowing Christmas was just around the corner really, really didn't help.

She accepted the tray of glasses of mulled wine Gabbie handed her and started toward the living room, determined to be cheerful. The smell of cloves and cinnamon and cabernet mingled in the air as she walked, passing the mirror on the way. Casey was surprised by the composed reflection that looked back at her. The sweater she was wearing was a vivid red that cast a rosy glow on her cheeks. Her emotions didn't show, except in her eyes. She looked like any other normal, healthy victim of unrealistic romantic expectations.

"How's your father?" Lucas McAllister inquired when Casey came in and placed the tray she was carrying on the table where he was seated.

"He's much better. Just beginning to champ at the bit, Mom said," Casey replied.

"A very good sign in a rancher," he chuckled.

"Which usually means they should stay in bed for at least another week," Meg said with a knowing gleam in her eye when she looked at her husband and then back to Casey.

"My mother would agree with you," Casey laughed, "but then I'm a bit like Dad—anxious to get things back to the status quo." A fervent wish that Casey knew secretly would never come true.

"Of course, it will be some time before your father can get around like he used to. He'll have to be content to do some armchair managing for a while." Gray eyes twinkled at her. "But then my son told me you think you could run the ranch by yourself."

"I don't *think* I can," she said with spirit, "I can, put it that way." The sharpness in her voice was more for the absent Flint than for his father.

"Still, it's a big responsibility for you." Lucas smiled, glancing at his wife. "Country gals are pretty tough, but there's nothing wrong in having a man around to lean on when the occasion warrants it." He winked boldly at Casey. "And even when it doesn't." Casey's cheeks flamed red hot as the teasing voice subtly linked her with Flint. "How are things at the ranch?"

"I really don't know," she answered haltingly.

"Oh? I understood Flint was here to see you this week." His head tilted inquiringly toward her. "I assume he came to discuss business. Guess it was more personal."

"Ah . . . I'm not sure why he came here. He didn't say. We, uh, met again under rather strange circumstances that brought him here," Casey stammered. She had no idea what, if anything, Flint had told his father. "Besides, he usually talks everything over with my dad."

"Yes, he probably would. No offense, Casey, but I can't really see my son reporting to a woman, even a pretty one," he chuckled.

"Flint has told us so much about your family that Luke and I are really looking forward to meeting them sometime." Meg McAllister changed the subject easily, drawing Casey's attention away from the older version of Flint.

Casey took the opportunity, now that the initial shock of meeting someone who looked so much like Flint had worn away, to study his mother. Her auburn hair was a shade redder than Flint's, even though it was elegantly peppered with gray, and when she smiled as she was doing now, there were two youthful dimples in her cheeks.

"Did you know that it was only after Flint met your father that he decided to take the job?" Meg asked. "Flint respects him a great deal."

"I know Dad thinks a lot of him, too," Casey admitted. "Just knowing he had someone as experienced and competent as Flint made it easier for

Dad to accept the fact that he would have to stay in the hospital. It eased my mom's mind, too, knowing there was a man in charge."

"You have a very rare trait, Casey." A voice spoke from behind her. "Praising a man behind his back and damning him to his face. Very unusual."

The blood washed out of her face at the sound of the voice. She nearly tipped the glass of mulled wine over as she spun in her chair to face Flint. He stood directly behind her, looking down at her with a smart-aleck smile on his face. She wanted to run, to hide, but she was hypnotized by Flint's mocking gaze.

"I brought Mark along with me, but I think he went down to the shore to explore. Too bad he can't go fishing. He really wants to." His eyes released her as he turned to his parents. "Mom, Dad, all set for a weekend of doing absolutely nothing? It's too cold to stay outside long and there's a big snowstorm predicted."

"Too bad. I catch my limit in summertime." Lucas rose and took his son's hand. "You caught us all by surprise. We didn't expect to see you." Lucas cast the still slightly dazed Casey a compassionate glance. Flint followed it.

"Don't mind her. She's usually this overjoyed to see me," he said as he turned toward his mother. "My ears have been burning for the last thirty miles. You must have been talking about me."

"What an ego!" Gabbie exclaimed, handing Flint a glass of mulled wine and indicating a nearby chair.

"You were only discussed indirectly." Meg included Casey in her smile, which Casey found hard to return. "We were actually getting to know Casey, so if your name was mentioned, it was inadvertent."

"What I'd like to know, Flint, is why you never told us how cute Casey was," Lucas demanded, leaning closer to his son. "I always thought you had quite a good eye for beauty."

Casey's face was suffused with color. She didn't know how much more of this family matchmaking she could take, especially with Flint regarding her reactions with so much interest. It wasn't any consolation telling herself it was only good-natured teasing. And it was all too apparent that no one was going to come to her rescue. But of course, they couldn't know the pain their innocent teasing caused. Flint was taking obvious delight in her discomfort.

"Hey, sis!" Mark breezed into the house, unzipping his down jacket, bringing the cold inside with him. His face was wreathed in a smile. "This place is awesome! Boy, I wish I could spend summer here. You can take my place on the ranch anytime."

Casey rose quickly to greet him, fighting off the desire to cling to him as if he were a life preserver. He was just too grown-up for any affectionate greetings. Just standing beside him gave her extra courage when Flint spoke up to introduce Mark to his parents.

"I've heard the fishing is terrific at Lake McConaughy," said Mark after Flint mentioned that his parents were here for that purpose. "Been some record-size catches here, right? I've heard people fly in from Texas to try their luck."

Lucas McAllister was quick to take up the change of conversation, which Casey was thankful for. It gave her a chance to check her sentimental heart while Flint and his father regaled Mark with tales of fish that got away. It was an opportunity to study Flint unobserved, to mark in her memory the leanness of his cheeks, the dark lashes that lazily veiled his eyes, and his brown hair that held a hint of fire.

But when her gaze strayed to the sensual curve of his mouth, shivers raced down her spine, leaving a burning trail of fire that spread throughout her body. The yearning to feel those lips on hers again was overpowering. Lost in thought and conscious of only one person, Casey nearly leaped from her chair when a hand touched her arm.

"It's lunchtime." Gabbie spoke quietly, her blue-green eyes sympathizing with whatever was going on with Casey. "Would you like to give me a hand?"

"Of course," Casey agreed, somehow avoiding contact with Flint's gaze as it narrowed on her.

"I'm sorry I startled you." Gabbie touched her arm comfortingly as they walked into the house. "But your face is transparent sometimes. I didn't think you'd want Flint to see. It's been clear to me since you got here that you have a lot of feelings for him, Casey."

"Thanks for telling me," Casey murmured, knowing how shamed she would have felt if Flint had looked up at her earlier and picked up on that look of love that must have been on her face. "But I'm pretty sure that he's not in love with me. It's just one of those things that happens or it doesn't."

"Some people get the measles, too, but they get over them a lot faster you know." The cynicism in Gabbie's voice was sisterly and touching.

"You make it sound as if heartbreak lasts forever."

Casey laughed weakly, trying to add lightness to the conversation that was threatening to bring tears to her eyes. But Gabbie just looked at her with a glance that plainly asked, *Doesn't it?*

They seemed to have a mutual understanding that it would do no good to discuss the situation any further. They were a silent team, retrieving the tray of already prepared sandwiches from the refrigerator, and the salads and chips. It only took two trips from the kitchen to the table in the dining room and practically everything had been carried out. Only a bowl of potato salad, the napkins, and the silverware were left to be fetched. Casey was a trifle mystified when Mark offered to help her. He wasn't usually so concerned about giving assistance even when it was his stomach involved. She became even more puzzled when, once they were in the kitchen, he shuffled back and forth on his feet nervously.

"This isn't like you, Mark," she joked, "volunteering for women's work again. I guess baking all those Christmas cookies had a permanent effect."

"I wanted to talk to you." His glance bounced off her face as he lowered his voice. "Mr. McAllister just offered to take me along on a drive to a hunting lodge, and I didn't know if I'd get another chance to talk to you alone."

"What's the matter?" Casey asked, the confiding tone in his voice startling her. "Reindeer aren't in season. Santa has nothing to worry about."

"Ha ha," he said flatly. "There aren't any reindeer in Nebraska."

"Santa still has nothing to worry about. It doesn't look like we're going to be having a good old-fashioned whatever."

"Yeah, but—"

Casey gave him a puzzled look. "You're certainly old enough not to ask my permission to go somewhere."

"I don't mean that." Her brother's forehead creased in a very determined frown. "You'll be coming back to the ranch in another week and there's something I think you should know. I thought it would be better coming from family than from a stranger telling you."

Casey longed to urge him to tell her what he was talking about, but it was so obvious from his serious, adultlike voice that it was difficult for him to explain and it embarrassed him as well. Not in her wildest imagination could she think of anything so dire that it would concern Mark, and it certainly couldn't be anything to do with Flint.

"Since you've been gone, Smitty has been seeing Brenda Fairlie," Mark blurted out in a rush, his cheeks a brilliant shade of red. Casey nearly sighed with relief. "The day you left, he took her out. They went to some restaurant and she started putting on airs like she always does. Smitty told her off, but she must have liked the caveman technique because she nearly fell in his arms apologizing. They've been inseparable ever since." Mark glanced at his sister to see how she was taking the news.

The tears in her eyes weren't for the loss of Smitty, but for the sudden attack of brotherly devotion Mark had just shown. She wanted to throw her arms around him and hug him tightly, but she knew she could never do that. He had no other option but to assume that those tears were for Smitty.

"Thank you for telling me." Her voice was husky, but her smile at him was quite sincere.

"Well, I knew you and Smitty were a pretty steady couple. And I thought . . . well, it'd be easier if you knew before . . ."

"It is," she answered simply. Casey glanced around her quickly, her eyes coming to a stop on the large bowl on the counter. "Here, you take the potato salad and I'll bring the rest in a minute."

"If you like, I can tell them you had to wash the silverware or something. I mean, if you need time to—"

"I'll be right there, Mark. I'm fine, really," she assured him.

Casey honestly thought she was. She even smiled at Mark as he walked out of the room. She told herself that she was glad for Smitty and Brenda as she leaned against the sink. Good old steady Smitty. Her lips trembled and her eyes filled with tears.

It finally hit her.

No matter what happened this Christmas, this time he wouldn't be there, not even as a friend, because Brenda would never understand. Not that Smitty probably would have comforted her anyway, she thought as a couple of tears trickled down her cheeks. He had warned her about Flint and would have been more apt to say "I told you so" than offer solace. Still, it was like removing another rock from the already shaky foundation of her life.

"Did Mark mention that he was going to drive to the hunting lodge with my father?"

Casey stiffened at Flint's voice, but she didn't turn around. "Yes, yes, he did."

"I thought we could drive up to visit your father." He was walking closer.

"Whatever you say." Her voice rang out harshly. She suddenly felt too tired emotionally to argue with him, so she busied her hands with the silverware spread on the counter top. "I'll be out just as soon as I get this silver gathered together."

His fingers touched her chin and turned her face up toward him. Casey summoned all her pride to stare defiantly into his iron-gray eyes. There was no way he could miss the trail of tears.

"I was eavesdropping," Flint stated unapologetically. "I didn't realize Smitty's defection would affect you this deeply."

"There's a lot of things about me and my feelings you don't know, Mr. McAllister." She pushed his unresisting hand from her chin, then wiped away the telltale marks on her face.

"Every time I think I'm beginning to understand you, you change colors like a chameleon." Irritation laced his words.

"First I was a prickle poppy, now I'm a chameleon." A brightly defiant gleam sparkled out of Casey's brown eyes. "Quit mixing your metaphors."

Chapter Fourteen

"Have you talked this over with Flint?" Lucille Gilmore inquired, her blue eyes studying her daughter's tension-filled face.

"With Flint? What's he got to do with it? What business is it of his?" Casey cried. "If I can't stay at Aunt Karen's, then I'll stay in a motel. But I'm not going back there!"

After an almost endless ride with Flint from Ogallala to the hospital in Scottsbluff, Casey had reached her breaking point. It didn't matter anymore if what she was proposing was cowardly, a form of running away. She just knew that she couldn't make that long ride back to Gabbie's with Flint. The prospect of being so close to him, of enduring the stilted conversations between them, was enough to drive her crazy. That was why Casey had lost no time in persuading her mother to walk with her to the lobby where she made her painful plea.

"Honey, it's not a question of whether Aunt Karen has room for you. Of course she does." Lucille moved her arm around Casey's shoulders in comfort. "That was a stupid remark I made, too, asking if you'd told Flint. Under the circumstances, that would hardly be likely, would it?"

Her mother's face blurred slightly as Casey stared at her. Did she know how she felt about him? Could she possibly have guessed?

"Now what kind of mother would I be if I couldn't even guess when my daughter fell in love? Here"—she rummaged in her purse and withdrew a set of keys—"these are for Karen's car in the parking lot. I'll make some excuse to Flint and your father. You run along and we'll talk later."

"Oh, Mom!" Casey hugged her tightly, clasping the keys to freedom in her hand. "Thank you," she whispered fervently.

Her mouth was pressed firmly shut as she disentangled herself from her mother's arms, but she managed to smile gratefully at her before she hurried down the hall to the hospital exit. The parking lot was full of cars from weekend visitors. Casey scanned the rows trying to locate her aunt's yellow sedan. Panic raced through her as she failed to find it. It had to be there.

The next thing she knew she was being taken by the shoulders and propelled toward the green station wagon that had brought her here. She had a fleeting glimpse of yellow in the next row of cars. Flint didn't waste time on politeness, but got Casey into the wagon on the driver's side. She grabbed for the opposite handle to yank it open.

"You sure must not like me," he said, getting in himself.

"That's not it—" He caught hold of her hand for

insurance and managed to start the car and reverse it with his free hand, driving out of the hospital lot.

"I don't want to talk to you! Not here and not now!" Casey demanded, digging her fingernails into the back of his hand.

He winced at the deep scratch and let go of her. "Okay, we don't have to talk. You could just listen." Flint gave her a cold look before returning his stormy gaze to the road in front of him. "I never thought you were one of those chicks who run off and hide when their feelings get hurt."

"Whoa. Back up. I didn't run off. I got sent away from my family's house so your sister could baby-sit me. The only reason I agreed to the plan, which isn't working, is because Dad asked, so don't get any big ideas. By the way, Gabbie thinks you're a pain."

"What else is new? Did you two have a good time discussing me over midnight bowls of popcorn?"

"Like I'd tell you what we talked about when you weren't there?"

"Don't. See if I care."

"You do, though. You got your boxer shorts in a twist when you found out I was talking to some other man."

"Oh, yeah. Him. Mr. Outdoors. What was his name again?"

"Sean. Sean Sorenson."

"Right. I sort of remember it was something Scandihoovian."

"Don't be rude."

"Just because some wet-nosed kid—" He inhaled deeply, but didn't finish his sentence. Flint went slower. They were on a graveled road now with the town behind them. There was a scattering of houses,

then the desolate countryside spread out before
them, fallow fields of cropland dusted with snow and
frost amidst the rolling hills. Finally Flint ground the
car to a halt on the shoulder. Casey riveted her gaze
to a distant sandstone bluff, fighting the powerful
pull as gray eyes ordered her to look at him.

"I know it was a blow hearing about Smitty." His
voice was low and controlled. "But it will pass, Casey.
You just have to give yourself time."

"Spare me the platitudes," Casey groaned, her
hands reaching up to cover her ears.

"Why do you huddle against the door like that?
I'm only trying to help." His gentle entreaty brought
a louder pounding of her heart and an increased
trembling to her body. It was nearly impossible not
to respond to his coaxing tone.

A hard, callused hand reached up and captured
one of Casey's hands, not roughly as before, but
tenderly as one would hold a frightened bird. It
would have been so easy to draw it away that Casey
left it there.

"You'll meet someone else," he said softly.

This time she turned to meet the shadowed eyes.
She stared into the face of the man she adored with
all her heart. A cry almost broke from her lips
before she pressed them together. Finally she
replied, "I don't think so. As the song goes, love
hurts."

Sparks from the fire in his eyes surprised her.
"It's still worth it," he answered with fierce determination.

"You're . . . you're being very kind, Flint." She
looked away, blinking hastily at the tears rushing to
fill her eyes. "But it just doesn't help right now."

* * *

He'd dropped the subject then and there, before he'd brought her back to the hospital again. Her dad had called and asked unexpectedly to see her. So be it. There were a few things that needed doing around the Anchor Bar, and it hardly seemed fair to the Gilmore family to leave tasks unfinished.

For starters, there still was no Christmas tree. If there was the least chance that Casey's dad might make it home—say, even after New Year's—it would make all of them happy. Playing Santa could be a tricky business, but that part of the job seemed easy. A tree was a tree.

That old cowboy, Sam Wolver, probably would know where to find one on the Gilmore spread— Flint sighed. He could buy a tree at the temporary lot in Marchand if it came to that.

He'd slowed down on his way through the tiny town to have a look at their offerings. A sketchy framework of two-by-fours held up a straggling line of bare-bulb Christmas lights around the unfenced lot, where a man in a grimy down jacket watched over the trees. No telling what the trees actually looked like. They were bound tightly with twine, leaning against each other, and even from a distance, seemed dry and withered somehow.

Of course the unceasing Nebraska wind could do that in a few hours, especially since the trees had most likely been brought down from far up north, possibly even Canada, and dropped off the back of a flatbed right into the lot.

Flint had driven away without getting any closer. Scarce as trees could be around here, he didn't want to go and cut a non-farmed one that'd made it through blizzards and scorching summers. But if Sam knew of a sheltered draw where there was a pine grove, they could take just one and leave more room for the others to grow even bigger.

He pulled off onto the road that led to the main house of the Anchor Bar, shrugged off his jacket, and made a huge pot of coffee. He fixed a cup for himself and sipped it while he poured the rest into a thermos for Sam, wondering if he should add milk and sugar. Hell, what did old cowboys take in their coffee?

He knew the answer to that. Flint looked around in the kitchen cupboards until he found a small flask of whiskey tucked in back of mostly empty bags of flour and sugar, and slipped it into his jacket pocket. Into the other pocket went a flat foil box of milk, the kind that lanky Mark still drank at lunch, and some sugar.

You're a walking chuckwagon, he told himself.

He made his way out to the trailer where Sam lived, hoping to catch him there or at the barns. The short winter days meant the older man came in early.

He saw nothing to indicate Sam's presence, not the bluish flicker of the TV he sometimes watched, or even a lamp lit indoors. Flint knocked anyway.

He was surprised to hear footsteps inside, a measured tread with just a bit of a scuffing sound to it. A cowboy's unhurried walk.

Sure enough, Sam still had his boots and his jacket on when he opened the door.

"Howdy," he said to Flint. "I just closed that door a few seconds before you knocked on it. Sorry about that. I didn't hear you arrive. My ears ain't what they used to be."

"No problem," Flint said, realizing he'd never heard Sam say that many words all at once. He held up the thermos. "Just thought I'd bring over some coffee and visit with you. I haven't had much of a chance to talk to anyone around here."

"Sure thing," Sam said hospitably. "Grab a chair. I'll get cups."

Flint took off his jacket and slung it over the arm of the chair he chose, seating himself as Sam opened a cupboard door and took out two thick mugs, then found spoons in a drawer. His accommodations were on the spare side, Flint noticed, glancing around. "Hope it's not too late in the day for coffee," Flint said.

"Just so long as it ain't dishwater or decaf," Sam replied. He set down the mugs on a small table near the chairs and hung his jacket on a peg rack that held a few other personal items: a pair of rough suede gloves and a worn, concho-decorated belt. Then he permitted himself a slow, deeply wrinkled grin when Flint pulled out the milk, sugar packets, and flask of whiskey. "Now you're talking, mister."

"I didn't know how you liked it," Flint said with an answering grin.

"Black, generally speaking. But I'll take a shot of that there whiskey."

Sam sat down as Flint uncapped the thermos and poured out the coffee, adding a healthy slug of whiskey to both cups.

The old cowboy took a swig of the coffee "Ahh.

Goes down easy," he said appreciatively. "Now, what brings you here?"

"Well, Christmas is coming. Thought I'd stop by, ask you how the Gilmores usually did things around the holidays."

The older man looked a little surprised. "Isn't Mrs. Gilmore still in Scottsbluff with John? I figgered he wasn't coming home. Somebody woulda told me if he was."

"Just in case he does, I want to be ready," Flint hedged. "And there's still Mark and Casey to think about. I'd like to surprise them with some kind of celebration."

"I see. Well, that's a right nice idea. 'Course, they ain't exactly little kids, but Christmas is still important."

"Do you know if there's a place on the ranch where we could cut a fresh tree?" Flint asked.

Sam nodded, sipping his coffee. There was a warm light in the eyes that looked at Flint over the cup's thick rim. "Yep," he said, holding on to the warm cup when he'd finished it all, wrapping his callused fingers around it. "John and I used to go there every year. We never did tell the two kids where it was."

"Guess you thought they'd find it themselves someday."

"That's right. Don't know if they have or not."

Flint laughed. "Maybe they thought the tree just appeared like magic."

"That's how it should be," Sam said solemnly. "Lights and all. And lots of presents. Santa Claus never skipped the Anchor Bar."

Flint finished his coffee, trying not to smile. So

a grizzled old-timer like Sam had helped to make sure, in his own quiet way, that Christmas had come to the ranch, and he'd help again. Good to know.

"Too dark now to go looking for a tree," Sam said. "Tomorrow morning okay with you?"

"Sure." Flint had a feeling that the visit was being tactfully brought to an end, and he stood up. "I'll leave that for you," he said, indicating the flask of whiskey.

"Much obliged." Sam grinned. "But you don't have to go just yet. If we're gonna git a tree, we're gonna need some dec-o-rations." He dragged out the first two syllables like he was trying to be funny.

"Really." Flint tried not to sound too amused. He could imagine Sam doing anything that had to do with ranches or horses, but not Christmas ornaments.

Sam pointed to an ancient leather cowboy trunk in the corner. Its tooled leather was worn and bumped, and one of the straps meant to hold it to a saddle was broken. "I got some old ones in there. Just dragged it out from under my bunk the other night—I was thinking about Christmas. Feeling sentimental, I guess."

"It'll be here soon."

"Yeah. Casey used to ask to see 'em even when it wasn't Christmas, but she didn't get around to putting them on the Gilmore tree in the last couple of years. I guess she forgot and then I forgot to remember to put them on myself."

Flint gave him a look of sympathy. "How old are they?"

Sam sighed as he got up a little creakily. "Antiques. Over a hundred years old, probably. Handed down in my wife's family, and when she died, I kept them. Now, I don't have anyone to leave them to, so when I go, they'll belong to Casey."

Flint hadn't even known that the old cowboy had ever been married. Casey hadn't mentioned it, but there seemed to an unspoken understanding around the ranch that Sam was Sam, someone who'd always been there and always would. Flint clapped him on the shoulder. "That's a long way off, Sam."

The old cowboy poured himself a shot of straight whiskey in the coffee cup. "Sure hope so." He tossed it down. "Ahh," he said again. "Anyways, Flint, I am glad you asked about the tree. Putting it up—that'll be like old times, but in a good way. A real good way."

"I hope so," Flint murmured. He followed the older man, who was dragging his chair by the back, over to the trunk.

Sam leaned over and picked it up easily—it wasn't very big—and sat down again with it in his lap. He undid one buckle and slowly pushed back the lid. The compartmented tray on top held odds and ends, and a few small hand tools.

The trunk itself was an antique, something that had been new when the first settlers arrived on the unbroken prairie. Flint wondered how Sam had come by it, but he didn't ask.

Sam set aside the tray and reached into the trunk, digging down past a garland of metallic greenery that was showing its age. He took out one of several items wrapped in tissue paper and carefully unwrapped it, showing the flat, handmade ornament inside to Flint with obvious pride. It was a colored engraving of a camel that had been cut and mounted to cardboard, with reins made of old shoelaces and real, tiny tassels.

"Got three of these funny fellers. Them humps always made Casey giggle."

"I don't doubt it."

"And I got three Wise Men to go with them."

Sam unwrapped those next, laying the old ornaments in the top of the trunk instead of putting them back. Then he found a star whose points poked through the tissue paper.

"And a Star of Bethlehem." He showed that off and then cut-out, somewhat battered Nativity figures of shepherds and sheep and oxen. "Yep, they're all here."

Flint nodded, genuinely touched. The ornaments looked like they had been made at a farmhouse kitchen table during the endless months of winter, by children who'd had the time to add their own imaginative touches. "That's great, Sam. It's a wonder that they lasted."

"Well, they ain't made of glass. That helped," the old cowboy said wryly.

"Got it."

"Anyways, me and Casey, we had a tradition—we didn't unwrap the Mary and Joseph until Christmas Eve. And the little baby Jesus, not until midnight."

"That's a fine tradition," Flint said quietly. "Let's keep it that way."

"Now, let me think. Casey was born in 1989," Sam mused. "Whew. That makes me feel even older when I think about it." He came to the bottom of the little trunk and took out an envelope, sliding out the faded Polaroid inside it.

Flint glimpsed a pretty woman in a bouffant hairdo, smiling for the camera—or at the person who held the camera. Her smile was warm and sincere.

"That's my wife," Sam said. His voice was a little shaky. "Thirty years now since I lost her to cancer. Seems like yesterday that she was by my side and we were planning a future together. Casey ain't never seen that picture. Seemed like a sad thing to explain to a little girl, so I never did."

Flint only nodded as Sam rewrapped each ornament one by one, his callused, work-roughened hands holding them tenderly. "I'll get the trunk to ya by Christmas Eve," he said.

"Thanks," Flint said. There was a lot of feeling in the single word.

The next day they rode out to where Sam had assured him there was a grove of pine trees. Flint wasn't expecting much. Nebraska winds had a way of keeping trees undersized as a rule.

The corn stubble in the fields they rode through was mostly covered in old snow, dusted with dirt, and wind-sculpted into frozen waves that never moved. They rode down through a draw into sheltered land that Flint hadn't ever seen. But then, he thought ruefully, he'd spent too much of his time at the ranch doing paperwork in John Gilmore's office.

The cottonwoods were bare, of course, their big, heart-shaped leaves dried and fallen long ago, like valentines to sunny days now gone.

Sam turned around a little stiffly in the saddle. "Almost there."

Flint wanted to ride up next to him, but the narrowness of the way prevented him. "Looks like an old Indian trail."

Sam nodded. "Likely so. The creek down there dried up more years ago than I can remember. But John told the kids not to come this way. Told them there were rattlesnakes here."

Flint looked at the jumble of rocks in the dry creek bed, and the snow that had drifted into every crevice. Still, when the summer sun was out, it would be an ideal basking place for snakes and lizards.

"They listened to their daddy, I guess."

Sam gave a shrug. "They were pretty good kids."

Flint didn't know if the taciturn old cowboy would tell him much more. He urged his horse on and kept up. In another minute, he saw a welcome sight: treetops, the deep green of pines. In a spot that was still lower, there was indeed a grove of trees, thick and fragrant and unexpected.

Sam reined in his horse and wheeled around. "I found this grove and then I told John. He said Santa Claus was making it easy on us."

Flint laughed. "All you had to do was pick the biggest tree and bring it on home."

"That's about the size of it." Sam rested his gloved hands on the pommel of his saddle, surveying the grove. "Hmm. Might even get me a little bitty one for the trailer this year."

"Was that an Anchor Bar tradition once upon a time?" Flint asked.

"Now, how'd you know that?"

"Wild guess," Flint said.

"Yep, you're right. We had one in the old bunk-house too."

They exchanged sheepish looks, not willing to admit to being sentimental, while the horses stamped and blew out philosophical-sounding sighs through wide-open nostrils.

"I expect they want us to get a mule for the job," Sam said, patting the neck of his mount.

Flint was eying the biggest of the trees. "I have an all-road truck that'd do just fine," he said. "Army surplus vehicle that I rebuilt. Drove it down from my folks'."

"That thing in the shed? I saw it," Sam said. "For the life of me, I couldn't figure out what that was for a few seconds. Looks like a tank crossed with a hay truck."

"It has four wheels and a cargo bed."

"Then it'll do. You'll have to get someone to help you besides me, though."

Flint gave him a questioning look before Sam filled him in.

"My old back won't take that much jouncing over open land." He clucked to his horse and wheeled it around. "But we could get a little tree now and bring it on home."

"Sounds like a plan," Flint said.

They headed home a different way to keep the winter wind at their backs. Being on horseback gave Flint a better view of the fields under the snow. They went on and on, like everywhere else in this county and the next. And the next. When you thought you'd ridden or driven through two more states at least, there you were, just a little farther along in the great state of Nebraska.

He glanced over at Sam, who had a small pine tree tied up and flopping over his saddle.

"Looks like you caught a big spiky fish, Sam."

"Kinda does." Sam looked pleased with it.

Flint suspected that the older man was happy to be celebrating again, in his own way. He hoped the same would be true for Casey.

Casey went back to the Scottsbluff hospital to visit her dad again, feeling a little better about life after stopping in at the Café Girasole. Marci had gone wild with a bunch of giant paper sunflowers from Mexico. She'd stuck them among swags of greenery, and the effect was crazy and cheerful.

Casey carried a large paper bag in one hand that she set down near the head of her father's bed.

"Hey, Casey girl," he said wearily, turning his head on the pillow and smiling at her approach.

"Hi, Daddy," she replied. "How are you doing today?"

"A little better, believe it or not. I'm just tired from the physical therapy session. We finished up about an hour ago."

"Good for you, Dad. That's wonderful that you're not letting yourself slide."

"Ginny doesn't let me," he said. "And once I get a grip on those parallel bars and start walking, I don't give up."

Casey bit her lip to keep from busting out crying. Fortunately, he didn't notice.

"All I want to do is get to the end of those damn

bars, Casey. And when your mom is standing there next to Ginny, cheering me on, I want to get there twice as fast."

She sniffed up her tears so hard her nose hurt. "That's great."

"So what's in the bag?" he asked hopefully. "Did you bring me a steak? I could really go for a steak."

"No. Look at the logo."

He did, and a look of memory warmed his expression. "Omaha Gals—hey, I remember that place. Your mom used to buy her square-dance dresses there. That place closed down years ago." He shook his head. "Doesn't matter. We're not going dancing anytime soon."

"I'd smuggle in a steak in a heartbeat if it'd get you back on your feet. Do you really want one?"

"Too much work," he sighed. "Besides, they gave me dinner. Three ounces of mystery protein, two lettuce leaves, and half a canned peach."

"Did you eat it?"

"You know, it wasn't bad." John Gilmore laughed. "I was starving after the physical therapy session."

"That's another good sign," she said encouragingly. "You feel like eating again. You were picking at your food for a while."

"I was picking at the hospital food," he corrected her. "If your mother cooked, then I ate it all."

"I see." Casey hoisted the bag and put it on the bed, trying to be careful and not bump him. "Well, this bag doesn't have anything from her. It's more like occupational therapy."

"Uh-oh," her father groaned. "Are you going to make me weave baskets?"

"No. So . . . okay, maybe this is dumb, but I

thought we could make a scrapbook together. If you want to," she added quickly.

Her dad chuckled. "That's your mom's hobby. You're getting more like her every day."

Casey made a wry face. "I wanted to do something a little different. You know how Mom always picks the photographs where we look perfect? Hair in place, smiles painted on?"

"Yeah," John Gilmore said. "Beats having your hair painted on, doesn't it?" He cracked up at his own joke, then ran a hand over his head. "Lying on this pillow is going to give me a bald spot."

Casey soothed him with a pat on the arm. "That's not true, Daddy."

He sighed and settled back down.

"I thought we could use up all the awful pictures she can't bear to throw out."

"She is funny that way," he agreed. "So that's what's in the bag. Did you sneak home to get all that?"

"Mark met me with it."

"Put it up here." He patted the bedcovers.

Casey lifted the old shopping bag carefully, praying the corded handles wouldn't rip out. She'd stuffed a new scrapbook into it, and some supplies.

Her father reached in and took out a random handful, starting to laugh right away. He held up the photo that had caught his attention. "You and your brother always misbehaved in front of a camera."

She leaned over and took the photo by its edge. "Let me see." Mark, a scrawny five-year-old, was making rabbit ears behind her head while Casey, being a good girl, simpered into the lens. "Mom took that. I remember her asking him to quit."

"He was quick," her father said. "The second she tried to find the shutter button, that little hand went up again. Okay, that's a classic. That's going in." He bent his good leg and made a shelf of sorts out of the tented bedcover, and set the silly photo on it.

He looked at the next. "This isn't."

Casey glanced at it. "That's you."

"Yeah, but I look fat when I wasn't. And my eyes are shut—no way, Casey."

She giggled. "The shirt caught the wind."

"That's right." He patted his stomach. "These abs are still in pretty good shape."

"And Mom says you're still the only man for her."

"Damn straight," John Gilmore growled. He reached into the bag again. "And there she is. Pretty as a prairie morning. I would say that was a perfect photo. I wonder why she didn't put it in an album."

"Daddy," Casey chided him. "The answer is obvious. Because her frilly dance pants are showing."

"How shocking." His eyes crinkled up at the corners from the way he was grinning as he studied the photo. It showed her mother at a square dance, wearing a fitted gingham dress with a full, swirling skirt that had undoubtedly come from Omaha Gals. Lucille was exhilarated, laughing as her strong young husband lifted her off her feet and twirled her in midair.

"Those were the days," he murmured.

"They're not over, Daddy."

"Yeah, but you're only young once. Make the most of it." He cast a glance at his daughter, giving her a considering look.

"What?" Casey hoped he wasn't going to ask her a whole bunch of questions about her love life.

"Nothing," he said. "I just hope you aren't too down these days."

"I guess you heard about Smitty."

Her father set the square-dance photo next to the one of her and her brother on the blanket. "Yes, I did. I thought it was too bad that he had to go and break up with you around the holidays, but that's how it goes."

"How come you don't sound surprised?"

"Casey, Smitty's a kid."

"He's older than me."

"Granted, but he's still a kid. So are you, but not in the same way . . ." He hesitated.

"Daddy, just say whatever's on your mind."

He looked up at the ceiling and not at her. "You're twenty-one. I don't get to tell you what to do."

"I'm not asking you to. I just want to know what you think." She actually didn't want to know what he thought about Flint. Her father seemed to instinctively understand that it was a sensitive subject for reasons his daughter couldn't begin to explain.

John sighed and searched for the right words. "Girls grow up faster than boys do. You're a few years younger than Smitty, but you're a lot more mature."

"I don't think so."

He fixed his disconcerting gaze on her. "If you were my age, you'd know exactly what I'm talking about."

"Whatever. I know we're talking in circles."

"Maybe so." He got himself into a more comfortable position. "Let's change the subject." He nodded at the bag. "Bring 'em on."

Casey reached in and took out another batch of photos, holding them like a poker hand as she looked at them. "Okay. Here's us on Christmas morning in our pajamas."

She turned her hand so her father could see all the photos at once.

He howled with laughter. "All I can see is Mark's butt and yours."

"We were hoping Santa got there early. We were looking for our presents."

"I think your brother was trying to climb the tree. He's only about two—look at the size of his rear end. Still in diapers."

"He did try," Casey said. "I remember that. I kept pulling his hands off the branches and hissing at him not to do it. He cried and Mom came running."

"That's right," her dad said. "And I was right behind her. I had to hold on to the tree while she dragged him out by his feet."

Casey plucked a photo from the bunch that showed a sobbing Mark with a few pine needles stuck to his plump cheek, cuddled in his mother's arm. "Two minutes later."

"Nothing a cookie couldn't fix. You know what they say: little children, little problems. Big children, big problems."

"We aren't a problem to you, Daddy."

"No, no," he said soothingly. "I was just saying that because it popped into my mind. You two have been great. Dear God, Casey—I'd give anything to be home."

She leaned over and gave him a hug, crushing the bag and scattering the photos. "Dad, you have to get better," she whispered. "But Mark and I will sneak a Christmas tree in here if we have to."

Her father gave her shoulders an affectionate squeeze. "Don't do it."

Casey heard the door open quietly. "Don't do what?" a female voice asked.

"Hey, Pamela," her father said to the nurse. "I was just persuading Casey not to spend too much at the mall. If I'm not home for Christmas, we'll celebrate in January. Everything'll be half-price."

"True," Pamela said. She tidied the room, picking up a photo that had fluttered to the floor. She smiled as she handed it to Casey. "Is that you and your brother?"

"Yes."

"He got a lot cuter."

Casey shrugged as she tucked the photo back in the bag. "I guess so. He's my brother. I just don't see him that way."

"How's my pal Mel Daniels?" her father asked. "Haven't seen him today."

"He got a tentative release. He might be checking out," Pamela said.

"What? He didn't call or come over," John Gilmore said indignantly.

"I'm sure he will. Believe me, Mr. Gilmore, he's not tap-dancing out of here. He's still waiting for the doctor's final okay."

"Hmph."

She tugged a little at his covers. "Visiting hours are almost over, by the way."

John Gilmore groaned. "We were just getting started on Casey's new project."

"Tell you what, Dad," Casey said. "I'll leave the bag here and you can sort the photos out for me."

He didn't seem too unhappy with that. "Okay. It's something to do." He reached for his daughter's hand and gave it a squeeze. "Thanks, Casey. For everything."

The young nurse picked up the bag of photos and set it on his bedside table. "I'll get you some small cardboard boxes. I use them to organize things myself."

"Okay, Pamela. And a pair of scissors would be great."

"What do you need those for, Mr. Gilmore?"

"So I can cut out the really awful ones of me. I'll be the empty place in the photos."

"Don't you dare," Casey said in a mock-threatening voice. "This is meant to be an album of us at our worst."

"Really? That's pretty funny." Pamela laughed. "I want to see that when it's done."

Her patient stopped grumbling and managed a smile at both young women. "All right. I promise to preserve every truly bad moment, no matter how unflattering."

"I love you, Dad," Casey said, getting a little misty.

He reached out and grabbed the bag, spilling all the photos onto the blanket and opening up the empty scrapbook. "Hmph," he said again. "I love you too. Now how do I put these in here?"

"Self-stick pages."

"Good thinking. Your mother will be happy that I have something to do besides beg her for back rubs." He hummed as he began to sort through the photos again and waved good-bye to his daughter with a fresh handful of them.

Casey shared an amused look with the nurse, said good-bye, and left.

Marci moved aside the tiered cake stand that usually held Mrs. Kreutzer's cinnamon-sugar doughnuts. The old lady had iced a last batch in bright red and green, then clambered into a Winnebago with her son-in-law at the wheel, and headed to Florida for a much-needed vacation.

Casey couldn't help noticing Marci's elaborate manicure. A white snowflake adorned each nail, set in clear polish and touched with a tiny rhinestone.

"Wow," Casey said, looking more closely at her employer's hands. "Those are . . . flakey."

Marci smirked. "And so festive." She waggled her fingers proudly.

"Big date?"

Marci shook her head, throwing Casey a disbelieving look. "In Marchand? No, I get my nails done just for me. I pretty much ran through the available men two years ago."

"I know what you mean."

"Casey, you're way too young to say that. Besides, I bet more than one great guy has his eye on you."

Casey scowled, thinking again of Smitty, a situation she planned to explain some other time. For now, she was going to stick with small talk. "I should get my nails done," she said. "If I had the time or the money, which I don't."

"You might be coming into a little of both,"

Marci said airily. She studied her snowflake nails as if seeing them for the very first time and didn't look at Casey.

"Don't be mysterious, Marci. I'll take a raise or a paid vacation. So who's your nail artist?"

"I went to the mall, y'all."

Casey looked around to see if anyone else was included in the "y'all." Nope. She and Marci had the café to themselves.

"Her name was Sunshine or Rainbow or something like that," Marci said finally.

"Aww," Casey said. "I wish I had a cute name instead of a boy's name."

Marci shook her head. "Casey is a cute name. And you should go get your nails done and get prettied up."

"Can't I be beautiful in my own scruffy way?" Casey complained. She hitched herself up onto a stool and investigated the iced doughnuts.

"Sure," Marci said agreeably.

Casey selected a red one that didn't look too lethal and nibbled on a side of it.

"If you're going to eat an iced doughnut, just go ahead and eat the whole damn thing," Marci said. "I don't know why women pretend they're not actually eating when they are."

"Because they don't want to look like big fat truckers in ten years," Casey replied. She pulled out a paper napkin from a counter dispenser and set the doughnut on it, trying to be virtuous.

"Good point." Marci pulled out a to-go container from under the container. "Want me to wrap that for you?"

Casey shook her head. "No. I want you to mail it

to my house with postage due, third class. That way
I'll never get it."

Marci put her elbows on the counter and studied
Casey. "Winter is a tough time, isn't it? All the
snacks and sweets you have to avoid—"

"Did I tell you that Mark and I did the Christmas
baking?"

Marci straightened. "No. I bet you did all the
work. Or most of it."

"No," Casey laughed. "He did. He's going to
grow up to be one of those guys who's in charge in
the kitchen."

"Can we clone him?" Marci asked. "I think Mrs.
Kreutzer is going to need more and more help."

"Just hire him. He could use the experience."

"Hmm," Marci said. "Your brother's pretty cute."

"The nurse at the hospital said the same thing. I
told her I don't see it."

"That's because you're his sister. Anyway, he
could work as a waiter," Marci said, making a sweeping gesture that encompassed the sunny space.

"The truckers won't care, I guess."

The older woman shrugged. "You know who
those guys really want? Mrs. Kreutzer. She gets
more proposals of marriage than any of the girls."

Casey thought it over. "I somehow can't imagine
that happening to me."

"It will," Marci said wisely.

"You sound much more sure than I am."

"That's because I've been married. You're the
kind men want."

"I am?" Casey looked at her, astonished.

"Yes indeed. You're tough but sweet. I know at
least one guy who has a serious crush on you."

"As if." Marci didn't say anything more. "So who would that be?" Casey asked at last.

Marci began to hum in an idle voice, looking everywhere but at Casey. Casey followed her gaze as it moved over walls that she suddenly realized were bare. Her sunflower photographs hadn't been up long enough to leave patches of brighter paint on the wall. That was why she hadn't noticed their disappearance right away.

"Hey, where'd my photographs go?"

"I sold them."

"And you didn't tell me?"

"I was waiting to see how long it would take for you to notice they were gone," Marci said.

"Well, I noticed. Oh, that must be the money you were hinting at, that I was going to come into—"

"That's right." Marci's eyes twinkled. "I have a check for you."

Casey watched as she went to the cash register and opened it, looking through the little drawers and picking up the wire gizmo in each one that held the bills down. "It's in here somewhere," she said absently.

Finally she lifted the tray and looked underneath it. "Here it is." She unfolded it and brought it over to Casey.

"But this is your check," Casey said, disappointed that she still didn't know who'd bought her photographs.

"I had the guy who bought them make out a check to me, then deposited it right away."

"Why?" Casey protested.

"I didn't know when you were coming back. You've been so busy, what with your dad and all, and having to go to Ogallala to stay with Flint's sister, and then coming back here—it seemed best."

Casey pouted. "I would've liked to have met someone who liked my photographs, that's all." She added hastily, "Just not the magazine guy. I'm not ready to pass myself off as a pro."

"Understandable. This other man did give me his business card. It's around here somewhere," Marci said vaguely.

"Wait a minute," Casey said. "Are you faking me out? Did you just buy them yourself because you feel sorry for me?"

"I really didn't," Marci replied. "No, the man wanted to buy them."

"And he wasn't the editor from *Heartland Home*."

"No. Casey, did you ever contact him?"

Casey gave a huge sigh. "Uh-uh. I just couldn't."

"Well, you still have the disc and the photos, right? You could e-mail him the set."

"Hadn't thought of that," Casey muttered.

"Or post them on a photo-sharing service and send him the link."

"Hadn't thought of that either. I guess"—she hesitated but only briefly—"I kind of like the idea of someone buying them outright. Like my sunflowers are going somewhere they'll get looked at every day, not just to a magazine that people flip through and forget."

"I have every copy of *Heartland Home* ever published," Marci said.

"Yes, and those old *Ladies' Home Journal*s that Helen insists are collector's items, and her *National Geographic*s from the 1950s on, and—"

"Can I help it if folks like something to read with their coffee and doughnuts?"

"No." Casey laughed. "C'mon, let's not argue. Aren't we supposed to be putting up Christmas decorations?"

Marci gave a disconsolate groan. "I think it may be too late. I did garlands. Could we go straight to New Year's banners and skip all that?"

"No again," Casey said firmly. "It's never too late to deck the halls." She looked again at the blank spots on the walls and hoped her sunflower photos were brightening up somebody's place. She felt secretly proud of them, knowing that someone had actually purchased several.

But . . . she had considered giving one to each member of her family, and now she would have to come up with something else. Or maybe not. There was a disconnectedness to Christmas this year that she couldn't fix. Nothing she could do was going to bring everyone together and make it all happen.

"I wonder how my mom did it," she said aloud.

"Did what?" Marci asked.

"The baking, the shopping, the decorating— none of it seemed to faze her."

"Oh, I think life was just easier then," Marci said. "Of course, the grass is always greener—or should I say the Christmas tree is greener?"

Casey slouched a little. "That's something else I haven't gotten around to."

"There's a tree lot right down the street."

"I know, I know," Casey said. "I keep driving by it. It looks depressing. And then I start to overthink it. What if I get the wrong tree? Stuff like that."

"There is no wrong tree," Marci declared.

"They're all beautiful. It's about the fun you have picking it out and decorating it."

"I guess I don't want to pick it out by myself," Casey said.

"Then grab your brother by the collar. Or Flint."

"They're both busy."

"Hey," Marci said thoughtfully. "Where did your parents get their tree? You could ask them. I just bet they cut it themselves."

"As a matter of fact, they did," Casey said, looking at her friend with surprise. "But I have no idea where. My dad and Sam, the hired hand, always tried to sneak in with this huge tree so Mark and I wouldn't see. But we knew it was them—we saw them ride over the road through the fields with it. They'd put it in a sled and have one of the draft horses pull it."

"That's nice. I bet that looked like a Currier & Ives print, coming over the snow."

"I never thought about it at the time," Casey said. "But it did. We never thought about where they got it."

"You should ask your dad."

"I will."

"How's he doing, Casey? I know you just saw him in the hospital, but I didn't want to ask—"

"Most likely he's not coming home for Christmas. So it doesn't really matter about the tree."

"Yes, it does," Marci said stubbornly.

Casey held up her hands in a time-out signal. "Not now."

"Okay. I guess I shouldn't bug you. I meant well, Casey."

"I know you did. Tell you what. Let's work off all

your insane decorating energy on the café. What else do you have besides sunflowers?"

"Gosh, Casey. I have so much stuff. From last Christmas, and the Christmas before that—I try to do a different theme every year. I was trying to keep it simple this December. The paper sunflowers were a real find."

"They're great, but—let's put it all up."

"Everything?" Marci asked, looking a little worried.

"Yup," Casey said decisively. "This year's theme will be Everything But The Kitchen Sink."

If she couldn't get it together to do her own decorating at home, she could manage to do the café. It was a welcome distraction from her moodiness and indecision.

Marci threw up her hands. "Whatever you say. I'm not arguing with you."

"Thanks."

"But I have to go out to the storeroom and find all that stuff." She looked toward the door. "Maybe we should close. Nobody's come in for an hour. The big rigs must be staying on the interstate."

"Christmas deliveries," Casey said. "I bet it's crazy on the roads."

"You're probably right." Marci went to the café's door, locked it, and turned the sign to *Sorry We Missed You! Please Come Back.* She looked at Casey, sighed, then headed to the back without another word.

Casey moved to a booth and slouched down so no one would see her and assume the café was open. She was glad she had a place like the café to come to, and a friend like Marci. Someone who knew when she wanted to talk and when she didn't.

Right now a lot of wistful memories were crowding in. Her dad hadn't mentioned it, but Casey had noticed the ornaments on the tree in the photo of her and Mark in their pajamas—they were Sam's, the old ones made of colored engravings that he'd let her put up every year, bringing that antique trunk to the main house and letting her unwrap each one.

Somehow that tradition had gotten set aside.

Casey vowed not to forget it this year. Or Sam, for that matter.

The next morning . . .

Flint took a deep breath and knocked on the half-open door of John Gilmore's hospital room.

"Come on in," said an absent-minded male voice.

He did.

John Gilmore looked at Flint over his half-glasses with surprise. "Hello, Flint. What are you doing here?"

"I was driving by. Then I thought I oughta stop in and say hi. We really haven't talked for a while."

John waved a pair of scissors at his visitor. "Sure. Casey's been doing the same thing. She finagles rides here from your sister or maybe Marci. I'm not sure why and she won't say. But I sure appreciate her coming by."

"I can understand why. That's good to know."

The older man nodded. "She fixed me up with a project so I wouldn't get bored. Clear off that chair and sit down."

Flint looked at the boxes filled with a miscellaneous

assortment of photos. He recognized Casey and Mark in some of them, and younger versions of John and Lucille Gilmore as well. "Got you going on the family albums, huh?"

"Yeah. How about that. Not exactly manly work. I'm supposed to be out on the range clearing brush and herding cattle, not doing this." He made a snicking sound with his scissors before he set them aside. "But it's fun."

"My mother does scrapbooking," Flint said diplomatically. "We all have our own set of albums."

"Well, good Lord. So does Lucille. We should get those gals together. I think my wife's done about forty albums so far. I built her a closet to hold them and her danged supplies. I never knew there were so many twiddly little things you could add to photographs."

Flint nodded in masculine sympathy. "I know exactly what you mean."

"Of course," John went on, "Casey is giving me free rein with this particular project. She only wants to use the goofy photos that her mother didn't like but wouldn't throw away. I think my little girl has an artistic streak."

Flint nodded. "I'd have to agree. I saw her photographs on the wall at the Café Girasole." He wasn't sure if he should tell John Gilmore that he'd bought several of them or not. Truth be told, he had no idea of how the man in the hospital bed would feel about him and Casey. John had expected Flint to take care of his ranch, not fool around with his daughter, after all.

"The ones of sunflowers?"

"Yes, sir."

"That takes me back," the older man mused. "When she was just a little girl, I told her about how the wagon trains would throw sunflower seeds to the side of the road so the pioneers coming through the next year would find their way by the flowers. She loved that story."

Flint smiled. "I can see that she would."

"Sit down, son. I said to clear off that chair and I meant it." There was nothing rude in John Gilmore's tone, just a blunt but friendly invitation.

Flint picked up the boxes of photos, looking at them again. "Do you want these anyplace in particular?"

"Pick a flat surface and line them up. The nurse doesn't mind. You're welcome to look at them if you like."

Flint set the boxes down on the deep windowsill and picked out a few at random. "I see what you mean about goofy. She grew up to be beautiful, if you don't mind my saying so."

John folded his hands over his chest. "Took a while. Crooked smile, shirt not tucked in, hair a mess—that was my Casey."

Flint smiled at the man in the hospital bed. "She still looks like that some days."

"That's because her fundamental nature didn't change. She always did like to do things her way."

Flint wondered if that applied across the board as far as Casey was concerned. What with one thing and another, he had a feeling that he'd gotten too close, too soon. Him being in charge of the Anchor Bar had brought them together, but not in a way that was necessarily to Flint's advantage.

His good intentions of helping her family were

getting in the way of his passionate inclinations toward her. But it wasn't his place to make demands, especially when her family had been pulled apart the way they had. Flint glanced again at the photo of Casey he held, smiling inwardly at her gap-toothed grin, then put it back.

"So how's things on the ranch?" John asked.

That was a much more comfortable topic of conversation. Flint pulled out a small notebook from his shirt pocket and gave the older man a complete rundown. While he was doing that, the nurse came and went unobtrusively, and John Gilmore asked a lot of questions about his stock and his operation.

Casey's dad might be flat on his back in a hospital bed, but he might as well be in the saddle riding over his land, Flint thought. He had nothing but admiration for the man.

"That about covers it," John said at last. "Now," he moved to get more comfortable, "how's things with you and Casey?"

"Ah—"

"Sorry to put you on the spot, son. But I had to know. She didn't say one word about you, but it was clear enough that something was on her mind when she brought me all these old photos."

"Really?" Flint didn't know what on earth to say.

"I had a feeling she was trying to make sense of things. Her life up to now, for one."

"I wouldn't know, sir. She doesn't exactly confide in me."

John Gilmore sighed. "No, she never really did confide in anyone much. She's too much of a tomboy to show her emotions. But God knows she's got 'em."

Flint only nodded. The subject was a tricky one.

"When she was growing up, she reminded me of a skittish colt." John's expression grew tender. "All big eyes and long legs. Curious as hell, and shy too."

"That does sound like her," Flint said. Surely it was safe enough to agree.

"I wanted her to venture out into the great big world after high school." John Gilmore shook his head ruefully. "It just didn't happen. You know how it is with young people around here. They up and marry someone they've known forever—not that it's necessarily a bad thing, but—" He broke off for a few minutes. "She was used to Smitty but that's not the same as really loving someone."

"Did you mind when you heard about them breaking up?" Flint sucked in a breath, not sure if he should've even asked a question as personal as that. But his own feelings for Casey required some clarification.

"Naw. Smitty's all right, but he's just a kid. And that girl he picked instead of Casey is a piece of work. But I'm not sure Smitty's smart enough to ever know what hit him."

Flint nodded.

"That's between us, by the way," the older man added.

"Of course."

"I was thinking that maybe asking her to stay with your sister wasn't a good idea," John went on. "I know how distracting Casey was to have around"—he waved away Flint's muttered protest—"she's headstrong and too pretty for her own good. Do you think I don't know that?"

Flint felt a little trapped. Admitting to his attraction for John Gilmore's daughter—hell, no. He couldn't. This wasn't the time or the place.

"But I don't think she's very sure of herself," John said.

"Maybe so."

John gave Flint a considering look. "I guess you've gathered that she hasn't been off the ranch much, or out of the state. Never did even apply to college."

"She'd do well if she did decide to go. Casey strikes me as highly intelligent." Flint paused. "But like you say, she's unsure."

"Yes. Taking photographs seemed to interest her for a while." John frowned. "But when I got hurt she just stopped in her tracks. I'm hoping that once I'm home, she'll be her old self again. Course, we have to get through the holidays somehow. But then it'll be a new year. She can make a new start."

"We?" Flint asked, wanting to be sure of the older man's meaning.

"Well, now, you don't have to stick around the Anchor Bar any longer than you want to once I'm home," John said. "But you're more than welcome to."

Flint got the point. John Gilmore was shrewd enough to figure out what was going on between the man who was running the ranch in his absence and his beloved daughter. Flint swallowed hard.

"Thank you, sir. If you need me to stay on for a little while after that, I will," he finally said.

"Glad to hear it. And I'll probably take you up on that. Lucille won't mind having an extra person around just so long as I get her a dishwasher."

"Thanks a lot." Flint chuckled at the other man's dry assessment of his wife's hospitality.

"Oughta be able to pick up a good bargain on one at the January sales, don't you think? We'll drive to Omaha or Hastings."

"Sounds like a plan." Flint understood that money was going to be tight for the Gilmores for some time. He could help, but John was far too proud to ever accept financial assistance. The two men talked a little longer, and then the nurse came in.

"Hello, Pamela. I believe you know Flint McAllister," John said.

"Yes, I've seen him around the halls," she said. "Hello, Flint. I'm glad you stopped by. Poor Mr. Gilmore is going stir-crazy."

"Just for the hell of it, I'm going to run somebody over with my wheelchair one of these days," John said teasingly. "You'd better watch out."

"We're all keeping an eye on you," Pamela said encouragingly, "and it says here you're doing really well with your physical therapy. That'll help your hip."

"Good. I have to get out of this danged place before I really do lose my mind."

Pamela winked at her grumbling patient. "You won't. It just feels that way, but you're too tough." She went through her routine of looking at his chart and checking his vitals as Flint rose to leave.

Then John Gilmore extended his hand in farewell, and they shook. Flint felt a reassuring vitality in his grip, something he hoped he could communicate to Casey. She must be more worried than she'd ever let on.

Chapter Fifteen

Casey knew what she had to do.

She couldn't keep driving from one stopping point to the next, at the hospital for most of day, back in Ogallala the next or crashing on the long-suffering Marci's couch. She was trying to outrun what was on her mind, but she couldn't keep relying on other people's kindness or their patience.

No, she was going to go home. And she was going to stay there. She belonged on her family's land and it was the only place on earth where she would be able to find solace, especially with the so-called season of peace only days away. She felt anything but peaceful.

Flint would just have to live with the idea of her presence, or work around her, because she wasn't going to avoid him. If she got sandbagged by the blues, she could find a private place to sit and cry. Living on a ranch gave her several thousand acres to roam over if she wanted to lose herself for a while and forget about the world. No way was she going back to Gabbie's, where she felt a little too watched.

That arrangement had been a well-meaning mistake from start to finish. But it was over. She'd insisted that Sam drive her car from the Anchor Bar to where she was with Flint, at an anonymous restaurant, coordinating the operation with a three-way cellphone call. Then she'd driven off without telling either man where she was going or what she was doing.

She wasn't going to let them stop her or boss her around. Sam wouldn't dare—the old cowboy would just shake his head and look sad. However, Flint was likely to offer his opinion and unsolicited advice into the bargain, and sound off about putting his foot down. Or, worse, get objectionably sympathetic over Smitty.

It had finally sunk in that a boy she'd pretty much taken for granted might turn around and do the same thing to her. But he was a boy. Chalk that hard-earned lesson up to experience, she thought grimly. It still hurt. Smitty had chosen someone as mean and petty as Brenda Fairlie, and they, the couple she hoped would be happy—when she was feeling charitable—would be living on the ranch next door—well, that was a fact of life and not a good reason for her to cut and run.

Her parents would have to understand what she was going to do and she very much doubted they'd make her go to her Aunt Karen's. Casey simply wouldn't. She'd had it. She was going home, if she had to break and enter to do it. Flint could say what he liked.

There wasn't going to be a Christmas tree in the usual place in the living room, and there weren't going to be family visits. The relatives who could find the time were heading to Scottsbluff to see her father and mother—even Mark was likely to show up at the eleventh hour on Christmas Eve, if he showed up at all.

Flint—now, he was a puzzle. He might just head on home to his family's ranch in Ogallala and leave the running of the ranch to Sam for a couple of days, come to think of it.

Her mind whirling, Casey pondered some interesting alternatives as she watched the sun set, a fiery red ball trailing uncertain wisps of cloud. What if she really did sneak in? It couldn't be called breaking and entering if you were getting into your own home, she reasoned.

But it would be a whole hell of a lot easier on everyone if no one actually knew she was there—oh, don't be an idiot, she scolded herself. Flint and Gabbie had practically sent a posse after her when she was walking by Lake McConaughy. Her father might be able to handle the idea of his headstrong daughter homesteading in her own bedroom, but if she disappeared it would be the end of him.

She sat in her car on the shoulder of the road, not far from Marchand. Even from miles away, the Café Girasole window shone warmly into the bleak night, making a bright patch on the solitary street. It was the only place open, besides the gas station outside of town, and that was a fluorescent-lit nightmare of a place. Clean, almost sterile, reeking of gasoline and diesel fumes and the defeated exhaustion of long-haul truckers, men and women alike.

Casey wanted to climb out of the car and howl at the stars. No coyote was ever as lonesome as she felt now—and even they were probably holed up in nice warm dens under what was left of the Nebraska prairie.

Ho ho ho, and to hell with the holidays, she thought glumly. Casey started the car, spun it around, and headed for the ranch.

Half a mile down the road up to it, she lost her nerve and pulled over, switching off the headlights. She still could not bring herself to walk jauntily in the front door and toss her cowboy hat onto the antlered rack that held Stetsons, rough-side-out shearling jackets, and a riding whip or two.

No, just for an hour or two she wanted to be alone and have a good cry on her own bed, before anyone—Gabbie, Flint, Mark, Sam, her mom and dad—had the slightest idea she'd gone missing.

Then she'd show her face and take the consequences.

She drove on, still with the lights off, letting her eyes get accustomed to the darkness. She knew every bump and furrow in the road almost by feel, and even starlight helped when the night air was this clear, and the heavens were so vast. She looked up, feeling privileged to see what most people no longer saw clearly at all: the Milky Way, poured across the sky in a sparkling wash.

Casey heard the gravel of the driveway crunch softly underneath her tires and she drove even slower. There were a few lights on in the ranch house—her dad's office, of course, where Flint probably was—but the bunkhouse, where Sam slept, was dark and so were the barns.

Feeling like a thief in the night, she drove toward them, intending to park behind the largest structure and shinny up to her second floor bedroom somehow. She rolled to a stop, turned off the engine, and put the gearshift in park. Then she got out, taking her handbag, and walked toward the house.

Her sneakers didn't make any more noise than the tires had. Casey had worn them instead of her creased, beat-up cowboy boots, and she missed the confident walk those gave her. Was that feeling gone forever?

Maybe so, she thought dejectedly. She made her way to the window of her dad's office and spied Flint, whose head was bent over papers held in place with one hand and a corner of his laptop. Even that was rugged, with an industrial-grade shell that looked like it could survive a trampling under a horse's hooves.

There was a look of concern on his face that touched her and made her stay there, watching him, cold as it was outside. It was hard to fault a guy for anything when he volunteered to help the way Flint had. It occurred to Casey that her father's recovery had been made easier by his simply knowing that Flint McAllister was here.

So why wasn't his presence simple for her?

She didn't want to explore the reasons for that and trudged on, heading for the ladder that usually got left against the side of the house. Roof shingles that peeled off and blew away were a frequent occurrence out here, where the wind was in charge and tempestuous weather was a fact of life. Casey shivered. She really didn't want to climb the ladder, not at night.

She went around the corner and there it was, propped haphazardly against the gutter along the edge of the roof. Casey put her handbag strap diagonally over her chest so it wouldn't get in her way and stepped onto the first rung, climbing up surefootedly. Once up on the roof over her dad's office, she stepped as quietly as she could and reached her bedroom window.

Using all her strength and breaking a couple of fingernails in the process, she lifted it smoothly and swung a leg over the sill.

Then she froze. She heard a light switch click and she blinked against the flood of light. Flint was standing there, looking at her as if he'd been waiting for a while.

"In the habit of coming in through the window?" he asked.

"It isn't the first time." Best to be honest, she decided. "My dad knew I did it, I guess."

He nodded. "I'm not even going to ask. But I did hear you."

"Good." She set her sneakered foot on the floor and swung her other leg over the sill. Then she jumped in, brushing crumbs of icy-cold asphalt from the shingles off her jeans-clad butt. His gaze dropped as he watched her do it.

"I ought to spank you."

"Sounds like fun," she said brazenly. Let him think about what he wasn't going to get. It would serve him right for whatever he was planning to do about announcing her unorthodox return home.

He made an odd sound halfway between a snort and a chuckle. A snuckle, she thought. Something about the amused glow in his eyes softened the lump of misery that had tightened her throat and she actually ventured a step, as if she were going downstairs.

Flint took a step toward her, but stopped.

"I was only kidding." She dropped her handbag on her bed and sat down on it. "Now, if you don't mind, I'd like to be alone."

He shook his head. "I think you should come downstairs. I have a surprise for you."

For a long moment they looked at each other, and Casey felt even more of her unhappiness melt away under the warmth of his gaze. "Okay," she said. "Obviously it won't be at gunpoint."

"Nope. Even though I thought you might be a prowler, no gun."

Casey stood up, checking her windblown hair in the mirror. Considering she'd been the unhappiest female in Nebraska, bar none, for the last several hours, she didn't look too bad. Her eyes were bright and her cheeks were nice and pink from being out in the cold, anyway.

"After you." He gestured her forward.

Was she giddy from the adrenaline rush of climbing a ladder to get in the house? Probably. Still, his old-fashioned courtesy tickled her. "Thank you, Sir Flint."

The stinging but appreciative slap that landed on her butt as she swept past him did more than tickle her. Casey had to hide her smile by staying ahead of him.

He was only a step in back of her all the way downstairs. She could almost feel his breath on the back of her neck. His arm curved around her waist from behind when she finally stopped on the bottom stair and she gave in to the impulse to lean back against him.

"Go on," he whispered into her hair. "Into the living room."

She broke free of his amorous hold and went on, taking just a few more steps before she saw the biggest Christmas tree ever standing—well, leaning slightly—in the corner. There were no decorations on it, but its needles were tipped with frost. Tiny spots of water on the floor showed where a lot of it had melted off. He must have just brought it in only minutes before she arrived.

The intense piney scent filled the room, suggesting dark woods and wild nights and something very magical.

"It's beautiful," she said softly.

"I don't know where the decorations are. But I wanted to get a tree, just in case."

"In case . . ."

He grinned at her. "You did exactly what I expected you to do. You galloped straight home. No saddle and no rider."

"Where else would I go?" she said indignantly. "I live here, remember?"

"I'm beginning to realize how much home means to you. You make it hard to forget. Even when you're all the way out in Ogallala." He turned her around to face him again and kissed her forehead. "Anyway, there's your tree. I didn't get time to wrap your presents."

"It isn't even Christmas yet, Flint."

He only shrugged. "I'm no good at wrapping odd-shaped objects. I can manage right angles okay, but I forgot to ask for a box. Shoot—how about if you sit down and close your eyes, and I just put them in your lap?"

"Them? Are they alive?"

"No." He brushed his hand lovingly over her cheek. "But they're for a girl who's so alive and so eager to have it all that she gets hurt sometimes. Yeah, I'm talking about you."

"Aw, Flint . . . I didn't get you anything."

He smiled slightly. "I think you need a present a lot more than I do. Go on, sit down."

She went over to the big leather armchair with rolled arms and studded trim, and sat, squinching her eyes shut. "I feel like I'm ten years old," she said.

"You act like it sometimes. Keep your eyes shut."

Casey obeyed as she felt two things land in her lap. She touched two tall columns of tooled leather and then her eyes opened, wide with delight when she saw the boots she'd admired in the store with Gabrielle.

"She told you!"

He shot her an exasperated look. "Of course. I asked her what you wanted. What kind of fool do you think I am? When it comes to buying presents for a woman, a man who shops alone, sleeps alone."

Casey burst out laughing. "I never heard that."

"That's because I just made it up. Try them on."

He dropped into the armchair she vacated, watching with barely hidden sensual fire in his eyes as she bent over to slip on the beautiful boots. He sat up straight when she strutted around, enjoying the new-sounding *thunks* of the heels.

Then she saw something else stacked in the corner. Rectangular objects wrapped in what seemed to be . . . tablecloths. Very familiar tablecloths. Bright yellow. The ones Marci used during the summer at the Café Girasole.

"What are those?" she asked. "Something else you couldn't wrap?"

"Ah—" He hesitated. "Those are your framed photographs. I have to confess that I bought several to give away. Not to you, obviously."

"You liked them that much?" she said with astonishment.

"Yes, I do," Flint replied. "And Marci has a check to give to you. I was going to be a mystery buyer, but the cat's out of the bag now."

"Uh, I got the check. But not the explanation. I wish everyone would get it through their heads that I like a straight story. And that I'm not a little kid who has to be protected." She went over and pushed away the tablecloth that swaddled one of the framed photographs, revealing the one of the sunflower at the end of the season, heavy and drooping, but laden with seeds that a small bird was feasting on. "Oh, right. I took that in September. So which one did you like best?"

Flint laughed. "Now how did I know you were going to ask that question? Actually, the one you just picked out. Something about that image really touched me. The sunflower seems to be carrying the weight of the world, but it's still going strong."

"Like my dad," she said softly. "And you, Flint. You've done a lot for us."

"Really, Casey? I would say that you're the strong one. I just don't think you know it yet."

"There's a lot of things I don't know," she sighed.

Flint nodded. "For one thing, that you have more talent than you probably think. As a photographer, I think you have a lot of potential. If you don't mind my sounding like a high school guidance counselor," he added hastily.

"You do," she replied. "But I don't mind. Do you know—" She broke off, just looking at him. "You just made me even happier."

"All right. And I haven't even given you your other present."

They exchanged a long, warm look, the feeling of attraction between turning into something like a magnet.

"Come here, girl," he growled. "Sit on my lap. And make me happy."

Her hands on her hips, Casey threw him a challenging look. "Don't mind if I do."

For the second time that night she obeyed him. And for a while he made sure that she knew who was boss in the most loving way he could.

Oh my oh my. Could I ever get used to this, Casey thought. Her hands threaded through his hair as she stayed right where she was for kiss after kiss.

He exhaled a long, long breath when that part of their reunion was over. "Now what?"

"Mmm. I can think of a few more things to do but not here and"—she winked—"not with my brother walking in on us."

"He's staying with Kyle and Kevin. We have the house to ourselves."

"Really?"

"Yup. It's just you and me and that great big tree."

"Wow."

He pulled her down to him for another kiss. Unseen above the roof, the stars wheeled in the infinite sky and love, sweet love, warmed two hearts below it.

In time, the feeling was almost too much to bear and she pulled away from him, remembering how it had been . . . and never would be again. Somehow the past seemed to intrude all of a sudden and her mind echoed with memories that didn't belong in the here and now.

What she was feeling must have showed on her face.

"Oh, God, Casey, please don't cry," Flint said, covering the small distance between them before Casey could protest and drawing her into his arms. "I can't stand to see you cry," he declared, burying his face in her hair as Casey struggled against the firmness of his embrace.

"Please, please let me go!" It was a breathless plea, one that her mind demanded she make while the rest of her reveled in his nearness.

"Why? I don't want to," he growled.

Her fingers reached up to still his voice and remained trembling on the sensual male mouth. "Are . . . are you saying you love me?" Casey murmured.

"Do you want me to say it?"

"Yes."

"I do."

She caught her breath. Her eyes closed to savor the glory of this moment before she spoke in a shaky but happy voice. "It's only fair to tell you that I wasn't crying for good old Smitty."

"I think I qualify as the old guy around here."

"No, you don't."

"Well, I'm older than Smitty."

"And thank God for that," she said feelingly.

His hand moved her chin upward so he could

stare into her face. "You sure you don't want him? I have to know, girl."

"Yes. I think I love you, Flint McAllister." It was unbelievable that those calm, composed words came from her. But they did.

There was a split second of utter stillness before Flint covered her parted lips with his, possessively taking all the love she was giving and returning it tenfold. The next moments were tempestuous, heat-filled ones that threatened to continue until Flint determinedly held her away.

"When I think of how I tried to do the right thing and keep you at a safe distance—hell, I could kick myself." The husky vibration in his voice shot quivering excitement through Casey. "I didn't know where to start or—well, I didn't want to end it."

"You charmed me out of my cowboy boots right from the start, Flint. Didn't you know that?"

"No. I didn't."

"Couldn't you tell what happened to me when you kissed me?"

"I've been told I'm a good kisser," Flint said smugly. "But—"

"Wow, you think highly of yourself. Are you asking for a smack?"

He grinned. "Do your worst."

"I can't. Smacking you would be like smacking a brick house."

He nodded thoughtfully. "Not that I would, ever, in a million years, raise my hand to you in return if you did smack me. I want you to understand that."

"Not a problem," she said cheerfully. "My dad would kill you instantly if you did, even if he had to run you over with his wheelchair to do it."

Flint sighed. "It doesn't look like he's going to be back at the Anchor Bar for Christmas, you know."

She shrugged, looking out the window at winter's bleakness. "Yeah, I'm getting that idea."

"You and Mark are welcome to stay with us Mc-Allisters. You know, I wanted so badly for you to know my family as well as I knew yours."

"They seem like really good people."

"My mom and dad are the best," he began to say.

"No, mine are," she replied quickly.

Flint laughed. "Well, we can figure that out later."

"What do you mean?"

He drummed his fingers on her thigh, then turned to give her an awkward smile. "Like, sometime during the rest of our lives together?"

"You . . . you don't think I'm too young . . ." Casey tried to answer.

"To marry?" Flint finished for her, smiling at the flush that filled her cheeks. "You might be. I'm not asking for a yes right now."

"And you're not asking for a no, ever," she said wryly.

He threw back his head and laughed. "Good comeback. Hey, I don't love the word no any more than you do. And I'm pretty damned determined to marry you when you're good and ready, my little prickle poppy."

"I thought the bride was supposed to arrange the wedding," Casey laughed breathlessly, enthralled by the love in his gray eyes.

"Usually," Flint agreed, pulling her back toward him to sprinkle kisses along the throbbing cord of her neck, pausing long enough to whisper in her ear, "but I'm afraid you might take too long."

Casey gasped at the desire in his voice as she turned her mouth to find his, managing to murmur, "Just this once, I might let you call the shots, Flint . . ."

The snowstorm hit several hours later. He still hadn't wangled a definite yes out of Casey, but she'd let him leave with no doubt in his mind that he was the man. Her man.

He'd taken the monster truck in case he had to tow stranded drivers with the steel-cable winch mounted in front, and headed out to help the county road crews and emergency teams, picking up a text alert on his cellphone.

Casey lugged umpteen boxes down from the attic, and looked inside to make sure no mice had taken up residence in the delicate ornaments packed in fine white straw.

Nope. Not one squeak. She lifted out a clothespin girl with a sweet painted face and a tiny crocheted hat and muffler, letting it swing in the air from the thin cord around her forefinger, thinking again of playing in the snow with her brother and their friends.

The local kids were going to have a field day, but some families from the areas that were likely to be hit the hardest were to be sheltered in the schoolhouse until the storm had blown through and the roads were cleared.

Flint would probably help with that too, she thought, just as her father had done in his time. He must have a snowplow mount on the truck. She went to the Anchor Bar office—the room that had

become Flint's bedroom—to call her parents in
Scottsbluff and reassure them that the animals were
taken care of, bedded down and fed, safely in their
stalls. Mark was going to stay with Kyle and Kevin,
and all was well in their little world.

For a wonder, it was. She hadn't gotten her
Christmas wish to have her father home, but that
was how it had to be.

Flint drove slowly over the dangerously slippery
roads, putting his cellphone in the hands-free
mount in case he had to answer it again. The head
of emergency services was organizing drivers to get
families into shelters until the huge storm was over.
Flint had volunteered as soon as the phone chain
reached him.

He'd been reluctant to leave Casey, but she'd insisted that he go. She'd weathered worse storms
over the years. Sure. With her parents in Scottsbluff,
and hired hands to help dig out—she wouldn't
listen to the arguments he tried to make.

Let her have her way, he thought. Despite the
danger, the driving snow made him peaceful inside,
but he drove with purpose.

He turned into a driveway almost obliterated by
the fast-falling snow, feeling the heavy tires grab the
rutted road underneath. Blinking the gigantic
headlights on and off to signal the family inside
and honking, he got out to help when he saw a
bundled-up woman open the door of a small, ramshackle house. She struggled out, keeping three
kids behind her.

They hung on to each other's mittened hands,

taking baby steps against the wind. Flint stomped through the soft snow to break a path to them and get them more quickly to the safety of his truck's big cab.

One . . . two . . . three . . . he lifted the kids in. Then he turned to assist their mother and realized that it wasn't just her heavy clothes that made her look so big—she was about eight months pregnant.

"Easy, ma'am," he said, extending a hand to help her up onto the running board and into the cab.

"Thanks so much for coming," she said, trying to get her breath. "My husband was deployed and we're way out here with no one to help—I don't know what I would have done with them three little ones. We would've been stuck for days—whew!" She undid a few buttons and her pregnant belly heaved. "Move over, Travis."

The smallest boy scooted over, crowding his brother, who was running his hands admiringly over the immense steering wheel.

"Cool truck," he said.

"Thanks." Flint grinned at the happy kid. "You all set, ma'am?" She was now struggling with the seat belt. He heard a click and she sighed.

"Just barely. Okay. Yes, I am. My name's Glenda Spark, by the way."

"I'm Flint McAllister."

"This is Travis, Cody, and Mike. You boys say thank you to Mr. McAllister," she said automatically.

"Hello, little Sparks." He heard a chorus of high-pitched, excited thanks and hellos as he shut her door and went around to his side. This was a great big adventure to them. But he was glad they weren't afraid. He sent up a silent prayer that their mother wouldn't go into labor all of a sudden.

"Ready?" he asked the kids when he got in and slammed the door on his side.

"Yes, sir," they said in unison.

"Glenda, you've got to buckle them up somehow, even if you do two together. Better than nothing."

The oldest boy took care of it and Flint swung back into the driveway. In only minutes, the snow was inches deeper and he prayed they wouldn't get stuck.

Grabbing and growling, his truck made it out and to the main road.

There were many more vehicles in the parking lot of the school gymnasium by the time they got there, and emergency workers were guiding the families inside and assisting the elderly as well. He took Glenda's arm and walked with her as her three boys scurried ahead.

"I didn't have time to get food or toys together for them," she said apologetically.

"I'm sure there'll be plenty to go around."

He caught a whiff of diesel and realized a generator was being tested somewhere nearby. For now they had power, but wires were likely to go down and soon.

The gym was brightly lit and the evacuated people were helping the volunteers set up cots while kids raced around. Glenda was met by other mothers, who thanked Flint profusely, then cast an experienced eye at her belly.

"You stay calm now, y'hear?" one said to her. "If that kid gets born on Christmas, he or she won't forgive you. Won't ever have a proper birthday."

"I'm not due until January fifth," Glenda protested.

"Good," her friend laughed. "I'm holding you to that. Now you come on over here and sit down."

Both women waved good-bye to Flint and moved

away. He walked toward the door, then turned for a moment to survey the scene.

Some of the parents already had the quieter kids settled down with coloring books and games, but it looked like there might not be enough to go around. A couple of granddads were organizing a relay race for the more active kids. They had the right idea: tire the youngsters out so they would go to sleep early. Good strategy in case they lost power, Flint thought. Hell. If they all had to hole up here right through Christmas Day, it wasn't going to be much of a holiday for any of them.

Flint saw an older woman dump the contents of a giant tote bag on a long folding table, making a small mountain of craft supplies. "Now who wants to help me make ornaments?" she called. Several of the children came over, and looked through bright scraps of fabric and paper, helping themselves to scissors and little bottles of glitter and glue.

She unfolded chairs for them and took out finished ornaments that were a lot like—he narrowed his eyes to see better from where he was standing—the ones Smitty had taken from his trunk.

Traditions. These people knew how to keep them alive. They were probably all neighbors, despite the long country miles between them, and Casey probably knew most of them. They were good people. The kind that looked out for one another and got through difficulties just the way she did: with a stubbornness that was sometimes cheerful and sometimes ornery.

He was glad to have been able to help them.

But he was damned if he would leave Casey alone with just Sam out in the trailer if anything went wrong. The old man would do his best, but he ought to stay hunkered down where he was and keep warm. Flint felt a powerful obligation to get back to the Anchor Bar as soon as possible—and then, just in time, he remembered that the lights had been on in the general store in Marchand when they'd driven through.

They might have a few things left on the shelves. He no longer had kids and a pregnant woman in the cab and he could make a run for it. Worth a try.

Casey was relieved to hear Flint's heavy boots scraping on the mat, and ran to him when he stepped inside, pressing her body against his snow-sparkled coat. He held her close, too cold to speak, but he managed to give her a remarkably hot kiss.

Thunk. He kicked off one boot and it landed in the corner, followed by—*thunk*—the other one. Then he shucked his jacket, scarf, and gloves, more or less in that order, and swept her up in his arms.

"To the bedroom, woman," he growled. "Warm me up."

Casey kicked her soft shearling boots in midair as he mounted the stairs, kissing him again and again.

Hours later, they were trimming the tree, looking at each other with eyes that were a hell of a lot brighter than the lights on the huge, fresh tree. Then there was a knock on the door.

The wind had picked up and was screaming around the corners of the house. Flint looked at her with surprise. "Expecting someone?"

She went quickly to the door, noticing the flashing lights of a cop cruiser outside the window even through the driving snow. "No. They must be starting to close the roads by now. Could be an emergency. God, I hope not. Oh, Flint—"

He was right behind her when she opened the door.

The deputy sheriff just touched the brim of his snow-laden hat. "Hey, Casey. I can't stay long but—" He looked past her to Flint. "We were searching for Santa."

Casey turned to give him an inquisitive look. "This isn't great weather for practical jokes, guys."

The deputy only smiled. "Let me explain. We saw a really banged-up old army-type truck of some kind drop off boxes of toys and games and snacks and canned goods at the school where those families had to take shelter."

"Really?" Flint said innocently.

"Yup. Seems the vehicle was not exactly street-legal, but it got through deep snow like nobody's business. Caught a glimpse of it myself, never seen anything like it. And it had expired plates and a few violations. Duct tape holding the brake light cover on, that kind of thing."

"Been meaning to get that fixed," was all Flint said.

Casey put her arms around his waist and looked up at him with pride.

"You do that. I just wanted to convey everybody's thanks. So if you see that Santa guy, you tell him he's very popular with us Nebraskans."

"Will do," Flint said.

The deputy beamed at him and Casey. "You two stay warm now."

"You bet."

They got through the good-byes in record time, because the snow was whirling right into the hall.

Flint kicked the door shut and bent down and kissed Casey again.

"Searching for Santa, huh?"

He looked embarrassed and pleased at the same time. "A man's gotta do what a man's gotta do."

"I really do think I love you," she said dreamily. "Now make my Christmas wish come true."

"I'm about to." He gave her a knee-melting kiss. "Mmm. How come you never asked me about the present you didn't get? And how come I never got my answer?"

"You keep distracting me, Flint," she murmured.

He reached into his pocket and took out a little velvet box. "Didn't have time to wrap this one either. But here you go."

Casey gave him a wondering look. "Is this—"

"Could be a this. Or a that. You won't know until you open it."

She pushed up the lid with her thumb. A perfect diamond solitaire set in platinum twinkled up at her. "Flint!"

"I still want you to take your time about answering me," he insisted. "You're young, but I'll be ready when you are."

"Oh, Flint . . ."

They didn't get out of bed the next morning until the snow had drifted higher than the first floor. The sun was shining. The world was totally white. There were record-setting mountains of snow to be shoveled.

But he'd gotten his answer from Casey in two parts somewhere after midnight. There were three letters in the first part, and three little words in the second.

Yes. And *I love you.* She didn't have to think about it. It was the truth.

Unwrap a Holiday Romance
by
Janet Dailey

Eve's Christmas

   0-8217-8017-4   **$6.99**US/**$9.99**CAN

Let's Be Jolly

   0-8217-7919-2   **$6.99**US/**$9.99**CAN

Happy Holidays

   0-8217-7749-1   **$6.99**US/**$9.99**CAN

Maybe This Christmas

   0-8217-7611-8   **$6.99**US/**$9.99**CAN

Scrooge Wore Spurs

   0-8217-7225-2 $6.99US/$9.99CAN

A Capital Holiday

   0-8217-7224-4   **$6.99**US/**$8.99**CAN

Available Wherever Books Are Sold!

Check out our website at **www.kensingtonbooks.com**

By Bestselling Author
Fern Michaels

__Weekend Warriors	0-8217-7589-8	$6.99US/$9.99CAN
__Listen to Your Heart	0-8217-7463-8	$6.99US/$9.99CAN
__The Future Scrolls	0-8217-7586-3	$6.99US/$9.99CAN
__About Face	0-8217-7020-9	$7.99US/$10.99CAN
__Kentucky Sunrise	0-8217-7462-X	$7.99US/$10.99CAN
__Kentucky Rich	0-8217-7234-1	$7.99US/$10.99CAN
__Kentucky Heat	0-8217-7368-2	$7.99US/$10.99CAN
__Wish List	0-8217-7363-1	$7.50US/$10.50CAN
__Yesterday	0-8217-6785-2	$7.50US/$10.50CAN
__Finders Keepers	0-8217-7364-X	$7.50US/$10.50CAN
__Dear Emily	0-8217-7316-X	$7.50US/$10.50CAN
__Sara's Song	0-8217-7480-8	$7.50US/$10.50CAN
__Celebration	0-8217-7434-4	$7.50US/$10.50CAN
__Vegas Heat	0-8217-7207-4	$7.50US/$10.50CAN
__Vegas Rich	0-8217-7206-6	$7.50US/$10.50CAN
__Vegas Sunrise	0-8217-7208-2	$7.50US/$10.50CAN
__Picture Perfect	0-8217-7588-X	$7.99US/$10.99CAN
__Payback	0-8217-7876-5	$6.99US/$9.99CAN
__Vendetta	0-8217-7877-3	$6.99US/$9.99CAN
__The Jury	0-8217-7878-1	$6.99US/$9.99CAN
__Fool Me Once	0-7582-1630-0	$6.99US/$9.99CAN
__Sweet Revenge	0-8217-7879-X	$6.99US/$9.99CAN
__Lethal Justice	0-8217-7880-3	$6.99US/$9.99CAN

Available Wherever Books Are Sold!

Visit our website at **www.kensingtonbooks.com**